BarbaraAnne Vincent
PMB 330, P.O. Box 7000
Redondo Beach, CA 90277-8710
(310/424) 378-9872

D0467356

Sun at Midnight

Sun at Midnight

A Memoir of the Dark Night

Andrew Harvey

JEREMY P. TARCHER/PUTNAM
a member of Penguin Putnam Inc.
New York

Most Tarcher/Putnam books are available at special quantity discounts for bulk purchase for sales promotions, premiums, fund-raising, and educational needs. Special books or book excerpts also can be created to fit specific needs. For details, write Putnam Special Markets, 375 Hudson Street, New York, NY 10014.

Jeremy P. Tarcher/Putnam
a member of
Penguin Putnam Inc.
375 Hudson Street
New York, NY 10014
www.penguinputnam.com

Copyright © 2002 by Andrew Harvey

Library of Congress Cataloging-in-Publication Data

Harvey, Andrew, date.
Sun at midnight : a memoir of the dark night /
Andrew Harvey.
p.   cm.
ISBN 1-58542-179-0
1. Harvey, Andrew, date. 2. Authors, English—20th
century—Biography. I. Title.

PR6058.A6986 Z44   2002   2002020364
828′.91409—dc21

Printed in the United States of America

1   3   5   7   9   10   8   6   4   2

This book is printed on acid-free paper. ♾

BOOK DESIGN BY AMANDA DEWEY

To ERYK, my husband and Love's warrior

To LEILA, beloved sustainer

To SANDRA, for herself and for her saving help

To DOROTHY, who always understood

To MY MOTHER, for her enduring love

Contents

✷

Part I

Prologue

W hen I came to live the long death of the Dark Night that destroyed and transfigured my life—and that I know now as its most profound blessing—three conversations with three spiritual friends of different religions and worlds kept returning to me. Their clarities circled my spirit like majestic tigers, protecting against despair, reminding, sometimes wrathfully, and with a certain scorn, of what it was to be brave enough to embrace and endure. Long before I could understand the value of the gift they were giving me, these three friends distilled for me the wisdom I would need when my killing came.

In the first conversation, I am a fierce, unhappy, intellectual twenty-eight-year-old, still uneasy with all things "mystical," stalking in old jeans and cheap army boots around Jerusalem. My guide to the mysteries of the old City is "Isaiah," a plump, bald, late-middle-aged Israeli poet and mystic who looks, as he himself says often, "like a semi-enlightened sunburnt frog" and who has, over two days, become a friend. I love his sardonic wit, his baroque flights of phrase, his Kabalistic learning, the way his eyebrows twitch asymmetrically when he gets excited, which he does often. Today he is wearing bright red sneakers and a Hawaiian short-sleeved shirt with great orange suns on it. Our talk is light, fact-stocked, and airy until we find ourselves in the early afternoon on the Mount of Olives, and stand, suddenly silent, in the stubbly ochre olive grove where Christ wandered on the night before His crucifixion.

"Even on a cloudless afternoon like this," Isaiah whispered, "this place is so sad. It is as if you can still hear Him weeping for all of us, for what must happen."

He stretched out his arm and pointed to the bricked-up golden gate in the wall of the Old City opposite us.

"Some Jews believe that the Messiah will come through that gate." He started to laugh. "Don't hold your breath. And suppose 'he's' a 'she'? Wouldn't that drive all the old boys in black out of their curlered heads?"

It was then that I noticed the faded black numbers on the bare arm sticking out of his Hawaiian shirt. I gasped; the afternoon before we had walked in silent anguish together through the Holocaust museum. Isaiah had said nothing then. Now, he turned slowly and stared at me, into me, steadily, as if weighing my soul.

Then he began to talk in a low, even voice I had not heard from him.

"Yes, I was in Auschwitz. As a child. From nine to thirteen. I don't know how or why I survived, but I do know what I learned."

4

I waited.

He opened his mouth, then stopped, and shrugged his shoulders.

"Words are hopeless. I want to say something so big, but I only have small words to say it with. That is why I speak of these things so rarely and to so few people. Perhaps the old Jewish prophets were right; some things are too terrible and too holy to be spoken of."

The afternoon darkened slightly. He paused, as if to gather strength, and went on:

"I am not going to dishonor the horrors we all lived through in that hell by going over them. You know many of them, and you have the heart to imagine more, although nothing you can imagine can come close.

"But it is not of these things that I wish to speak to you. I want to tell you what I discovered in hell. It may shock you.

"In Auschwitz, I discovered that there was one thing I was even more terrified of than death. When you live in an atmosphere of terror, you realize that all the fears you shrink from in 'normal' circumstances are relatively minor and that there is one terror that everyone has which is overwhelming, and that hardly anyone ever talks about because very few have gone through enough to find it out."

"And what is this terror?" I asked, a little afraid by now.

"The terror of Love, of Love's embrace of all things, all beings, and all events. Everyone pretends they want to know and experience Love, but to know and experience Love is to die to all your private fantasies and agendas, all your visions of 'right' and 'wrong'; even 'good' and 'evil.' Everyone who comes to that death is dragged to it kicking and cursing and screaming and weeping tears of blood, just as Jesus was in this garden."

He breathed deeply as if to steady himself.

"I was twelve years old. It was mid-winter. I was in despair. My mother, father, and sister had all starved to death. I knew by then that the chances of surviving or of being saved were very slim. There was a guard who was particularly sadistic who used to beat me with his leather strap until I bled.

"I was only twelve. What did I know about anything, about God? All I knew was that I had to decide, once and for all, whether the horror I saw around me was the ultimate reality or whether the joy and tenderness I could still feel stirring inside me was the truth. I knew that they couldn't *both* be the truth; if the horror of the camp was the reality about human nature and life, then what was stirring in my heart was some kind of mad joke. If what was stirring in my heart was real, then it was the horror that was the mad joke.

"I thought about this for months. 'Thought' is too polite a word. I *bled* about this, I wept over it, I wrestled with it as Jacob must have wrestled with the angel, for my life. I had to know, or I would drown in the darkness. For the first time, I started to pray. My prayer, which I began to repeat at every moment, was only four words: 'Show me the truth.' Nothing came. Not a single insight, not a single vision, no dream with any comforting angel. Nothing at all.

"But I went on praying, more and more desperately, and then early one winter morning I heard a quiet voice say to me, 'You must decide.' What did it mean? For a week, I wrestled with this. What could the voice mean? How could I, a child, decide the truth of the universe? Was this the devil laughing at me? Was I God in disguise? The maddest thoughts swirled round my brain.

"Slowly, I began to understand. I understood that I was always free to decide whether the world I was being shown was the real one or whether the world I felt in my heart was the truth. When I really thought about it, the second choice seemed even more frightening than the first. What if Love was the real choice? Would I have to love the guard who had beaten me? Would I have to forgive the apparatus that had killed my parents and hundreds of thousands of others? Would I even have to forgive in some mysterious way God Himself for having allowed these horrors to take place?

"I lived through indescribable torment, much worse, even, than what I had suffered in the camp at the hands of the guards. A twelve-year-old soul, let me tell you, has abysses some of the angels would be scared of.

"Then, one morning, I awoke and knew quite simply what I had to do. I had to choose what was at the bottom of my heart, the fire I felt there when I thought of my mother, or our cat at home, or the flowers and vegetables in our kitchen garden. So I went out into the camp yard, covered with snow, with a gray lowering hope-less sky overhead and, closing my eyes, I screamed with my whole being silently, 'I choose Love! I choose Love! I choose Love!'

"And then it happened. When I opened my eyes, a sun not of this world had come out and was blazing in glory all around me; the snow along the barbed wire glittered like diamonds, and the air was sweet and hard like the skin of a cold apple against my cheek. The guard I hated at that moment came out of another building, smok-ing a cigarette. He didn't see me, but I saw him and—this was the miracle—I felt no fear at all, and no hatred, only a burning pity that scalded my eyes with tears. I did not feel vulnerable as I had feared; the Thing in me that was crying was stronger than anything or any-one I had ever encountered. It or He felt like a calm column of fire that nothing could put out.

"Somehow I survived for another year until release came. Whenever I could, I would gaze at the way the ordinary light changed on the ground, along the wires, on the roofs of the huts and the crematoria. I knew now Whose light it was a reflection of. The fire in my chest did not leave. It has never left. I have tried to live and breathe and act from it and from its laws.

The sun was setting in a riot of rich red light in the sky, setting the gold dome of the Temple Mount alight. Isaiah took both my hands in both of his.

"I doubt if we will meet again. You are leaving tomorrow, and I am in the last stages of cancer. I am not afraid. The Glory is here always. I see it with open eyes, every day; I am not unique; there are thousands of us, maybe millions, all over the world, of all kinds, classes, sexes, and religions. The Glory gave me life and It is giving me now my death; but through another death long ago It gave me a Life beyond all dying. And it is into that Life that I am going.

"You have a long journey ahead of you. I have a feeling it will be a difficult and wonderful one. Remember always three things— forgive me for being so 'rabbinical,' and in such a shirt and wearing such sneakers—but write these down in that black notebook of yours. (And you don't have to worry about your ideas being stolen, not even the seraphim could read *your* writing.)

"Pain can be terrible beyond any human description, but it is transient; Bliss is eternal.

"Evil is real, but only in its dimension that includes this world; the Glory shines forever here and everywhere in a way evil cannot stain or defeat.

"Horror has its day, or year, or decade, or century; the Sun of Love has never, and will never, set.

"And here's a fourth: *Whatever* you have to go through to come to know this beyond any shadow of a doubt is worth it.

"And now I am going to buy you a dinner of the best sheesh kebabs in Jerusalem in a little place off the Via Dolorosa."

"I thought you only ate kosher food!"

"Are you mad? Arab cooking is wonderful. One way to start making peace with your neighbor is to eat his food. Don't they teach you anything in that university of yours?"

Prologue

———

Paris, 1992. I am forty, living in a gussied-up maid's flat in the seventh arrondissement, working in the mornings on English re-creations of the Persian mystic Rumi, and, in the afternoons, on a book of conversations about him with Eva de Vitray Meyerovitch, Europe's leading Rumi translator and scholar; she had become a friend.

Ten years before I had found Eva's French translations of a thousand of Rumi's Odes in a second-hand bookstore in Saint Germain. I still remember sitting by the Seine reading them, shattered and astonished, my chest thumping. When I met her in 1991, at lunch in the country with mutual friends, I warmed to her—immediately. She was in her early eighties, tiny, plump, moon-faced, with slanting melancholic eyes, a feisty, sometimes savage, wit, and an old-world way of talking in perfect soaring sentences, rich with her learning in Arabic, Persian, Latin, Greek and all the major European languages. She moved me with her paradoxical mixture of French grande-dame hauteur and girlishness, of extreme, even contemptuous, authority and vulnerability of heart that often brought a catch into her voice, especially when she was talking about the one she called "our Master."

The day after we met, Eva rang me. I heard her precise voice pouring down the phone, "It was marvelous yesterday! Our Master has brought us together! We are two pearls on the same string, you and I! With you I don't have to edit myself! I'm too old to edit myself! We have the same culture! I saw from the fire in your eyes that our Master is for you as he is for me, the Light of my life, my journey, my soul! I have decided we must do a book together! We must do it soon, because I am about to die! Let's start today!"

In fact, we started the next afternoon. Every afternoon after lunch, for five months, I would race across Saint Germain and the Luxembourg Gardens to the fifth-floor poky, dingy flat where Eva lived that always smelled of old books and vegetable soup, and which had the kind of antiquated kitchen straight out of a nineteen-thirties French film that makes you fear for your hostess's life every time she gets up to make a cup of tea. There Eva and I would sit on her sagging gray-brown sofa, strewn with yellowing manuscripts, with a microphone between us, and talk and talk; sometimes she would tell stories of her first researches into Rumi, when no one had ever heard of him; sometimes she would recite one of Rumi's Odes in Persian, and translate it word for word and pour out for hours all her love and learning and inner knowledge of what she called "the Path of Fire," the Path of Love.

She was always precise, scholarly, obsessed with dates and textual accuracy; sometimes, though, another Eva would surface, the Eva who, although she would never claim to be a mystic, had had what she called, somewhat dramatically, her "hours of lightning" and longed more than anything to come into the Divine awareness of the being she had worked on and lived with for so many years. "So you think He will be waiting for me when I die?" she would ask often, not expecting an answer. After a while, we both realized that we would never be able to finish a book; we went on recording but, as Eva said, "Something more important and wonderful than a book is happening between us." She was handing me, naturally and with an aristocratic abandon, the jewels of a lifetime's search; I was giving her the ardor and inquiry of my own journey and love of Rumi.

One particular afternoon I shall always remember as the most profound hour of our friendship. I was late for our daily appointment; it had been raining. Eva met me at the door, her hair unraveled from its usual tight gray bun, tears racing down her face. This was so unlike her usual slightly sardonic self that I was momentarily speechless. Staring wild-eyedly at me, she broke into sobs; I took her hands and steered her gently onto her sofa in her living room.

"Eva, what on earth is wrong?" I asked, sitting down close to her.

"Don't you know? It's November 29th."

My mind went blank.

She became impatient and started to shout. "November 29th, 1244, is the day Shams is supposed to have met Rumi, the day when Rumi met his Beloved and his killer, the day when he met the one who would bring him death and resurrection."

I had never heard her speak in such a way. The sobs grew louder. Her sobs grew so violent I was scared she'd choke herself.

"Shouldn't we be celebrating?" I suggested, trying to calm her down. "Shouldn't we dance and sing? The mystical love story of Rumi and Shams has lit up the whole world."

"I'm not crying for us, you idiot." She was almost shrieking. "I'm crying for him. I'm crying for Rumi! I'm crying for how much he had to suffer! Don't you see, don't you understand? Everything we have been given by our Master—all the glory of his Odes, his 'Mathnawi,' his table talk, of the life he lived as an enlightened being for thirty years—all of this comes to us perfumed by a terrible death, an agony and grief that would have killed you or I. I have Christian friends who on Good Friday weep for what Jesus had to suffer to leave us all that He left; well, today is the day I always remember the sacrifice that our Master made."

It was both more than a little absurd and extremely moving— seeing, behind the facade of her fifty years of scholarship, the wild, personal, protective love she still had for Rumi.

"I know that one day I will understand. Perhaps he will tell me himself when I see him, and it won't be long now. But why did Shams and their love have to be so fierce and terrible? Why did

Shams have to meet so much jealousy from Rumi's disciples? Why did Shams have to be murdered after only three years of their being together, and almost certainly by Rumi's oldest son? And why did Rumi then have to go mad with grief, to be wrecked and ruined, before there could erupt from him the burning fountain of Glory that is his work? Why is God so terrifying? Why must there always be Gethsemane and the Cross before there can be Resurrection! I'm eighty-one, I've seen two world wars, Dachau, Hiroshima, Pol Pot, and now Nature burning to death. What does all this horror mean? What will it birth? There are days when all I want to do is beat against these walls and howl with rage. Don't try and give me any answers. I know all the answers. Just sit with me."

An early Beatles song, "She loves you, yeah, yeah, yeah," floated up from the student flat below and we both laughed. Eva, quieter now, wiping her eyes, turned to me and began:

"I want to tell you about the afternoon I first arrived in the city where Rumi spent most of his life—Konya, in southern Turkey. It was twenty-five years ago, and Konya was a quiet, ancient, civilized place: wandering around it you could almost believe you might meet Shams and Rumi or at least glimpse them, sitting by candlelight in an upstairs window, deep in love. All that has gone now, of course, like almost everything else sacred and beautiful.

"That afternoon, I arrived about four, went immediately to my hotel, left my bags, and asked directions to go immediately to visit Rumi's tomb. I had wanted to kneel and pray to him there for fifteen years. As I walked toward the museum where it is, down the main street of Konya, I seemed to enter a dream state. Street noises reached me, yes, but as if from a distance; the air seemed to be shining. I thought to myself, 'Watch out! What will they say back at the university if you return a little weird in the head!' As I approached the tomb, the whole sky seemed to split open in the cries of the muezzin for afternoon prayers; everything in me and around me rang with that wild sound. Blessing after blessing seemed to be raining down on me from the ringing sky and something in my chest opened and I felt a pain like a spear going through my heart.

"I found my way to the tomb. You have never been, I know, but you have seen pictures, no? It is large, fifteen or twenty feet long, indescribably magnificent; that evening it was hung with gold brocade, emblazoned with verses from the Koran, and ringed by hundreds of lamps that made the gold brocade melt and swim before my eyes. I stood by the tomb, and the strangest thing happened. I started to laugh wildly. Thank God there was no one else around. I laughed so hard I doubled up."

"What on earth made you laugh like that?"

"Here I was coming to pray to our Master at his tomb as if he was dead, and yet—" Eva paused, groping for words—"and yet, as I stood there, I felt that the tomb was a volcano erupting again and again covering me with the boiling lava of a Fire and a Presence that had never died, never been born, and would never die. I wanted to laugh and shout and dance.

"I went back to the hotel still in ecstasy and couldn't eat dinner and retired early. I prayed to Mevlana, and then opened my copy of the Odes at these lines:

'My heart is a vast tablet of light;
An ocean of agony drowned it again and again.
It has become a warrior, after being martyred a hundred
    times;
I venerate each one of the waves of this ocean;
I'm at once the feast and the disemboweled victim.'

"The pain in my chest that had started with the cries of the muezzin now became almost intolerable. I cannot explain what happened next and I have never before talked about it to anyone. Paris isn't exactly made for mystic confessions, is it?"

She paused for a moment, looking frightened.

I squeezed her hand. "Please go on, Eva."

She stood up and started to pace around the room.

"What happened after I read the lines I told you was that I entered into the pain of Rumi's heart. That is the only way I can say it. Suddenly, I was made to feel without any mask as much as I could stand of the agony that he had endured after Shams died. I had been given the Glory first, I see now, so I would be strong enough to stand this. It was greater than anything I had ever felt or imagined feeling. I have suffered in my life. My life has been hard. But what I felt on that night and throughout the night was a kind of pain I didn't know existed. I know now what Teresa of Avila means when she writes in *The Interior Castle* that 'there is a spiritual pain so great that when it possesses you, you would not mind if your body was cut to pieces.'

"Even as I was wriggling on my bed like a stabbed animal, I knew that I was being given a gift; I was tasting just a tiny fraction of what my Beloved had to go through to be changed into the being he became, the volcano of Divine Love whose blessing had poured eternal gold over me in the afternoon. I had spent years translating his Odes; now the Divine was giving me a glimpse of the furnace the Odes had been forged in.

"I wish I could tell you that the experience transfigured me and that I spent the rest of those two first weeks in Konya walking around in bliss, having conversations with the risen Rumi in my head. That is not true. In fact, what I experienced that night made me frightened and furious, more furious than I knew I could be. As dawn came, I found myself screaming at God (thank God, the room had thick walls and heavy Turkish carpets). Words, filthy words, poured out of my mouth; I didn't know I could curse like that. I hated God for torturing Rumi so. How could Love really be Love and ask and demand so much so horribly?

"I was so angry I stayed in my room for two days, eating very little. There were many times I feared I would lose my mind. At last I had the presence of spirit to start to pray; I have never prayed like I did then. I begged to be helped to understand why Rumi's annihilation had been necessary, why annihilation itself is necessary on the Path of Fire. The Sufis call this stage 'fana,' you know. Al-Hallaj wrote, 'Take away the me so only You remain.' 'Fana' is when the 'me' is utterly unraveled, burnt down to its roots, so the 'You' of God can take over the whole being and use all the operations of the ego and senses as its expressions. Oh, I know the theory, you see! You should hear the lectures I give on 'fana' in Ibn Arabi and Al-Hallaj and Lahiji! They are miracles of precision and textual corroboration! You can have read all the texts, Andrew, and know the theory, but when you begin to taste the awfulness of the reality, all of your learning becomes dust and ashes in a whirlwind.

"I prayed to be helped to understand. No peace came. I prayed for twelve days, in my room, at Rumi's tomb. Nothing. Each day I understood less. I couldn't even read our Master; the letters would swim before me and become meaningless. Then, on the last full afternoon of my visit, I met someone who helped me more than anyone has helped me in my life, who gave me, gently, a few simple keys to help me understand the necessity of annihilation. I still wrestle with that necessity as you saw when you came in, but I think that I know the truth, even if I cannot wholly accept it. One part of me accepts it; the other, you know now, still screams in the night."

Eva went to the window, opened it, breathed in deeply the

freezing rain-wet air. Turning, she said, "Never forget what I am about to tell you. If you come to 'fana' and enter the dark hurricane, it will help you. It will not save you—only you and the Divine Grace can do that—but it will help you on those many, many days when nothing will make sense and your whole being will be a cry.

"I had gone, worn out and miserable, to say goodbye to Rumi at his tomb. I was still desperate, too—how would I return to Paris after what I had experienced? I was in pieces, like a pot thrown against a wall. I talked to our Master then as I had never talked to him inwardly before. I was direct and abrupt. I remember, I said, 'You have plunged me into this chaos; it's your fault; you have to do something about it now.'

"I came out into the late afternoon air and sat down by one of the fountains in the museum's courtyard. I noticed an ancient, wizened, old Turkish gentleman sitting by my side with a face like a big-eared elf. He was dapper, with brilliant black shoes, a pin-striped suit with a red tie, and smelled heavily of rosewater cologne. Normally I wouldn't have spoken to him. For no reason I can think of, I turned to him and started to tell him everything that had happened to me. It all tumbled out, just as I have told it to you. At the end I looked at him and asked him, 'Are you a Sufi?'

"He replied, gazing at me directly, 'One day I hope and pray I may be.'

"I noticed for the first time how beautiful his deep rich brown eyes were. He took my hand and began to talk quietly and gently as if to his own daughter. This is what he told me:

" 'To accept that Divine Love will ask us in the end to die into it—that is, for everyone, even the greatest of saints, the hardest of all things on the path. Even Jesus in Gethsemane begged, "Take this cup from me." Even Jesus, Who had seen God, heard God, healed with the power of God, been seen transfigured by His disciples on Mount Thabor. Even Jesus wept tears of blood at what had to be. So you should not be surprised at your rage or your fear. They are natural. They are inevitable. They are part of the process.

"'Divine Love begins by seducing you, by kissing you on the inside of your heart. That is how it hooks you. Then it feeds you with ecstasy and vision and revelation, drawing you deeper and deeper into a devouring longing to be one with it. When your longing is great enough and you are surrendered enough to it, Love changes into a Black Lion and tears you limb from limb. Then when you have been scattered to the four quarters of the universe and not a scrap of "you" remains and darkness reigns, the Lion turns golden and roars and "you" are reassembled, resurrected, and your whole being shines with the Glory of the Lion's own Light, the light of the Sun.

"'All this is natural and logical in the dimension of Divine Nature and Divine Logic. You cannot begin to understand it through human reason or through the intellect or even through contemplation; you can only begin to understand it through Love. Love itself will teach you what you need. But to be able to learn at all, you will have to have made yourself open through many years of prayer, meditation, and service of all living things and beings.'

"He smiled and pointed to a rosebush near us with one full luscious red rose on it.

"'The whole meaning of the planting of that bush in the first place was to obtain that open fragrant rose shedding its perfume in all directions. The whole meaning of the Creation is to birth beings like Rumi and Jesus, the full, open, Divine human roses, who inebriate us all with the fragrance of Divine passion. Isn't it written in the Koran, "I was a hidden treasure and I wanted to be known; that is why I created the world." Those who know "the hidden treasure" of their innate divinity are those who have opened completely in the Sun of Divine Love. To birth that opening is the secret meaning of the Creation, its goal, its justification.

"'Look at that fragrant rose, open so abandonedly, giving itself with such purity and truth to us! Just imagine what has to happen before that bush can produce that rose! First, a clipping must be taken from a healthy original rosebush and planted in good earth; then, it must endure living underground and pushing its way upward in the dark; after that, when it finds the sun it has been dreaming of and longing for, it has to protect itself against predators, grow thorns, and struggle to create a solid stem; and after that, it has to fling out from its secret sun-kissed depths such energy and passion that from that stem branches start to grow, branches on which the roses it dreams of making begin, slowly, to appear as bigger and bigger buds. All this takes a long time, constant effort, focused passion, season in, season out. Everything has to follow natural order and logic; you cannot go from a clipping to a branch thick with buds directly. All the different stages have to be honored one by one.

"'Imagine now that you and I had been sitting here a week ago. What would we have seen where that full rose now is? We would have seen a big, juicy, still-enclosed bud. What has to happen before the bud can become a rose?'

"I was at last beginning to understand. 'The Sun has to break it open.'

"'Yes,' he whispered. 'The Sun has to train its fire on it and break it open so everything that has been carefully, over many stages, enfolded within the bud can now be unfolded for everyone and so that the perfume the bud is keeping secretly hidden within itself can be given now to everyone who wants it.'

"His rapt calm voice had spread a carpet of peace over my mind. 'You see, my child,' he continued, 'God as the Sun and the gardener knows what He is doing and what must be done. Before Rumi met Shams he had already, through prayer and study and inner aspiration, grown a solid stem; falling in love with Shams drove him to fling out branches; the ecstasies and agonies and revelations that loving Shams brought him grew the buds along those branches, buds juicy with knowledge and hidden Divine fragrance. Then the moment came when all of those buds had to be broken open otherwise all the long alchemy of the growth of the Rose of Glory would have been wasted. Shams was killed; what had been "Rumi" was destroyed by grief. A being both "Shams" and "Rumi" and neither was born. Now, at last, all the buds could break open. The entire world is still reeling in their perfume.

"'Yes, this is a terrible alchemy. But it is natural in Divine Nature; the shattering of the bud is the condition of the flaring open of the rose. How can the secret dream of the rosebush and the gardener who planted it be realized if that does not happen?'

"We sat silently and then, still in pain, I said harshly, 'What you have told me is fascinating, but there is something too pretty about it all.'

"My wizened, shining-eyed elf laughed out loud. 'Pretty? Have you asked a bud how it feels when it is shattered open? But I know what you mean. Let me try again. All that I can offer you anyway is analogies, images. I think I know how much what I am stammering to convey to you means to you. I think I know that it is a matter— how shall we put it—of life and death.'

"'Yes it is.' I had not admitted that to myself and my nakedness shocked me.

"'You already know enough,' my new friend went on, 'to know

that fana, or annihilation, the Dark Night, is the ultimate mystery in this life. Mevlana has taken you to the time when you can start to see the Black Lion prowling in the distance and hear perhaps some of his growls in the night. That is already a blessing. Most people die without even suspecting that there is such a thing as a dying in life that makes you eternal.'

"'Have you been through this dying?'

"'Yes,' he laughed gaily like a child. 'Yes, thank Allah. And I am only a baby in the new life. Eighty-five years old and a baby. It's silly, but it's true. Blame Rumi! It is all his fault! . . . And now, I'm going to try once again and share with you what Rumi has taught me, and this time I will ask your forgiveness in advance, now that I know how hard you are to enchant.

"'Another way of coming to contemplate the mystery of anni-hilation is to see it as the pangs of a great childbirth. I will explain this slowly.'

"He took my hands in his and patted them tenderly.

"'Ten years ago, when my time came to be killed by the Lion, I, too, came every day to pray at this tomb and I was just as lost, angry, and desperate as you. If you are not lost, angry, and desperate the Death cannot happen. But there is always protection—you will find this out, perhaps you are finding this out already—and there is always direct guidance for anyone who asks for it. This I know as I know the name of the man who made these black shoes for me. Perhaps the greatest paradox of all the paradoxes that dance around "fana" is that while you imagine you are at your furthest from God, you are actually so close that you are blinded by His Glory and think it night. Stare into the sun, after all, and your eyes will in the end see only dark; they cannot stand too much Light. What the Darkness really is is the dawning of a Light too immense for your yet-untransformed senses to register.

" 'But it isn't metaphysical paradoxes that I want to share with you; I want to tell you of what happened to me ten years ago after I had been praying to Rumi for guidance for a long time. My wife sent me out to buy some bread at about five o'clock one evening. I took the long way round to the bakers, stopping off here at the tomb. I came out, and when I walked out of the front door I saw a young woman lying on the pavement and screaming horrible screams that tore the air and made my blood curdle. I immediately imagined the worst; she must have been raped or stabbed. I ran to her, held her up, and started to look for some telltale wound or bruise. She was too far gone to understand anything I was saying to her, and her screams got worse and I got more desperate. Suddenly, I noticed that she had spread her legs, and then all of a sudden it struck me: she is screaming because she is giving birth! She wasn't dying at all, she was having a baby! I ran and found an old woman who knew how to deliver children, and the child, a healthy boy, was saved. The woman had been shopping when labor pangs started and had made her way in a hallucination of pain to the entrance of Rumi's tomb, thinking that there she would be safe and find help.

" 'The screams of the self being torn apart in annihilation, the screams that you hear in Rumi's poetry as Shams rends his false self limb from limb, the screams of Rumi's madness—all these are not the howls of death but of birth. And Rumi must somewhere have known that; he must have known that what was killing him was also helping him to give birth to the New One in him, the Divine Child.

" 'Remember what he said in his table talk:

" ' " This body is like Mary. Everyone of us has a Jesus within him, waiting to be born. If pain appears to be our midwife, our Divine Child will be born. If not, our inner Jesus will return to the Origin by the same secret way He came, and we will be deprived of His mystic joy and splendor."

"'Annihilation, then, is the dark birth canal the inner Jesus has to pass completely through to be born in the Sun. If you can hold to that knowledge and have faith in its reality, through everything, then the Rose of Glory will be opened in you.'"

Eva finished, stood up, and poured us two stiff brandies. We sat in silence a long time. Then she asked me, "Where do you think you are on the Path?"

I tried to answer her as precisely as I could. "I have been through many minor deaths. Each of the stages of the Path, after all, demands a death which is a metamorphosis. What I wrote about in my book *Hidden Journey* was the passage through the first purification on the journey—what the Christian mystics call, I think, 'the Night of the Senses'; when the senses one by one are transformed so that the Divine Light can come up in consciousness and start to use them for its own purposes. This Light has come up; I see it normally; with it has come energy, vision, a totally different level of longing for God. It is strange that we are having this conversation today, because last week I read for the first time the Ode of Rumi that begins:

'You've endured many terrible griefs!
But you're still under a veil
Because Dying to yourself
is the fundamental principle!
And you haven't adhered to it
Your suffering cannot end
Before this death is complete
You cannot reach the roof
Before climbing up the whole ladder.'

"These lines pierced me like so many swords and I saw just how far I still have to travel."

"And did you pray for 'fana'?"

"No," I said. "I didn't dare."

Eva laughed drily. "I don't blame you. I have been too proud, too rational, even with everything I have been given, to risk 'completing my death.'"

She got up unsteadily, went into her bedroom, and came back with an open red rose. We stood together and drank in its rich heady perfume.

"You know what the Turkish Sufis like to say? 'Isn't God amazing?' Remember today and this rose and the old Turkish man when your time comes. I have a feeling it will. Something in you has fallen in love beyond reason with the Beloved and the 'something' will drag you beyond yourself in the end."

She stroked my cheek for the first and last time.

"There are two questions I have," I asked unsteadily. "How do you know when your Divine Child has been born?"

"I asked the old man that. He said, 'You know when you no longer hate or fear anyone or anything, and when your deepest desire is to serve all beings with everything you have forever.' Your second question?"

"What was the old man's name?"

"I thought you might ask me that. I asked him, too, when the time came for us to part. I asked him also for his address so we could stay in touch. He looked amused. 'My dear,' he said, 'we have been talking beyond names and addresses. I have nothing else to give you than what I have given you. Seeing each other again would only ruin the perfection of this meeting.' Then he turned abruptly and walked, surprisingly fast, off into the night of Konya. Sometimes I have thought . . . no, this is too crazy . . ."

"Say it." We were both smiling now.

"That it might have been . . . No I am *not* going to say it. I have already said a great deal too much."

In many ways, the third conversation, whose gift of wisdom was to guide and steady me, was the most significant; in it I learned of the Dark Night from someone who had lived it consciously, as the most decisive part of the long and passionate search for God. Only two weeks after my talk with Eva, I found myself sitting with the man whom I came to think of as my deepest spiritual friend and father-in-God—Father Bede Griffiths, an eighty-six-year-old Benedictine monk and mystic.

An Australian film director had rung me in Paris and asked me to go at short notice to South India to interview Father Bede in his ashram for a television documentary about his life. I said yes at once, dropping whatever else I had to do: I knew and admired Bede's books; I had heard him speak the year before at the Camaldolese monastery in Big Sur, and he had made an indelible impression on me by his gaunt, white-haired, austerely radiant presence and by the reverent but no-nonsense precision with which he spoke of the mystical life. And now here I was—sitting with Bede alone in his small bare hut after our first day's interviews—with the sounds of the tropical south Indian night whirring and clicking around us, and its perfume of wind and moist grass scenting the air.

Bede lay back in his orange robe on his bed, gazed piercingly but tenderly at me. There was an almost full moon, and thick silver light poured through the open door.

"I am happy you have come," he said softly. "I feel we are already friends and that you understand what I have lived. I feel we have come together now for a purpose. I do not have much time left. I feel well, but I *am* eighty-six, after all." A bright, almost mischievous smile lit up his face. "I feel only eleven or twelve, of course, but I know that is an illusion."

Bede had the authority, even grandeur, of a sage but also the sweet artlessness of a child. As I gazed at him, I drank in the grace of being with him, here, in India, in the place he had lived and prayed for almost forty years.

"What are you reading these days?" he asked.

It was such a deliciously "English" question that I chuckled. Bede had, after all, like me, been educated at Oxford, at Magdalen College. Englishness was another force that drew us together.

"I'm reading St. John of the Cross's *The Dark Night of the Soul*," I replied and explained to him how absorbed I had recently become by the subject. I told him, in detail, about my conversation with Eva, about the old Turk and his remarks.

When I finished, Bede sat up straight, leaned forward, cupped his face in his hands, and remained silent for a long time, as if listening to something behind my words.

Then he began to speak, in his clear, serenely precise, and cadenced voice. "*The Dark Night of the Soul* is the supreme mystery of the Path and the true passage into Christ-consciousness. Jesus lived, you see, the entire Path out for us, both externally and internally. All of those who wish to follow Him will have to go through what He did—Gethsemane and the Cross and the Descent into Hell and the Resurrection. What I am telling you is not new. All the great lovers of Christ have known this. St. Francis knew this; Teresa of Avilá knew this; and St. John of the Cross, of course, knew it with a wonderful precision. To come into the freedom and deathless joy of the Christ-consciousness you have, as St. John makes clear, to go through two deaths, in fact, two 'nights': the first Night is that of the senses, which enables you to ascend from ordinary 'psychic' consciousness into what modern transpersonal philosophers call 'subtle consciousness'—the consciousness open to Divine knowledge and inspiration. When I read *Hidden Journey* I realized that you had lived through this first Night; that is what your book is describing.

"What happens in this first Night of the senses is, as you know, that each of the senses is purified one by one so that they can all become instruments of Divine awareness and Divine Love and no longer the servants of the false self. But—and this is what St. John of the Cross makes clear—the old false self still survives in a subtle form. Amazing experiences now happen to it, all kinds of visions and illuminations, but it still remains as the 'witness' of these experiences and as their 'focus.' In other words, you still think you are Andrew although you know by now that you are one in your depths with the Divine Light and the Divine consciousness.

"The logic of the transformation into the Christ demands that another and far more drastic death now takes place—the death of this false belief in personality itself and this focus, however subtle, on the still-'existent' false self. This is the Death of the Dark Night of the Soul. St. John of the Cross says that while the first Night cuts off various branches of the tree, the second pulls the whole thing up by the roots, systematically, and with terrible precision.

"What the Dark Night of the Soul makes possible, in fact, is the transition from 'subtle' consciousness, where the false self is still a subtle focus, to 'causal' consciousness, where the Cosmic Christ is known and felt as the 'cause' or 'experiencer' of all things and events. This is the stage which opens onto the Resurrection and Resurrection-consciousness; it is this awareness that Saint Francis lived in at the end of his life and Teresa of Avilá describes in the seventh mansion of the *Interior Castle* and that Saint John of the Cross celebrates in *The Living Flame of Love,* and it is this consciousness that all of us who love the Christ must aspire to realize here on earth while we are in the body. Jesus had to abandon and leave behind everything He thought He knew or believed in, even His understanding of who God was—even His most precious mystical awakenings—in order for Him to discover and become the One beyond all form and name and understanding, and so do we. Just as He did, we have to undergo the crucifixion of everything we believe we are and know before we can come into the radiance of the Resurrection. This is the essential mystical process that Christ came to live out, embrace, and reveal to all of us, and it is because the churches have lost its secrets that they are mostly now so narrow and soulless, and largely impotent to birth the living Christ-consciousness."

He paused and began again, more softly this time, his voice hushed as if by the grandeur of what it was recounting. "I don't just want to talk theoretically to you, Andrew. Please listen with your heart because I have the feeling you will one day come to need what I say. I shall pray for that, in fact."

I shivered slightly at his words and waited, watching his hands folded in his lap.

"Something absolutely new has been taking place within me these last three years through the grace of God," he began. "In my early eighties, I have made more profound inner progress than during the whole of my life. I hardly recognize myself as the person I was before.

"On January 25, 1990, I was sitting meditating on the veranda of this hut as I usually do at six o'clock; suddenly, with no warning, a tremendous force came and hit me on the head. It seemed like a kind of sledge hammer. Everything went fuzzy. Then this force dragged me out of my chair. It was coming from the left and pulling me out of my chair. It was terrifying. I don't know how, but I managed to crawl on top of the bed. One of the monks came and found me about an hour afterwards.

"For the next week, they tell me, I didn't say a word. I don't know what happened during that week. I was immersed in a vast darkness. Slowly, very slowly, I started to come round.

"Then on February 25, exactly a month later, I had another death experience. I had about five or six altogether in those first two months, but this was the most significant. I woke up at about two o'clock at night and felt that my time had come to die and that Christ was coming for me. I began to pray to the Virgin and the angels and waited for death. Nothing happened. Then after an hour or two, one of the monks came in and massaged me, and I started to get back to normal.

"I had a little breakfast but was still feeling restless, not knowing at all what was happening. Then quite suddenly, I seemed to hear a voice inside me. Its message was totally unexpected but very clear, 'Surrender to the Mother.' Somehow I *did* surrender to Her. Quite suddenly, I was overwhelmed completely by an experience of extreme love. Waves of blazing love flowed over me and into me. Judy, my great friend, was watching and so were other friends. I called out to Judy, 'I'm being overwhelmed by love.'

"It was the most extraordinary experience of my life. Looking back now, I can see that it was a breakthrough to the feminine. It had to be violent; I had to be hit, as it were, and then immersed in fear, bewilderment, and darkness because I had been so masculine and patriarchal and so continually left brain. I loved India from the moment I arrived here in 1955, loved the sensuousness of the people, their animal grace, the way in which in the villages every hill and river and field is sacred; I had recognized with my mind how in India the feminine is adored as sacred, and I had been moved by this but it had never truly permeated me, never really transmuted the depths of my being. Now India and the Mother had decided to intervene; the right brain—the feminine, the earth power, the glory of Creation—came and hit me.

"It is a very strange thing, Andrew, but when I thought of surrendering to the Mother I naturally of course thought of Mary—I often say the Hail Mary—but it was Mary as the Black Madonna that came into my mind. For me the Black Madonna is the Mother of the earth as well as heaven, of the body as well as the soul, the Mother of the subconscious, the hidden, of all those powers that the 'masculine' mind represses, the Mother of the sacred darkness. In Her the Western Christian vision of the Divine Mother and the Eastern one merge and meet; you can think of Her as both Mary and Kali, both preserver and destroyer. From that time on, I have turned to Her again and again: invoking Her strength and grace, I find, makes the 'birth' go so much faster and more cleanly. None of this knowledge was accessible to me before the strokes. She has changed me."

His face seemed almost to shine in the darkness.

"How exactly?" I asked.

Bede smiled at my boldness. "It is hard to put these things into words, Andrew, but I know you really want to know, and so I'll try." He turned and gazed directly into my eyes. "After the stroke, I could no longer think in the old way; my left brain and the whole rational system was knocked down. At first I panicked. It was as if everything I had relied on all my life was being taken away. There were many, many moments of terror in which I felt I had been abandoned. St. John of the Cross speaks of this. All those who go into the Dark Night to have their entire being broken down, dissolved, and remade necessarily feel this way. Then, very slowly, I realized that nothing had been destroyed. It was just that the stroke had opened up—like a can opener—my right brain, the intuitive in me. What I was now living was a far deeper and richer experience of reality than I had ever had; it was an experience of what in India is called 'advaita'; non-duality. The divisions between things started to melt away, and everything was flowing naturally into everything else. My left brain was still there, but now it was the servant of this amazing experience, its interpreter, and not the force that prevented it happening.

"During the days after the experience of the stroke I felt extremely close to the death of Christ. I realized in the core of myself that what happened to Him on the Cross was that through intense psychological and physical suffering He came to the point where He, too, had to lose everything He had ever understood of God. Facing the darkness of death, He had to abandon his mind. Then He entered into the darkness beyond the mind, that is the darkness of Love.

"One of the greatest of all the Christian mystics, Saint Gregory of Nyssa, said that beyond the purgative and illuminative way, which is the way of Light, there is the unitive way, the way he said 'of love in the darkness.' Jesus went through the darkness into total Love. He became total Love because He surrendered everything. His whole body and His whole soul. Both were swept up and taken completely and together into the fire of the Spirit. This is the real meaning of Resurrection."

"So," I said haltingly, "the body as well as the soul is transformed. Both are transformed together in the sacred marriage in the darkness."

Bede clapped his hands. "Yes, this is so important. John of the Cross understands everything there is to understand about the psychological and spiritual torment and radical adjustment of the Dark Night; he knows every nuance of fear and abandonment. What he doesn't understand and so few people do, because of the almost complete ignorance of the feminine not only in the Christian traditions but also in the others, is that, in this fire of the sacred darkness, the body is also transformed, the body is also, in a sense, broken down and remade.

"It is as if there are two related Dark Nights—one of the soul, and one of the body. Both soul and body have to be refashioned in the sacred marriage if we are to come into the dimension of Resurrection and know ourselves in every way non-dual both with the Creation and the Transcendent, just as in the ancient Mother mysteries, and just as the Christ did, after the Crucifixion and the Descent into Hell.

"All my life, I imagined that Awakening would come from freedom from the body. This is, after all, the patriarchal way, and I have been celibate. What I realized after the stroke is that the body, too, must be transformed. The body, too, must be possessed and taken over and divinized in all its centers and desires by the spirit. This is an immense, deep, slow, rich work, and since my stroke it has been going on all the time. I feel that at every moment spirit and body are marrying within me more and more intensely. Before the stroke, I lived largely from the head; then after the stroke, I got into the heart. But now the Force of the Mother is going from the heart center down to all the others. The spirit is constantly coming down, first through the center at the top of my head—which the Indians call the 'sahasrara'—then through the heart center to every other center. It has entered my sex region also. I am rediscovering the whole sexual dimension of life at eighty-six, imagine that! A wholly new power of Love has entered my life because of this; I find I love all beings more fully and tenderly because my love is now *in the body* as well as the heart and spirit.

"Although I pray continually to the Mother, the Black Madonna, and know that in this luminous darkness I have been taken into She is gradually taking over, I also know that it is not the Mother alone. Both 'Mother' and 'Father,' the transcendent and the immanent, are integrating themselves within me. They are having their marriage within me, and this inner marriage is slowly birthing a wholly new being."

"The Divine Child."

"Yes," he smiled. "It is strange to be becoming a child in your middle eighties, but the Divine can do anything after all! And God knows the process isn't completely realized. Sometimes it is very bewildering. There are always forces opposed to the marriage taking place that try to interfere with it, but they don't win, and the integration continues. And when I get bewildered and confused, I enter into the silence and the emptiness and I allow the confusion to settle. The order comes out of the chaos again and again. I have all the time to try and *not* control what is happening. I have been so used to controlling myself. But if I do succeed, everything stops."

His humble and guileless precision brought tears to my eyes. Trying to control my voice, I said, "And what are you seeing as this marriage deepens in you?"

"Let me tell you first what I am *not* seeing. I do not see all things and beings as being *One Thing*, undifferentiated. Each thing and each being seem, and are, unique and holy, far more unique and holy than I ever understood before. The universe in this state does not disappear into a kind of radiant Whole. And yet while each thing is differentiated, they are also, obviously and profoundly, related, contained, in fact, in a deeper unity and always part of it. Let me give you an analogy. Mozart, apparently, could conceive a whole symphony in one note. In such a symphony, the notes are not confused; every single note and every sophisticated shift of harmony is there, separately, but still all contained in one moment. This is how I am coming to see the world—everything separate but present together in each moment. In Christian mystical terms you might say I am coming to see and know the truth of the universe as the body of the Cosmic Christ and of myself as a living cell of that body, part of all things, yet not lost in them, but completely 'myself.' We are all one in God and one in each other, but the miracle of this relationship is that we are not dissolved in it; we are found in—or born into—our total being 'as persons within the Person,' as St. Augustine said, or, if you like, as different-shaped flames of the One Fire.

"The great mistake some Indian thinkers—both Hindu and Buddhist—have made is to see this state or union as one in which the Creation and all beings are recognized as dreams or illusions. This is not true. I cannot say it strongly enough: In this state, every being and thing is recognized as sacred. Every bird and slug was holy to St. Francis. That is why when you come to this awareness you wish to devote your entire life to serving and honoring and protecting not only human beings but all of the Creation. Why it is so important that as many people as possible now come to know something of the holiness of this inner marriage is that through it they will be inspired to do and give everything to start saving the environment."

"Because they will know who they are and what the world is at last?"

"Yes," said Bede. "You know that you and everyone else is the Child of the Father-Mother and that the Creation is the Dancing Ground of the Glory. Or, to put it in the terms of the Christian mystical tradition, you know the whole universe as the 'display' of the Trinity. Everything flows out eternally from the Father, the Godhead beyond name and form, the Ground of Being, in the Son, the Word of the Father, the Creation and all its forms, and returns in the Spirit. The Father is pouring himself out eternally in the Son, and Father and Son return to one another, unite with one another eternally, in the embrace of the Holy Spirit. We are enfolded forever in that eternal Love, and we have come here to experience that eternal Love in all of its facets, in our transfigured bodies as well as our illumined souls."

"To be born twice, in fact."

"Yes," Bede said. "And in the second birth we are born as sons and daughters of the Living God."

We sat a long time in silence.

Then he said, "Your generation will be able to go further than mine did. The world's mystical teachings are available to you; you haven't inherited so hysterical a split between mind and body as we did. You will be able to bless your sexuality more completely."

Then he said, "I am going to pray that the Holy Spirit comes to you."

I smiled. For the first and last time, Bede was stern with me. "Do not smile. I mean what I said. And, believe me, when the Spirit descends, it changes everything."

Again, something in his voice made me tremble slightly. I got up to go, and took his hands.

Looking deep into my eyes, Bede said, "One last thing. . . . Remember that to participate in the birth of the Child what you most need is a direct relationship with the Divine. Many of the gurus now are not enlightened beings but black magicians, occult Masters manipulating millions of seekers; what Jesus calls 'wolves in sheep's clothing.' All the serious mystical systems know of the existence of these occult powers, but modern seekers are naive and uninformed and so vulnerable to them. These 'Masters' are not actually helping the Great Birth but working against it, aborting it. I have never had a guru; the power of the Living Christ and the Black Madonna is enough. I am not saying anything for or against your guru, Mother Meera. But remember my words when your time comes."

I turned at the door to smile back at him, but his head was bowed in prayer.

Part II

My Dark Night

[in seven acts]

＊

In this cure God will heal him
of what through his own efforts
he was unable to remedy.

St. John of the Cross

I will lead you by a way you do not
know to the secret chamber of love.

St. John of the Cross

W hat now follows is the story of my Dark Night, of the sacred marriage that took place at its heart, and the birth that resulted from them. My "time" came far sooner than I had expected only a year after my conversation with Eva de Vitray Meyerovitch and Bede Griffiths—and, of course, in a way I could never have imagined.

I have written my story to help, encourage, and inspire all other seekers who come to this ordeal. Everyone will go through the Dark Night in their own way and in terms of their own temperaments and circumstances. But everyone will experience what St. John of the Cross describes in the *Dark Night of the Soul:*

Since the Divine strikes in order to renew the soul and divinize it (by stripping it of the habitual affections and properties of the old self to which the soul is strongly united, attached, and conformed), it so disentangles and dissolves the spiritual substance—absorbing it in profound darkness, that the soul at the sight of its miseries, feels that it is melting away and being undone by a cruel spiritual death. It feels as if it were swallowed by a beast and digested in the dark belly, and it suffers an anguish comparable to Jonah's in the belly of the whale.

In other words, everyone who comes to the Dark Night will suffer similar terrors and desolations, a similar destruction of all of their life-illusions. Had I not already known something about this great transformation, through the conversations I have shared with you, and through my reading, I believe I might have gone mad or killed myself. While insight and information from others cannot much mitigate the necessary anguish of the Dark Night, it can show you why and how and for what purpose that anguish is necessary and so give you the courage to surrender to the logic of the experience.

The telling of my story, too, will show all of you who come to this rite of passage just how much Divine guidance and protection · are offered at every stage of the "disentangling" of the soul. St. John of the Cross only mentions these in passing, but I found that these are showered upon the person willing to undergo the experience, and in ways that, in the end, permanently heal and exalt. And, as you will see, and as Bede Griffiths hinted to me, the body, too, is given a great blessing and revelation: in the night of despair is unfolded its true tantric glory.

It is my belief that many seekers are now being taken to the gates of this death and this birth. The world itself is going through a crucifixion. Toward the end of his life, Bede Griffiths wrote in *The Marriage of East and West*:

Christ had to go through death in order to enter the new world, the world of communion with God. . . . We have to go through death with him. It is the only way. This is the challenge that faces the world today. We are passing out of one world, the world of Western domination, and entering a new age in which the logical, rational mind of Greek philosophy and Roman law, the economic and political order, the science and technology of the West will pass away. . . . Something new is emerging. Nobody knows what forms it is going to take. It is a moment of trauma, of birth.

Mainstream culture and most of the so-called New Age is in denial of this "trauma"—the trauma of a world in environmental, cultural, and spiritual holocaust. But many seekers are also waking up to the extent of the disasters that threaten humanity and Nature. Those who dare to wake up to the worldwide "trauma" wake up also to the necessity to die to all old forms of acting and being, to the necessity of being reborn in a dimension of authentic joy and wisdom and power from which they can be of real help and of real service.

True rebirth can only come about through a death, the death of the Dark Night; there is no other way. We have come to a moment when a great many people will have to die and be reborn in this way if humanity is going to be preserved and Nature saved from unimaginable destruction.

What my story will make clear, I hope, to all those who read it with a critical mind and open heart is that this death is also a revelation and that the Divine threads each of Its agonies with the gold of Its all-transforming grace.

ACT I

Disaster

✴

The opening up of our deepest interior center may be likened to an underground explosion, wherein all parts of our being are sent flying out of control and scattered in every direction.

BERNADETTE ROBERTS, *The Path to No Self*

In a vision that I experienced during the psychic shattering, the image that came to me was of the earthquake that shook Jerusalem at the moment Jesus died and how the curtain of the temple in Jerusalem was torn in two from top to bottom. It was that type of horrendous, even cosmic, type of psychic rendering.

JIM MARION on the Dark Night,
in *Putting on the Mind of Christ*

A s I look back at the series of events that together make up this story, I keep returning to a dream I had in Paris only a week before the day I call "Black Monday," the day when my universe was burned to the ground, December 27, 1993.

I had just finished writing my book on Rumi, *The Way of Passion*, and went to bed feeling relieved that the work was over.

I fell asleep quickly and found myself in a large, fragrant, wooden room, which looked like the square drawing room of a mountain chalet. A voice said, "Go to the window." I opened the wooden shutters and there in front of me, curling from one end of the horizon to another, was a vast, brilliantly blue wave, almost transparent with a cloudless sun-washed sky adazzle above it.

Wonder turned to terror when suddenly the entire wave reared like a vast cobra, turned boiling black. A tremendous storm began in the center of the rearing wave in front of me, and from its threshing core sprang a bolt of the wildest and most brilliant imaginable lightning, so wild and bright that I fainted.

Eryk, my lover and companion of nine months, was sleeping calmly by my side when I awoke. Still shaking, I got up and went to my copy of Rumi's Odes and prayed for a sign from his work to help me interpret the vision I had been given. I opened the book at the following lines:

> One breath of the Lover would be enough to burn away
>   the world,
> To scatter this insignificant universe like grains of sand.
> The whole of the cosmos would become a Sea,
> And sacred terror rubble this Sea to nothing.
> A smoke would come from heaven.
> Out of this smoke, flame would suddenly flash out across
>   heaven.

Shaken, I shut the book and glanced down at my desk, lit up now by the thin gray rays of a Parisian December dawn. I remembered, suddenly, how Bede had said, "I am going to pray that the Holy Spirit comes to you." The week before, two postcards had arrived of the same photograph of Kali that illustrated the exhibition of a friend in Zurich. Kali, killer of illusions, Queen of the thunderbolt that shatters all our beliefs . . .

"With Kali in the house, anything can happen," I'd said to Eryk.

I awoke very early that morning of Monday, December 27th. I was in a small bedroom in Mother Meera's large house in Thalheim, a village in Germany near Frankfurt where she lives. The morning was gray and cold, and fresh snow covered the fields. Eryk was not with me in the house; he was staying in a hotel nearby. I had an appointment to see Meera at eleven o'clock. I would see Eryk afterwards for lunch.

I had met Meera fifteen years before in a white room in Pondicherry, South India, when she was a silent and serene eighteen-year-old and I was twenty-seven. I described the experiences and initiations that arose from that encounter in my book *Hidden Journey,* which made Mother Meera a household name in spiritual circles and brought her thousands of devotees. For the four years since its publication I had been regarded as her spokesman, and I had spoken of her, of what I believed to be her mystic power and universal, unconditional love, all over England and America. I had, in fact, consciously devoted my entire inner life and art to her. In *Hidden Journey,* I had announced Meera as an avatar of the Divine Mother, a Divine being come on earth to guide and save humankind in the worst moment of its history. I felt extreme gratitude to her for having, as I believed then, saved and illumined my whole life, loved her with my whole being, and was prepared to die for her. For Meera I had risked the derision of the academic world I had moved in, the mockery of my fellow writers, the jealousy of fellow disciples furious at the intimacy of my relationship with her.

With what I believed then to be the best part of myself, I thought that no humiliation or suffering or sacrifice was too great if it could help Meera's mission and enable her truth to be born. From the beginning of our relationship, Mother Meera had claimed to be bringing down the Light of the Absolute to effect a massive transformation in the human race; because of the extreme and vivid mystical experiences I had had around her I believed her.

If I was certain of anything that freezing winter morning, I was certain that the rest of my life would be spent in Meera's service. I had just finished two major books dedicated to her—my book on Rumi, *The Way of Passion,* into which I had poured all the revelations my Path of Love with her had opened me, and *Dialogues with a Modern Mystic,* in which I had for the first time tried to outline the changes I believed she as the Mother was trying to effect everywhere. I had also finished a film about my life for British television, *The Making of a Modern Mystic,* which had featured Meera prominently and had, in early November, been shown to considerable interest in England.

A great part of the spring and summer of 1993 had been devoted to arranging a complicated American tour for Meera. It was the details of this event about which I was expecting to be talking to her. I had managed to persuade the California Institute of Integral Studies in San Francisco, where I was teaching, to invite her and to prepare for her an entire festival and conference on the Divine Feminine. From April 1994 onwards for fourteen weeks, I would teach a course on the Divine Feminine in all the world's major religious traditions; in late May, the Institute would host some of America's leading visionaries in a conference devoted to the Divine Mother in different religious traditions and the return of the Sacred Feminine; in mid-June, Meera herself would appear and give her silent darshan both in the Institute and in other places in San Francisco, including Grace Cathedral. Nothing like this visit had ever occurred; it had required a vast amount of time, energy, and passion to prepare; I was grateful that so far everything had gone well. At last, I believed, Meera would come to an audience primed both intellectually and spiritually, to receive the wonder of her power.

I felt, that December morning, that the consummation of years of hard work for Meera was going to be realized soon; I was fresh with the joy of the two latest books I had created for her, delighted that through the television film millions more people would now know her, elated at the prospect of her coming to San Francisco. I felt that fifteen years of love and service were about to be fulfilled.

The other joy that flooded me again and again that morning as I thought of my interview ahead with my Master was gratitude for Eryk. Three days earlier, as he slept opposite me in the train to Germany, I had written, "For nine months now I have had the grace of having this wild, brave, wounded, poignant, beautiful young man in my life, fifteen years younger than me, who has loved me with his whole truth and begun to teach me—against all my fears and evasions, against all the evidence of my past—that I am lovable, desirable, that I can allow myself to be loved. I never believed that I would find my heart's companion in this life, and when he appeared at last in Eryk (and when I was almost forty-one), I had long, long ago given up hope of him arriving. I know this is *her* Grace. After the long mystical journey I took with her out of my body into the world of pure spirit, the Mother is allowing me to return into my body, helped and supported by Eryk and his faith and warmth; the Mother is giving me what I always wanted and hungered for so much—a lover, a friend, a real *companion*. After healing my spirit, she is healing my body. And with so much to do for her still I am overjoyed at having someone with whom to share the struggles ahead."

I felt certain that morning that meeting Eryk was part of Mother Meera's plan for me—and part of the great healing that the Mother was effecting in my life—that I went into the empty darshan room near my bedroom and prayed to her for an hour, deliberately remembering everything I could about my nine-month relationship with Eryk and offering up everything to her, in gratitude.

Everything about our first meeting was magical, and we fell in love fast, almost immediately. Eryk and I met in Paris on March 30th, 1993, near midnight, on the Rue Saint-Benoît opposite the La Hune bookshop, only a few hundred yards from the small, fourth-story flat where I then lived. I had just said goodbye to the English television crew, who made a television film of my life and spiritual journey, and was walking home slowly, relishing the cool, fresh, cloudless spring evening. Suddenly, Eryk walked past me, almost touching me, tall, broad-shouldered, with the fierce and starkly chiseled face of a Nordic angel and the body of a dancer, wearing a black leather jacket, black shirt, and tattered old jeans; we turned to each other at the same moment, and both laughed. I can see him laughing now with his whole body, his molten blue-green eyes wide open in amusement, the wind flinging up his shaggy dark hair in a wild halo. Shaking a little, I went over to him; we shook hands shyly; I plucked up my courage and invited him to come and have a drink with me at home. He was then twenty-five years old: I was nearly forty-one.

In my flat we talked for hours excitedly—about Rilke and Rumi, my passion for India, and about his long, extraordinary friendship with Marlene Dietrich, whom he had never met physically but with whom he had spoken on the telephone frequently during the last five years of her life. I had always loved Dietrich, especially as a singer; cassettes of her rough, burnt voice had accompanied me often on my travels; seeing her just once, on stage, in London in 1975, had been one of the most haunting artistic experiences of my life. Eryk told me later that he hardly ever spoke about Marlene to people. That night, however, he spoke of her with a hilarity, passion, and nostalgia that often brought me to the verge of tears; he told me her oddest and most extravagant stories; imitated her voice; summoned her, in fact, to be with us. Marlene had been a kind of mother to him, and had infused him with her cosmopolitan culture, making him read Dostoevsky and Goethe and, above all, Rilke. Since my early twenties when I first discovered him, Rilke had been the closest of all European poets to my heart, because of his reverence for all life and sacred knowledge of solitude; it was amazing to meet in Eryk someone so much younger who loved Rilke's work as much as I did, and for the same reasons. Where had he come from, this passionate boy-man who knew Marlene Dietrich and could quote "The Panther" and whose electric grace and idiosyncratic turn of phrase were so exotic and startling?

We made love that first night and it was as if our bodies had always known each other, always known how to give each other complete and tender pleasure. Eryk made love with a mixture of abandon and purity of soul that I had never encountered. After our first night, after we had drunk our morning coffees and he had left to fly to Barcelona for the day to sell a Miro drawing for the gallery he was then working for, I wrote: "So much *beauty* last night. I cannot express it any other way. Eryk and I have the same culture, the same odd loves; I *recognize* him and he *recognizes* me and already we have found a way of talking in lightning shorthand that usually only old friends or lovers have."

I had to leave for San Francisco in four days to take up my teaching job at the California Institute of Integral Studies. Eryk and I spent every remaining evening and night together, sleepless, talking and eating and drinking wine and reading poetry and making love. During our second night, Eryk told me that he had been sketching a face obsessively for years, on napkins in cafés, and on the backs of newspapers; it was, he said, looking away, my face.

Next morning, as I sat alone, thinking about him, I happened to look up at the large red, black, and gold guardian angel an American friend had painted for me five years before and which I had placed above my bed; I almost shouted out loud. The angel could have been Eryk's portrait; it had, unmistakably, uncannily, Eryk's face, the sometimes stern fierce purity of his gaze, his high Slav cheekbones. That night I pointed out to Eryk the resemblance he had to the angel. He told me that he had noticed it immediately when he had come into my flat, but said nothing for fear of scaring me. He said, "Two things reassured me the moment I came into your room. The first was that the walls were covered with icons of the Virgin; the second that you had an angel with my eyes and face above your bed." And then he told me that the night we met was the first night he had spent in my quartier—the seventh—for over a year and half; he had only made the long trip from where he lived in Neuilly that evening because he had wanted to find a book on the Marian apparitions. "I didn't find the book, but I came into your room and there she was smiling at me from every corner."

We were both miserable at having to part so soon after we had met, and we wept and held each other. When I reached San Francisco, I rang Eryk immediately and shook with joy, hearing his voice. We rang each other every day. Eryk flooded me with letters written on different colored paper in his large handwriting—letters of a naked tenderness that I had never before received from anyone. All he could think of was how to get the money to join me; he went to work at nights in a garage and sold autographs of Sarah Bernhardt from which he had sworn, he said, never to part. "I want to be with you more than anything," he wrote again and again, "I know you are the love of my life."

In our letters and phone calls we talked incessantly about God and especially the Mother. He told me of his long passion for the Virgin and I told him about my journey with Mother Meera. One of the things that had made me trust him immediately was that he quickly embraced and accepted my faith in Meera. On our first night together, he had pointed to the photograph I had of her above my desk and asked, "Who is that?"

I had taken my courage into my hands and replied, "My Master, Mother Meera, the Divine Mother on earth."

He didn't flinch or drop the subject but said, "You mean she is something like the Virgin come back to earth in a body?"

"Something like that," I said.

"Anything is possible," Eryk said slowly, taking my hand.

Released by his acceptance, I could then tell Eryk about my mystical journey with the Mother. He was not skeptical. "I have had my own strange experiences," he said. "I know that God exists and that death is only a door to another world." The fact that he had listened to what I had lived around Meera with such reverence convinced me that our relationship was direct Grace, *Her* Direct Grace in fact.

After I had been alone without Eryk for a month in San Francisco, the producers of the television film decided they needed a few extra scenes and flew me to London at the end of April for a long weekend. Eryk joined me from Paris, and we spent an ecstatic three days in a slightly sleazy, khaki-walled bed-and-breakfast in Kensington. He started to trust me with some of the details of his early life, and I began to realize how extremely he had suffered.

Although Eryk had been born and brought up in privilege—his childhood was a long nightmare. He had been battered, and repeatedly, savagely, abused by his father from an early age, with the full participation and consent of his mother; the first time he was hospitalized—with a fractured skull—was at five months old; by the time he was four and a half, he had lost the hearing in his right ear. When he was seven, his parents were killed in a car crash in Belgium. Because he had been praying every night for over a year that they would die, Eryk went mute with guilt and did not speak for ten months. After two miserable, lonely years of being shuffled from orphanage to orphanage and "lent out" at weekends to foster families to be used as an unpaid farm hand or domestic, Eryk was sent to Paris to live with a great aunt, already in her seventies. She confined him to the servants' quarters of her chilly flat in Neuilly, never officially adopted him, clothed him in the too-big castoff clothes of her grandson, treated him as an idiot and dead-weight, exploited his hunger to be loved by using him as a slave to do her shopping, drive her to the theater, and correct the manuscripts of her interminable autobiographies, and systematically, with brilliant malice, destroyed all his efforts for years to create or get a job or believe in himself.

Shattered so young, so brutally, and so repeatedly, Eryk never stayed at school long, drank Johnnie Walker at eleven, and by four-teen was an alcoholic and drug addict. Nobody cared whether he lived or died; he would leave Paris for months at a time to wander aimlessly around France. When he returned, his aunt would hardly notice; she never even asked him where he had been. At twenty, his elder brother by two years—who had also been abused by their parents and who could no longer live with the memories of what they had done to himself and Eryk—committed suicide; it was Eryk who found him, and had to clean his flat and him. At twenty-three, Eryk was diagnosed with a rare and potentially fatal form of throat cancer; only several fearful bouts of chemotherapy put his cancer into remission; his body was still weakened and shaken.

When Eryk first unfolded for me in one sitting that May in London the whole account of his life, I could not speak for a long time. It was, in almost every way, the most shocking story I had ever been told. I understood at last how he could be at once so young, and so preternaturally, almost scarily, experienced and astute. Then I asked him how he had survived so much horror.

"Only through the Grace of the Virgin," he said, and added, "When I met you at the end of March, I had already decided to go back to drugs and slowly—or not so slowly—kill myself. What did I have to live for? For me, Paris has always been a sick, evil place and I had long ago lost all hope. But you and our love gave me hope. For the first time in my life."

On the last morning in London, Eryk came and sat, sad-eyed, in his shirt and underpants on our bed. He was looking so serious I thought I had hurt him.

"Are you alright?" I asked him. "Have I done anything?"

He didn't answer. He was holding something tight in his right fist.

Tears glittered in his eyes.

"I want to give you this," he began, "so you will always remember me and remember this weekend and know how much I love you."

"You don't need to give me anything. You've already . . ."

He cut me short. "No," he said, almost harshly. "This is important. I want to give you something that will always protect you."

Eryk went on to tell me, with his eyes half-closed, the story of a relative who saw the Virgin as a small boy in a village in Belgium. "He is a wonderful, simple man, married and with a family now. I hope we will meet him together one day. When he was six or seven, the Virgin appeared in a tree in the schoolyard of his school for forty days each afternoon to four children of which he was one. When I asked him once how she looked, he said, 'Seeing her spoils you for a lifetime. Nothing—not even the most beautiful things or people in the world—comes close to Her beauty. She glowed like the light of summer lightning.'

"At first the four children were not believed by anyone. The local nuns and priests called them liars; their own families were skeptical. One day my friend asked the Virgin sadly when She appeared if She would do a miracle to *prove* to everyone that she was really appearing. It was the middle of a raw, slate-gray Belgian winter; the next afternoon, the straggly hawthorn tree was covered with white blossoms."

Eryk uncurled his clenched fist slowly to reveal a small blue-edge envelope.

"What is it?" I asked.

Eryk smiled and stroked my face and said nothing.

"What is in the envelope?" I asked again.

"Take it and open it very gently."

I took the envelope and, slowly, calmly, pried it open. Inside it was a tiny dry hawthorn petal.

I knelt in the empty *darshan* room in Thalheim and went on thanking Meera for having, as I believed, brought Eryk into my life. I remembered Eryk's tense nervous face as he walked through Customs a month after our meeting in London to spend five weeks with me in California, the five weeks that sealed and deepened our bond; I remembered how strongly kind he had been to me in all the months since then, first in Paris and then in India and New

York, when my back had been out severely and I had hardly been able to do anything, sometimes not even sit without pain. I remembered all my fears that his love could not be real, that I could not be worthy of it, and how he had, again and again, dissolved them. I remembered how, one afternoon, Eryk had walked several miles from Neuilly to my flat on the Left Bank with a large board to put under my mattress so I could sleep at night.

I thanked Meera, too, for what I had seen our love had already given to him—confidence, courage, a joy in his walk, the sense for the first time in his life of belonging to someone. When Eryk came to San Francisco, he started to take photographs and I had immediately seen how gifted he was; now he had already half-completed a superb and original series of photos of Paris cemeteries. On our first night together we had spoken of his friendship with Marlene Dietrich; in the months since then, Eryk (who had never thought of himself as a writer) had written the first—and direct and beautiful—draft of what was later to become his memoir *I Wish You Love: Conversations with Marlene Dietrich*. My love for him had helped him begin his life as a photographer and writer; his love for me had started to heal the loneliness and humiliation of my past, and to cure me of the hatred of my body and fear of sexuality and intimacy that early betrayals and a procession of miserable love affairs throughout my twenties and thirties had bred in me.

I remember that morning as I knelt, speaking to Meera under my breath and smiling, "You knew how lonely I had been for so long and you sent me Eryk, knowing that he would be perfect for me, in his great wild clarity, in the tenderness that his suffering has birthed in him, in the strange mixture he has of youthful beauty and maturity, and, most of all, in the intensity of his devotion to the Mother and so to you."

Eryk and I had visited Thalheim before going to India last August. Eryk had loved Meera at first sight and accepted her. Some of the disciples had tried to humiliate him (talking about him within earshot as "Andrew's gigolo"), but these slights had not disturbed him. I had gone to Meera and asked her if she blessed and accepted my love and she smiled broadly, which I assumed meant acceptance. Then I asked her if Eryk and I could visit her in her house in India, in Andra Pradesh, where she would be at the same time as he and I were in India. Initially she said yes; the next day Adilakshmi, her companion, a tall, big-boned Indian woman in her late forties, had come to me and explained that Eryk was not yet "ripe enough to be in the Mother's presence directly." Even this disappointment had not annoyed him or put him off. When I told him, he smiled, "Well, then, you must go alone." His lack of rancor and possessiveness had only convinced me more that Eryk was the right companion for me; if he was going to be with me doing the Mother's work, he would have to be strong-hearted, able to weather jealous disciples, able to accept the sometimes unfathomable decisions of the Mother herself.

It was five minutes to eleven. I walked up the stairs to Mother Meera's flat, composing myself and saying her mantra as I always did before I came into her presence. Adilakshmi, smiling dazzlingly, in a sun-bright green sari, opened the door. Meera, smaller, slightly round-shouldered, stood behind her in a white sari covered with pink and blue roses. Her huge dark eyes stared at me expressionlessly. She had not done her hair; it hung black and lustrous around her shoulders. "Oh Ma," I said, catching her eye. "Just to see you makes my whole being race with joy. I feel like a small boy."

Meera smiled a little distantly, shaking her hair from her shoulders and taking a long sip from the mug of tea she held in her right hand. "It has been fifteen years now since you came to Mother," Adilakshmi said. "We have total faith in you, Andrew. Total faith."

"Well I hope so," I said. "I have total faith in you."

"And now," Adilakshmi said. "We must go into the front room, sit down, and have a serious talk."

Something in her tone—a slight harshness—made me nervous. "Is anything wrong?" I asked. "Did you dislike the film?" Adilakshmi and Meera had seen the television film of my life, and I was afraid that they might not like some of the rather garish special effects the director had put in, against my wishes.

Meera spoke for the first time: "Oh no, no, the film is good."

I stood awkwardly looking from one of them to the other. There was a silence. Then we went together into Mother Meera's drawing room. Herbert, Meera's husband, a gruff large German in his mid-forties, was whistling from the kitchen.

I sat down facing the large window that looks out across the fields behind her house. I had always loved being in this room with her: It seemed to me like a junk shop of a Divine Child, with its garish gray-pink marble floor, the marzipan Indian representations of Gods on the walls, the various childlike presents from devotees on display everywhere, a red bear with "I love you" in large gold letters on the sofa, crudely but vividly painted flower mandalas grouped in crooked clusters on the walls.

"I am so happy to be with you here again," I said, turning to Meera, who sat facing me with Adilakshmi by her side. She smiled, and gazed down studiedly at her hands. Clearly something very important was going to be communicated to me. Was it to do with the American tour? Was it perhaps that Meera wanted to go to Canada or England as well, as we had often discussed?

Meera started to talk in a soft but inexorable voice, on and on, in Telugu, the language of the state she comes from in India, Andhra Pradesh. It was unusual for her to speak to me in Telugu, as her English had improved in recent years. I supposed that whatever she had to say must be so important that she did not want any ambiguity in our communication. Adilakshmi would translate; her command of English has always been more exact. Meera at last finished and Adilakshmi looked at me.

"Well?" I said, smiling.

Adilakshmi did not return my smile.

"What Ma has to say to you is very delicate," she said, drawing out the word "del-i-cate."

A sudden fear struck me; Ma was sick. Her allergies had worsened into something more serious. She was trying to prepare me and through me the other disciples for a long and perhaps fatal illness. For a long time, I had been secretly obsessed with her health and its fragility.

"Yes, Andrew," Adilakshmi said, her voice deeper and harder this time. "It is time for a very delicate discussion."

"Well, Adilakshmi," I said. "I have known you and Ma for fifteen years. If we can't speak heart-to-heart without fear, who can?" I looked across at Meera. She continued to gaze intently at her hands.

Adilakshmi began, "Mother says she has been receiving letters. Many letters. These letters come from the article written about you last month in *The New York Times* and from the film that was shown in England in November. In these letters, people are writing to the Mother, 'Are you the Mother only of gays? Will my son become gay by following you?'"

I laughed out loud. "Oh my God," I said. "What craziness!"

Neither Meera nor Adilakshmi laughed.

"Obviously," I went on, "Mother is the Mother of everyone. There were only passing references to my homosexuality in the article, and besides, I am frank about myself in *Hidden Journey,* and that has been out for years now. How could anyone believe that the Mother is only the mother of gays!"

I started to laugh again. Obviously the thought was ridiculous.

"I don't think you are understanding," Adilakshmi was saying. "There are letters, *many* letters."

"Can I see them, Adilakshmi? Perhaps I would see their seriousness more clearly if I could read them myself."

"You don't believe me?"

"Of course I believe you."

"I haven't got time to go and get the letters now," Adilakshmi almost barked. "What I am meaning to say is this. Mother is giving you a choice."

Everything was getting steadily more bewildering.

"A choice, Adilakshmi?"

"Yes. The time has come. You have a choice. The Mother has just said to me, 'Tell Andrew that he has a choice. He can either become celibate or he can get married.'"

My mind went blank. I asked Adilakshmi to repeat what she had said.

"You have a choice," she said. "Either give up sex and focus totally on Mother or get married. Isn't that clear?"

I stared at the wall, trying to control the sob that was rising in my throat.

Adilakshmi went on. "Mother prefers that you get married. When you are married, Mother wants you to write a book about how her force transformed you into a normal person, into a heterosexual. Mother says that single-sex love—man-man or woman-

woman—is not good, not healthy, not wise, not in the spiritual way at all, not healthy."

Adilakshmi repeated the word "healthy" with a swoop on the first syllable to give the word special emphasis.

I felt as if my stomach had been shot away, as if all the blood had drained from my body. Adilakshmi went on: "You must get married, Andrew. It is the time. You are in your early forties, no? That is a *wonderful* time to marry, no? You are mature now. Mother is saying that your great consciousness must go on now, must be transmitted in the blood, to children and grandchildren." And she repeated, "And you *must* write now Mother is saying this in *Hidden Journey II*—about how the Love of Mother *healed* you of your homo-sexuality and made you heterosexual. You must write this *wonderful* and *healthy* book, you must, this is your task, your mission, your duty. This is the will of the Divine Mother." When she said, "This is the will of the Divine Mother," a shattering pain went through my heart and I felt as if I would faint or die.

Adilakshmi held out a box of Kleenex.

"Cry if you want," she said dryly. "We all cry sometimes."

For a long moment, the tears streamed silently down my face. Then I turned to Meera, who was looking impassively at me, and I said, "I must know." I said, "It is very important if what Adilakshmi has said represents exactly what you said to her in Telugu."

"Adilakshmi says exactly what I say," Meera said in her low, slightly singsong voice.

"Exactly?"

"Exactly." She smiled slightly. "No doubt."

After a long pause, I managed to frame the question I had never imagined that I would have to ask her, "Are you saying, Ma, that you want me to leave Eryk? Is that what you want of me?"

Adilakshmi added, "And Ma wants you to get married and

write a book about how Mother changed you. This book will protect the world from homosexuality."

I tried to keep as calm as I could and repeated the question to Meera.

Meera said flatly, "Yes. You must leave him. You must leave him soon. You are going to the U.S. at the end of March to arrange everything for my visit? Leave him by the end of February. No, by the middle of February, that is better." She spoke coldly, mathematically, as if Eryk were a piece of luggage I could simply deposit somewhere. Just the night before after *darshan,* Eryk and I had embraced on the road to Dorndorf under a cold sky of stars and I had said to him, "Here at last we are safe, for we are in Her hands."

All I could do at that moment was to repeat mechanically in a small-boy voice, "So I must leave Eryk before I go to America?"

"Yes, yes," Meera said a little impatiently, though smiling this time.

Looking directly at me, Meera went on, in English, "It is essential the family is protected. Homosexuality does not honor the family. It destroys the family. It is not in nature. It is not Divine. There is AIDS everywhere due to the homosexuals. Children are not obeying their parents and the family is in danger. The Mother wants families to flourish. What I am asking you to do I am asking you to do to protect the world."

"To protect the world, to protect the world"—the words repeated meaninglessly in my mind. Even as I sat there frozen with panic, they made no sense. Protect the world from Eryk and myself? Protect the world from our honorable and passionate love? I did not dare to take in the enormity of what she was saying.

"But you have always known I was homosexual," I said. "I wrote it in *Hidden Journey.* I have never hidden it, never been ashamed of it. Many people have said to me that one of the reasons they are with you is because your most public disciple is a homosexual and that makes them see how free you are from the prejudices of the past."

"I am not prejudiced," Meera said smilingly. "I love all beings equally."

"But you want me to give up Eryk, give up my homosexuality, marry, and write a book about how your force transformed me. All this to protect the world?"

"Yes," she said smiling less. "It is my will."

For a moment I did not recognize the small woman sitting in front of me with a mug in her hand. I felt my mind was dissolving.

Adilakshmi began again, leaning forward so far I could smell her sandalwood scent, her voice suffused with what seemed like warmth.

"We love you, Andrew. We accept you. You are a son for us. It was you who wrote the book on Mother. It was you who signed her will last year. Now you must be a hero, Andrew. You must do what the Mother wants even if it kills you." Her voice rose. "The way of the Mother is death after death. The Mother is asking you to die for her and into her. But you will be dying into life. How can you die into the Mother and not die into life? Yes, what Ma is asking of you is a death. But so what? What is a death to a true lover of God? It is a necessary death, Andrew, your duty, your destiny, your future. Your life has brought you to the moment where you can die, die for her. How many times I have died! And what is it? Nothing, nothing at all."

Adilakshmi sank back in her chair, exhausted.

I suddenly wanted to vomit. I tried to bring the conversation back to what Meera had said.

"Let me get this quite clear," I said, sounding far more lucid than I was. "You want me to marry and write *Hidden Journey II* to protect the family."

"To protect yourself, too," Ma said. "If you go on being gay, you will die of AIDS. What you are writing now is great. Your consciousness is needed. You must hand on your consciousness in the blood. It must go on."

"Why can't my consciousness go on in the people I teach, in those who read my books?"

"No, no," Meera said firmly. "It must go on in family. You must find a nice good woman to look after you, to see to your every need. You are not getting younger. You need a woman to look after you."

I gazed at her, feeling sicker and sicker to my stomach, thinking, "Who could have looked after me these last months with more care than Eryk? Who could love me more tenderly than he did?" But I was too terrified to say anything out loud.

Meera must have mistaken my stricken silence for the beginnings of consent or understanding, for she went on: "Of course I know that women are very difficult." She smiled, "Oh yes, women are very difficult. More difficult by far than men—always wanting, wanting, always asking for more. But you will find a good woman."

"And then there is AIDS," Adilakshmi interjected shrilly. "What a terrible death! You will die of AIDS if you do not marry. I feel this."

It would be many weeks before the full cruelty and folly of this conversation would sink into my brain. At that time, I could only follow it moment by moment, as if I were in the middle of a hopelessly tangled dream.

For a few minutes I was seized by what I can only describe as an absolute fear. It was not focused; it simply possessed my body. It took my entire power of British self-control not to shake. I felt I was going mad, that nothing of what had been said could possibly be true. There must be some deeper meaning I was simply not getting. How could the Mother of all beings ask me to destroy the greatest and healthiest love of my life? How could she ask me this, and for what? To appease the prejudices of a few half-baked disciples? Hadn't she come, like Christ, to bring a love that burned away all barriers between beings?

I could say nothing. I smiled and got up to go.

"Thank you, Ma," I said idiotically.

Adilakshmi was evidently satisfied that I had completely understood and accepted everything that had been told to me. She slapped her knee and said, "I knew you would see the truth of the Mother. I knew it. You have always been faithful—and obedient."

I felt like vomiting again.

"Thank you, dear Adilakshmi," I found myself saying.

I walked slowly to the door.

Meera said, "Don't say anything about this to anyone. This is private. Just for us, no?"

"You know how I have always kept secrets," I said. "I won't tell anyone."

"Oh yes," said Adilakshmi warmly. "You are a good child. You have always been a good child."

I staggered downstairs, retching, and managed to get to the bathroom near the bedroom I was occupying, and vomited again and again. I lay on the floor and held my head down into the toilet bowl afraid that pain would explode it. Meera's voice—"You must leave him by the middle of February"—and Adilakshmi saying, "The way of the Mother is death, death, death," circled around me; in my shattered state I seemed to hear them reverberating from all sides of the gray beige bathroom full of the smell of soap and wet towels.

The pain I felt was far too intense for me to be able to think. I could only feel, feel so fiercely my whole being seemed to be bleeding. Meera had taken an axe and split my entire identity right down the middle. Help me understand, I kept murmuring to her, help me, help me.

I don't know how long I lay on the bathroom floor or how many times I vomited. Time and mind had ended. I seemed to be falling, falling continually; nothing in the world was solid. Even the floor I was lying on seemed to be undulating. For long, hideous, timeless seconds I felt the boundless absurdity and panic of real madness; its black wing swept over me again and again. The whole bathroom became a mouth, a large black mouth that only awaited a secret signal from me to swallow me up.

The moment I dreaded arrived. Jake Long—my then manager—drew up in his car into Meera's drive, with Eryk leaning out of the window. I stared at Jake's chubby stubbled face but didn't dare to catch Eryk's eye, and got into the car with my head bowed.

"Is anything wrong?" Eryk asked immediately.

"Nothing," I replied, still looking down, my voice too high and unsteady. "Nothing at all. What could be wrong?"

Jake said in the deliberately soft "blissed-out" voice he used on "spiritual" occasions, "You've just been with the Mother, right? What could be wrong about that? To be with her is to be in heaven on earth."

"Jake," I almost shouted, "would you mind leaving Eryk and me at his hotel. We need to be alone for a while."

Jake left Eryk and me at the Hotel Christine, in Dorndorf, where Eryk was staying.

"I have to walk," I said to Eryk. "I have to breathe. Let us go out into the snow."

The whole of the world that day was white; everything was covered with snow. Thick gray clouds covered the sky.

"You look terrible," Eryk said. "What's happening?"

I walked on and turned, "I have something to tell you."

I started to sob uncontrollably.

Eryk's face became the color of the fields around us.

"Oh my God," he whispered. "Oh my God."

I said, "Mother has told me to leave you. By the middle of February. Before the American tour."

Eryk ran to me and held me fiercely in his arms, burying his head in my neck. "How can she ask this? Doesn't she know how much we love each other? How can the Mother be so cruel? I don't understand. I don't understand anything."

I couldn't say anything.

Eryk stopped, stepped back, and took my face in his hands, holding it so hard it hurt.

"Answer me, now. Whatever you do, don't lie to me. I can bear anything but being lied to. Are you going to obey her?"

I said nothing.

Eryk screamed this time, "Are you going to obey her?"

"What else can I do? What else can I possibly do? What choice do I have? I have been with her for fifteen years; everything I have ever wanted for her is now about to blossom. She must know what is right, Eryk, however hard it is for us—"

Eryk interrupted me. "Are you crazy? Are you out of your mind? Are you really going to ruin the love of both our lives because some crazy Indian woman—"

His voice trailed off as he studied my face nervously. We had walked by now into a vast open field. We stood facing each other in a meaningless, featureless white wilderness.

"Please Eryk," I wept. "Don't make it even harder than it already is."

My voice sounded so hard, so surreal. I winced and looked down at my feet.

"Please Eryk," he started to mimic my English accent. "Please Eryk, please Eryk."

Eryk started to stagger, and then broke into a run. Then he started to scream, a horrible visceral scream that seemed to echo from one end of the landscape to another. As long as I live I shall remember that scream.

"I can't bear this," he screamed. "I won't bear this. Whenever I found anything beautiful it was always broken afterwards. Always. When I found you . . . I can't bear to lose you. I've been beaten, used, and thrown away all my life. I can't bear it, not now, not you. I will die."

Eryk fell to his knees in the snow and started pounding the earth with his fists. Then he began to roll, still howling, in the snow, his face a black crushed ball of anguish. I watched, paralyzed with anguish and guilt. Then, I found the strength to run to where he was and fall onto the ground before him.

"I love you," I said, grabbing his shoulders and shaking him. "I love you, do you hear? I love you more than I have ever loved anyone. You mean more to me, far more, than anyone else."

"Don't lie," Eryk said with tremendous bitterness and rage. "Don't lie in your calm English voice. You love her. You are going to obey her. You are going to let her kill us both."

He sobbed in my arms, no longer bitter now, utterly broken.

"Eryk," I started again. "You must help me. You must understand that I have no choice. Tell me what else I can do. Tell me what else I can do."

Eryk stopped sobbing. His face was small now, the face of a savagely beaten child. I couldn't look at him.

Through my closed eyes I heard him saying, "I'm begging you. I've never begged anyone for anything, but I'm begging you, Andrew. Don't leave me. Don't abandon me. Don't throw my heart away. I will die. You have saved my life, don't destroy it."

"You have saved my life," I found myself saying. "You know

how much you have given me. We have been wonderfully happy. Everyone who knows us both has seen how good we have been for each other."

"Everyone but that madwoman you believe is the Divine Mother on earth. Open your eyes, you idiot. Can't you see she must be crazy?"

"Stop there," I shouted. "She must see something we cannot see now. This must be a teaching for both of us that we cannot understand now. We will understand. I know it, one day we will understand."

"You're as crazy as she is," Eryk wept furiously. "You're as crazy as she is. Are you so blind you cannot see what is before your eyes? She's homophobic, Andrew, and she is trying to murder love."

I put my hand over his mouth.

"You must never speak of her like that again. We must calm down. We have to, otherwise we'll understand nothing. Let us go back to your room. We'll talk and pray there."

We stumbled back through the fields, clinging to each other.

"You must be joking," Eryk kept saying. "She can't possibly have told you to leave me. You must be joking. You can tell me now. I won't be angry. I won't hold it against you."

I could say nothing. All I could do was stroke his head.

We went back to Eryk's room. Eryk curled up on his bed like a broken child and started shivering and whimpering with fear. I found myself saying, "There are fifteen years between us. I have more mystical experience than you. This must be a test. I have heard of such terrible tests of disciples by Masters. This is a test and if I—we—do not obey her we will both be destroyed."

"Why would the Mother destroy?" Eryk said bewilderedly. "Why would the Mother of Love want to destroy Love? What possible reason could she have for separating us but homophobia?"

I didn't want to hear what Eryk was saying. I found myself going on in a surreal, detached, fakey calm voice, the very "English" voice that I had feared most in my education in England.

"You are a beautiful young man. You have had relationships with women. Perhaps the Mother is saying that it is your destiny to marry, live a normal life, have children, be happy. Perhaps she is doing all of this to save you from a life you are not suited to."

"Are you crazy?" Eryk started sobbing again. "Listen to yourself. What is this 'normal life' rubbish? You and I live a normal life, Andrew. We eat, walk, wash our clothes, go to films, worry about money, make love. If she doesn't think this is 'normal life,' that is *her* problem and not ours. I don't want to marry a woman; I want to marry you. You are my husband and wife. You are man and woman and child to me. You are my Beloved. I know this as I know I am lying here, as I am breathing. Nothing that witch can say can alter that. Nothing. And there are no explanations about 'teachings' that are going to satisfy me. All that is manipulative bullshit. She is homophobic, that's all, and you have to face it or kill us both."

"She cannot be homophobic," I found my voice rising. "Please, I beg you, pray, compose your heart, keep it open to the Mother. She will feed us the wisdom we need, the strength we will need to understand and endure."

Eryk cupped his face in his hands. "You are more lost than you can possibly know," he whispered. "More lost even than I am. And God knows . . ."

We sat on the bed together, cradling each other, a long time in silence.

"*Darshan* is in an hour," I said. "Please come. Please come and offer your pain to her."

"I cannot," Eryk said. "I could not stop myself screaming. I will wait for you after *darshan*."

I went out into the darkened afternoon, shaking and sick to my stomach, and started to walk down the drive of the hotel. I heard a noise behind me. Eryk had come out into the snow behind me, holding Balthazar, our toy tiger, and wearing only socks on his feet. Tears were pouring down his face.

"Oh my darling, don't leave me. Don't leave me. Don't leave me."

I walked to him and silently walked him back into the hotel.

"Don't leave me," he kept whimpering.

"We must pray and wait," I kept saying. "We must pray and wait."

Eryk stopped crying and looked at me, "How do you really feel? How do you really feel behind the words and explanations?"

"Totally destroyed," I said.

That night in *darshan* I came closer to wanting to die than at any other time of my life. The silence of what had for fifteen years been for me the holiest of occasions rang only with Eryk's feral howling in the snow. I stared at Meera, as she took head after head into her hands, and tried to feel the old adoration for her; all I could feel was a panic so immense that it seized and shook my whole body. Help me, help me, Mother, I prayed to her, trying to control my shaking, help me survive this, keep my heart open to you, don't let this panic dissolve and make me mad.

Eryk was waiting for me after *darshan* in a small side room by the stairs in Meera's house. He looked dreadful, distraught, disheveled, hollow-eyed. Adilakshmi was with him. I entered the room to hear Adilakshmi saying in an eery singsong voice:

"This is not a drama! Human beings so love drama! This will pass. You are a beautiful good boy. You will get married, you will lead a normal life, you will have children. You will bring them here to the Mother and everything will be wonderful. So what is there to cry about?"

Eryk sat staring sardonically at her as she rattled on and on.

As we walked back over the frozen roads to Dorndorf and Eryk's hotel, Eryk said, "What you saw in the room was nothing. Adilakshmi found me waiting outside and came up to me and started squeezing my muscles, kneading them like bread, saying with a mad look in her eyes, 'Oh what a strong boy!' She had already given me the marriage speech in two different versions before you arrived."

Back in a banal, badly lit hotel room, Eryk told me that he had rung our best friend in New York, Leila L., and told her everything. They had wept together over the phone.

"Leila said to me that she had heard of cases where Tibetan Masters tested lovers in the way we are being tested to see if they really loved each other."

Neither of us could speak. We sat on the bed and held each other. "I don't understand anything," I said. "I've never understood less in my life. I've been on the Path consciously for fifteen years, and I feel I know less, far less, than when I started."

"Perhaps you don't want to understand," Eryk said bitterly. "Perhaps a part of you wants to leave me and our love. Perhaps you want to return to your long empty days and solitude and prayer and living safe from everything."

I grabbed him and hugged him "Are you crazy? I was rotting in that life. You brought me back to life, you brought me to life for the first time. Your Love is my life. We have to believe in what we have lived and built together, or we will be destroyed."

"We are being destroyed. Look at me. Can't you see the destruction in my eyes? Look at yourself. You look dead."

We lay in each others arms, feverish and agonized all night, crying and wiping away each other's tears, hardly talking at all, both abandoned to our private world of pain and memory. Just before dawn Eryk at last fell asleep with Balthazar, our tiger, in his arms and all the lines of his face blackened and smudged out with grief. Every time I looked at him, a wound opened further in my heart; he had suffered so much in his life and now, through no doing or will of my own, the most beautiful thing that life had given him— our love—was being destroyed.

I got out of bed and, kneeling on the floor, prayed in animal wild anguish to her: "You have to say soon that you did not mean what you said. You cannot mean it. You cannot want Eryk's annihilation after all he has already been through. You cannot want me to go on as your Messenger and talk of unconditional Love while stepping over—and making me step over—the corpse of the person I have loved most. What kind of being or Messenger would I be, married and conventional and castrated? I would be a robot, a deadened idiot, and not a human being anymore. How could you want that? And who would believe me if I wrote that I had been transformed into a heterosexual? Who would believe such nonsense? Why would you want me to lie about Love? I would be ridiculed and all the honesty in my work derided and discounted. You are tearing out the heart from my heart in asking me to abandon him; you are tearing out the life from my life. How can I inspire anyone and guide them to you if I am dead?"

My back was in agony and wave after wave of vomiting seized me. I dragged myself to the bathroom where, as I vomited again and again, I saw in my mind's eye very vividly a painting of Abraham and Isaac that had always scared me. In it, Abraham is gazing up to heaven as Isaac kneels submissively waiting for death. This time, however, Isaac was not compliant and composed as he knelt, tied to the rock: He was writhing so furiously the cords that his father had bound him with were biting into his flesh and making rivers of blood stream from his side. For one terrible moment I thought the scene was happening in the bathroom itself and that the blood from Isaac's side was flowing all around me and rising in a great tide. Isaac had Eryk's face.

"I can't do it," I cried out loud. "I can't be Abraham. I reject a God who wants the sacrifice of the one dearest to me. I will not do it."

I prayed to her again, "How could the Divine Mother want to repeat the horror of the Father? How can the Divine Mother want the death of any *real* love? How could the Queen of Love demand the death of a young man? And you know he will die . . ." As I railed against Meera, I kept seeing her as I had seen her once, fifteen years ago in Pondicherry, standing in the doorway of her bedroom, her eyes on fire, the Light, the Divine Light streaming from her body and hair. "It was to you," I said, "that I brought Eryk, in the faith that you could help him rebuild his shattered self and strengthen his great powers of love. And now you are shattering him worse even than his father and mother shattered him."

The wild wrangling voices in my mind went on and on circling round each other, egging each other on, contradicting each other . . .

Eryk had awakened when I returned to bed. He looked at me with hollow eyes. "You must do something," he said. "You must refuse or we will both die."

I returned to Meera's house, went into my room, lay on the floor staring at the ceiling for hours. Then I wrote down everything that had happened, in as exact and clinical a way as possible. I knew I had to be clear about what had been said and demanded or my mind would dissolve in chaos.

A Sufi story I had been told a month before kept swimming back into my broken mind. Before a group of witnesses, a Master killed a disciple. As the Master hacked the disciple with his knife, the disciple just stood there smiling quietly with his hands folded in prayer until the moment when they, too, were hacked off and he was nothing but a mess of blood and bone. The disciple died. The Master cleaned his knife, laughed once loudly, clapped his hands and the disciple sprang back to life with not a single knife mark on his body. The Master said nothing and went on to the veranda of his house to read the morning paper.

Why was this story returning to me? Was she "sending" it to me to help me understand? Was I simply to surrender totally, blindly, to her against everything I thought I knew or understood? Was what I was being put through a spiritual "murder" that she knew would make me wiser than I was now?

Rumi had written, "Be in love with the friend's tyranny, not his tenderness." Was Meera staging this atrocious drama to see just how far I was prepared to go for her, to see if I was prepared to sacrifice everything to her, even the deepest and subtlest human love? If she wanted me to sacrifice human love to her, why did she in her *Answers* stress the necessity of warm and tender bonds between people? And why would she want to sacrifice Eryk as well? In the Sufi story, there was only *one* disciple; in our story, hers and mine, Eryk was also involved. And how could he possibly "submit" and "surrender" to what she was asking of him? Was it only my lack of faith that did not see how she would miraculously also sustain Eryk if I "gave in" and did what she wanted, how she would enfold him with her grace and marvelously give him the courage not to die?

At noon, Jake Long came with Eryk and collected me to go shopping for food. When I got into the car, Eryk smiled at me and said, "I saw last night that your old black shoes had holes in them. I walked to a shop where I got you these new German walkers. Aren't they butch?"

And, laughing, he held out the ugliest but strongest pair of German walking shoes I have ever seen. Even in the depths of the misery in which he was drowning, Eryk was still thinking of me.

Later that day, as I walked down to Thalheim alone, what seemed then like a wholly new understanding began to dawn in me.

Going down in the gray, late-afternoon light to the Mother's house it became clear to me what Meera had been doing. Meera had done what she did, not as I had thought earlier as a savage test of surrender to her but far more beautifully (and here my heart leaped) as a test of my surrender to Eryk. In pretending to want me to separate from Eryk, Meera was forcing me to confront my own inner homophobia; in mirroring it so blatantly and so flatly she was compelling me to exorcise its last remnants in myself and to turn with my full being and claim my right to be homosexual and to love Eryk and to live with him in a dedicated spiritual union and in gratitude to her. Asking me to get married and to write a book about how her force had changed me into a heterosexual was, I saw clearly, a ploy; if I had simply said yes, she would know that my love for Eryk was still not complete, not Divine enough. What Meera was clearly doing was driving me to the moment when I would be prepared to fight her for him, to fight her love for his; by this she would see whether or not I had really learned her lessons of sacred Love. And when she saw that I had—that I was prepared to give up fifteen years of devotion, my position as her Messenger, any power at all that accrued to me from that position, and any influence in the spiritual world—when she had really seen to her satisfaction that Love was the deepest and most essential value in my heart, then she would smile and call the whole madness off, like Jehovah in the Abraham and Isaac story. Why hadn't this explanation arisen before to me?

I went up the stairs to Meera's room, strong in my love for Eryk, brimming over secretly with joy at the new formulation of what was happening that had just come to me.

Meera opened the door herself, unsmilingly, and led me with Adilakshmi into her room.

As soon as we were seated I looked at her directly, my heart singing, and said, "I think you know what I am going to say, don't you?"

She said nothing and continued to stare at me unsmilingly.

"Well," I said triumphantly, "I am not going to—I cannot—leave Eryk under any circumstances, and I am going to tell you why."

I turned to Meera, leaning forward and smiling, "You said yesterday, Ma, that I needed someone to look after me. Eryk is that someone. My back has been in pain for six months. Any other young man would have left me; Eryk not only stayed with me but made it possible for me to travel and work. He has done everything for me these last months, with complete tenderness, and he has never complained."

Meera coughed and looked at her hands.

"Ours is a Divine Love, Ma, his and mine. Our relationship at its deepest truth is holy; it is one of profound mutual respect. I love his soul, Ma, his spirit, the courage he shows every day. He is the bravest, truest, most naturally spiritual human being I have ever known, different from anyone I have loved before. The men I loved before were scared of love or too weak to embrace their true sexuality; Eryk is unafraid, uncomplexed, free, despite everything, to love and give without holding anything back. When he came into my life last March I knew it was you who was sending him to me, sending him to me to heal all the emotional and sexual wounds I know you know I have."

Meera coughed again and did not raise her eyes.

"Ma," I started again. "You taught me to open my heart. It was my years with you, loving you and the Mother in you and you as the Mother, that gave me the strength and the power to love Eryk without fear, that gave me the passion to open to another human being. Haven't you always said that there is only one Love, Divine Love, that manifests in a million different shades and forms? My love for Eryk is one of those forms, I know it. I love Eryk, Ma, with the heart *you* opened in me, with the truth *you* strengthened in me. I love him with *your* heart, with the Divine heart *you* gave me. How can I accept that same-sex relationships are 'unhealthy' and 'unnatural' when I am living one that is restoring me to a health I never had before, that is awakening me to a depth of beauty and glory in Nature and in Life that I never knew before?

"You say people are writing you letters. Write them back and say that they must lose their prejudices once and for all. You said yesterday that my consciousness must go on. Won't I be stronger in every way if I bless my nature and Eryk's love and write and act from the wholeness that must bring me? I will be able to work even more whole-heartedly for you with him by my side.

"Can't you see, Ma, that whoever or whatever I was there would always be complaints. If I was a Jew, or black, or Indian, or married or unmarried, there would be complaints, difficulties. People are crazy, as you have often said; they are never satisfied with anything or anyone. Why should my being with Eryk matter?"

Meera smiled and spoke for the first time. "I am not against homosexuals."

"But you said yesterday—"

Adilakshmi cut in harshly, "Yesterday is yesterday. How can the Mother be against anyone? Is she not the Mother of universal Love?"

There was a long silence as I tried to make sense of Adilakshmi's abrupt denial of what had been so clearly said the day before.

"Look, Andrew dear," Adilakshmi went on, her voice smooth as honey now, "we do not like to see you suffer. You were in such pain last night at darshan. So many saw it and told us about it. We love you so much."

Meera said something, in Telugu.

Adilakshmi smiled broadly, "Oh you are a lucky boy today! You are a lucky child." She spoke each word slowly. "The Mother says you can take your time."

By now I was completely panicked and bewildered.

"Take my time in what, Adilakshmi?"

"Why," she smiled broadly, "take your time in leaving Eryk. You cannot leave him now, just like that. We see that. You can leave him *slowly*. Take your time. Take your time. No need to go fast. You don't make a good meal by throwing everything into the pot at once, do you?"

A part of me was still so desperate to hear Meera relent that I believed her "take your time" was, in fact, a reprieve, a complete about-face. The thought even crossed my mind that Meera was deliberately stalling to "protect" me from those in her entourage who were actively homophobic. Taking my time, after all, could mean a lifetime. Crazily, I started to smile inwardly at her "wisdom."

"So I don't have to leave him immediately?"

"Not immediately," said Meera smiling. Was I imagining it or was there a special brilliance to her smile, a special intensity that signaled that I was beginning to "understand"—or was I going mad?

"Thank you, thank you," I heard myself saying. "I am so happy."

"Yes," said Adilakshmi. "You can always come to the Mother with whatever Tom, Dick, or Harry you want. Yes, come with whom you want. You are welcome."

Why was Adilakshmi mentioning "Tom, Dick, or Harry" when I only want to be with Eryk? Why was her voice still so full of contempt?

Meera went on smiling broadly. My earlier "perception" now blossomed in that surreal atmosphere into another full-fledged "theory." It was clear to me that Meera had staged everything to go along with the provincial homophobic outrage of Adilakshmi and the other disciples; now that I had defended myself before Adilakshmi, she would be able to say "take your time." I and Eryk would now be protected, protected by the Mother herself! Sublime Master! I wanted to fall at her feet and kiss them, but restrained myself. I would play the game poker-faced.

Then Meera spoke again in Telugu to Adilakshmi. Adilakshmi translated: "Ma is now saying, go and do whatever you want. But always remember what we told you yesterday. Keep returning to it and meditating on it and one day you will see the truth." I was bewildered again. I was being told to "take my time," and yet I was also being told to go over in my mind continually the very urgent message to leave Eryk and become a heterosexual that I had been given the day before. I decided that this too was a "ploy" of Meera's to protect me even more completely from Adilakshmi and the others. The Mother couldn't be seen to "let me off" lightly, after all.

"Of course, Adilakshmi," I said. "Of course, I will."

Adilakshmi continued, "You must remember, Andrew, that to do the Mother's will we have to go sometimes against our own. I never imagined, for example, that I with my philosophy degree would have to work for months in the Indian hot weather building a house. But Mother told me to go to Andra Pradesh, to Madana-palli, and supervise the building of her mansion there. And I did."

I stared at Adilakshmi in disbelief. How could she begin to be-lieve that supervising the building of a house as a philosophy grad-uate was a comparable ordeal to having to give up the person you loved most and change the whole orientation of your life? I was too exhilarated, however, at what I imagined to be my "reprieve" that I did not challenge her.

"Of course we have to sacrifice for the Mother," I said glibly, my heart dancing. "I have sacrificed quite a lot for her, you know, Adilakshmi."

"You can never give enough. Never. Never." Adilakshmi's voice was once more shrill, fervent.

I got up to go and gazed at Meera, who returned my look enig-matically saying nothing.

"Bless you, Ma."

"Relax now!" Meera said in a rich low drawl. "Now you can just relax."

I avoided analyzing what had just happened because I wanted to cling to my belief that Meera had intervened subtly to "save" me. I walked as fast as I could back to Eryk's hotel. "We're saved," I said as I opened the door to find Eryk, unshaven, haggard, with his head in his hands.

"We are saved," I repeated.

Eryk looked out at me doubtfully.

"What do you mean?"

"Mother relented. She smiled and said, 'Take your time.'"

I did not dare add "in leaving him." Didn't I now think, after all, that the Mother merely added those words to protect me in Adilakshmi's and the other's eyes?

Eryk started shouting, "Take your time? Take your time in leaving me. . . . Isn't that it? Take your time, don't do it messily all at once, especially now and here, since everyone is beginning to suspect something dreadful is up. Take your time and leave Eryk when you are back in Paris, where there will be no witnesses. . . . How can you still not see the ways you are being manipulated? A small child could see it, Andrew." He started to sob angrily.

I was so certain of my crazy interpretation of the "secret meaning" of what was unfolding that I knelt and embraced him round the knees. "I know that everything I have said seems not to make sense. But Masters teach in mad ways sometimes, and I'm beginning, through her Grace, to see my way through."

And for the next half hour I explained my new analysis of what she was trying to teach us and of how she was actually "protecting" us.

I said to Eryk, "Don't you see? You have always been terrified of being abandoned; Meera is making you face that fear head-on. So you will see that this time it is unfounded. I'm *not* leaving you; I've stayed; I will stay. I will go fighting for you even against what she is pretending for the game's sake to be her position. And every time I fight for you I will be doing what she secretly wants me to do—convince you in your depths that you are loved and wanted."

Eryk looked at me coldly and said with icy irony: "And what is this subtle, paradoxical teaching doing for you?"

"It is obvious, don't you see? Meera is facing me with my greatest fear—my fear of real love, of success in love. She's forcing me to destroy in myself anything on any level that could block me from opening to you completely. She is pretending to be homophobic so I can destroy what is homophobic in me by opposing her so that I—knowing you as I do and the wonderful power and beauty of our love—can finally claim you and my sexuality and my body and my full life."

Eryk leaned forward and held me tenderly against him. A month later he told me that what he had wanted to say at this moment was, "If she wants to bless our union so much and open you so completely to our love, why doesn't she simply say so?" But Eryk knew that at that moment I needed to believe whatever fevered fantasy could protect me from the hideousness of what was unfolding; I was still too fragile not to be shattered by the truth. Besides, he told me later, he did not argue with me then because he did not want to make me angry; I was so thrilled, so childishly delighted by the "mystic subtlety" of my new diagram, he was terrified that if he opposed me, I would find him stupid or "blasphemous" and leave him.

That evening, Eryk and I talked the whole situation over again with Jake. Other disciples of Meera now knew, too, what had happened. Eryk and I spoke at length to John and Jim, a gay couple who happened to be in Thalheim with us. John is in his eighties, a distinguished avant-garde filmmaker and poet; Jim is forty years younger and a photographer. They were, of course, furious and horrified; they had seen me hardly able to move when I knelt before Meera. Jim, especially, was shaken by the depth of Eryk's misery. "I have never seen anyone in my life suffer so much," he told me. "I cannot believe this is any kind of teaching."

"She is just a homophobic witch," John raged.

We told Jake of the reaction that Jim and John and other disciples who now knew were having.

"Oh my God," he groaned. "We need some damage control around here."

After a few gloomy rumblings, he started to perk up. Then he laughed and clapped his hands. "I've got the perfect solution. I haven't spent all these years in showbiz for nothing. Showbiz is quite a good preparation for the spiritual world, in fact, as it turns out. Why didn't I think of it before?"

"Think of what?"

Jake leaned forward conspiratorially, lowering his voice.

"A film-star policy."

"A what?"

"A film-star policy," he repeated annoyedly. "It's simple, Andrew, wonderfully simple. You keep your life totally private, do whatever the hell you want with Eryk or anyone else. If the press asks you anything, you'll smile like Tom Hanks or Barbra Streisand—you know the smile you've see it a million times—and you'll say you are Ma's messenger and you are only interested in answering questions about her."

Jake turned glowingly to Eryk.

"No access will be given to Eryk whatsoever. His name will not be mentioned. No photographs of you and him together will ever be let out under any circumstances. The most rigid control will be kept up at all times. This will not mean, of course, that you and Eryk cannot be together. He can travel with you, as your personal secretary, or something."

Just as I had grasped Meera's injunction to "take your time" as a sign of her secret desire to free me from the whole situation, so I took Jake's proposition as something divinely "suggested" and "transmitted" by Meera to him so that the rapidly developing and agonizing drama could be defused.

"Why not?" I said, when Jake had finished. "Why not have a film-star policy, whatever that is? It sounds doable."

I was sounding like Jake and I winced.

Eryk had been sitting intensely still. He turned to me. "Are you crazy?" he said softly. "I can't just be your secretary and walk like

Prince Philip six paces behind you. I'm not your secretary; I'm your life-partner. You may believe that you can enact this charade, but I refuse to. Why should you have to keep your private life secret? What is shameful about us and our Love?"

"Eryk," I said pleadingly. "Please listen. This policy is our one real hope. It shows them that we appreciate *their* side of things." I started to ramble. "Whatever we do in public, we can go on doing what we want in private."

"What we want?" Eryk drew out the words sardonically. "Are you listening to yourself? You've been going on and on about how all this is supposedly purifying you of your inner homophobia and now in desperation you are ready to agree to a film-star policy that will keep your real life secret and make the man you love a prisoner of secrecy. I could not bear it."

"Please think about it, Eryk," Jake said a little roughly. "You're still young. It's good to be young, to be fierce, to be honest. But things don't always follow the lines we want."

Eryk got up calmly and walked out onto the balcony. I joined him.

"Some great religious movement, this!" Eryk snorted. "The Messenger of the so-called Divine Mother has to have a film-star policy. Excuse me, but are there contradictions in this picture?"

"Eryk," I said, "we need to get out of here. Let's say we accept this solution for now and leave early, on Saturday or Sunday."

"Okay," Eryk said. "I'll say we accept it if we can get out as soon as possible."

"I promise. Besides, I trust Jake."

"Once more and yet again, my darling, you are blind. I never liked him, not from the first moment I saw him. You know what Jake said to me this afternoon when we went shopping in Limberg? On the steps of the cathedral he drew me apart and said in that blissy-wissy voice of his: 'You're just the cock of the moment. Last year there was someone else, next year there will be someone else. Don't fool yourself.' He is lucky I am completely exhausted, or I would have knocked him out. I think the man is a homophobic vulgarian, and all he cares about is his position with Meera and making as much money as possible out of you. You'll find out."

I felt sick. I knew Eryk could not be lying.

"Whatever Jake's reasons for arranging this policy," I said finally, "I must go along with it now. The whole situation is turning completely crazy. We've got to get out and get somewhere where we can really think."

"On that at least we agree," Eryk smiled. "Okay, let us try this if you want. I'll support you. But we have to leave soon."

I walked back into the room and asked Jake to go to Meera and Adilakshmi and explain to them exactly what a film-star policy was, and what it would offer them. "Now there will be peace," Jake said. "Thanks for that."

I did not sleep at all that night. The full agony of the conflict that possessed my being broke over me. For hours I could not move at all but lay on the floor in the dark, feeling with each breath that another part of my heart and body was being pierced, flayed, and broken.

As I tried, increasingly desperately to "understand" (praying to Meera incessantly, "Help me, Help me"), waves of the fiercest and most protective love for Eryk kept washing over me. As the anguish of confusion deepened, that love seemed also to grow more absolute, as if the confusion was a black acid that was stripping layer after layer of rust from my heart to expose and uncover there depths of gratitude to and compassion for Eryk, which shook me with their power. At moments I seemed almost to become him, to become the small three-year-old left by his father to starve for four days alone in a cupboard. Suffering peeled me of barriers I had subconsciously been placing between myself and what Eryk had suffered. Two images returned again and again, driving me deeper into his agony: the image of a seal I had seen on a Japanese documentary being clubbed to death on the ice, and that of a dog I had discovered in a forest in South India years before, tied to a tree and horribly beaten and starving to death. Both the seal and the dog had Eryk's eyes, the eyes he had turned to me howling in the snow. My whole being convulsed now in love and heartbreak, and I rolled over and over on the floor, as if reaching for him and crying out, "Oh my darling, my darling."

Even as I wept and cried out, I knew that something had forever been saved in me, because, finally at last, I loved another human being more than myself. I knew that I would rather die than cause Eryk any more suffering, and not from guilt at all, but because we had now become, at some depth impossible to articulate, one heart, one body, one being. The blood of both of our lives and hearts had run into one cup and I was drinking that blood that night, that bitter-sweet blood, and nothing from that awful, and marvelous, moment on would be able to obliterate its taste in me.

On Friday, New Year's Eve morning, Jake went to see Meera and Adilakshmi to explain to them the film-star policy he had decided we needed to pursue.

We met in his room afterwards.

Jake was smiling broadly, "Mother was so beautiful this morning. She looked so sweet and wonderful. I explained the policy to her perfectly. You would have been proud of me."

His wife, Delia, stroked his hair, "You could talk the monkeys down from the trees, honey."

Eryk smiled, "So now I must begin to practice walking three steps behind you, Andrew. We'll have to buy a briefcase and some boring glasses."

"Stop it now!" Jake said aggressively. "Don't go and ruin everything."

Delia went on stroking his hair. Then she look straight at Eryk and her face broke into an ecstatic smile.

"Jake has something else to tell us, don't you, Jake?"

Jake looked coyly at his rings. "You say, Delia."

"Well," Delia began, "Mother has granted us what we most desire. She has seen the depth of our true devotion to her and she has allowed us—" Delia was now crying with joy—"she has, I can hardly believe it, she has invited us to travel with her on the tour. To go with her together everywhere."

Eryk sat frozen with pain and contempt.

Delia paused, "Isn't that the most wonderful news?"

Neither Eryk nor I could speak.

Then after a long pause, while Jake and Delia gazed tenderly and gratefully into each other's eyes, Eryk said, "And where will I be during the tour? Locked up in jail? Sent off to Hawaii for three weeks? We mustn't see the Messenger is a queer, after all, must we? And you, Andrew, are you going to wear gray and speak in a deeper voice than usual?"

Delia purred, "Oh Eryk, you are always so extreme. Don't ruin everything. Everything is being slowly arranged. You'll see. Jake can do wonders."

Eryk whispered to me, "Get me out of this room before I murder this woman."

I coughed and got to my feet unsteadily.

"Thank you, Jake, for everything you are doing. I am delighted you and Delia can travel with the Mother in June."

Jake clapped me on the back, "You see what a little calm perspective and patience can do?"

"We see very clearly, don't worry," Eryk said.

Jake and Delia beamed at him, unaware he was being ironic.

"We knew that everything would be fine," said Delia.

Outside in the snow, Eryk said, "We have to leave as soon as possible. Neither of us can bear this much longer."

"I can't face returning to Paris in winter just yet," I said. Then suddenly and very clearly, an idea came to me. "Let us go to Belgium," I said. "Let us go to the places where the Virgin appeared. You have told me of them so many times . . ."

Eryk's face blazed with relief. "You mean Banneux and Beauraing. Oh my God, what a marvelous thought!"

"We'll go this Sunday," I said. "I promise."

"I will feel safe there," Eryk said in a quiet voice. "I will feel safe with the real Mother. And Mary will bless and protect us." He stood and closed his eyes, breathing in the cold air. I remembered the morning seven months before when Eryk had given me in London the miraculous hawthorn blossom from the tree in Beauraing in which the Virgin appeared.

"Remember when I gave you the hawthorn in London?" Eryk said.

I started. "I was just thinking of that."

Tears filled both our eyes.

"The thought of being away from here," I began, "fills me with relief. I never imagined I would say that."

"Who could have imagined what is happening?" Eryk shrugged.

"I must see Mother one last time," I said.

Eryk said nothing, but his face turned ashen.

"Nothing she could say could make any difference to us now," I said.

"Swear," Eryk said. "Swear."

"I swear."

I had to see Meera before I left. A part of me was still clinging to the ever-fainter hope that what had happened was a teaching, despite increasing moments of clarity which were so frightening that when they came my eyes started to spasm and I could not breathe and felt the same panic I had as a child before an asthma attack. What would it mean to undo so many years of passion, to dissolve in the acid of oblivion so many—as I believed—unique moments of shared sacred tenderness, of walks and conversations and dreams and exalted silences in *darshan*? Who would I be when—and if—I extracted Meera from my being?

Awaking early after hardly any sleep on Saturday morning, the image came to me of being trapped in a vast black web like a human fly. The fly had legs and arms and a face like mine, but its torso was rotting and it was paralyzed and could not move. Horrified, I saw that it could understand enough to register every nuance of what the spider had done to it—and what hanging there paralyzed in the darkness waiting to be eaten further was doing to it—but it could not move or cry out. The vampire-spider had sucked out not only its physical but also its moral and spiritual strength; not only its body but also its heart and mind were stripped bare, hollow, hovering on the edge of total dissolution into nothingness.

Meera herself opened the door of her upstairs flat, in a brown sari.

"I am going tomorrow," I said. "I have to. I wanted to see you before I left."

"Yes," she said calmly.

Adilakshmi appeared, smiling a little too insistently, and we went again into the drawing room.

I had no idea of how to begin to describe what I was going through and so asked Meera what she thought about the film-star policy.

"Oh, it is a very good idea," she said, laughing gaily. "Next time, do not send Jake to negotiate. We must talk between ourselves. Why do we need anyone else?"

Her voice was soft and honeyed.

I leaned forward. "Can Eryk come with us on the tour in June?"

Adilakshmi coughed nervously.

Meera's face darkened momentarily, "So much can happen between now and then."

A chill went through me. I heard her voice say inwardly, "Take your time in leaving him."

"You know how much Eryk is suffering."

Adilakshmi and Meera waited.

"He is suffering horribly, Ma. You must help him. After his childhood and all its torments . . ."

"What torments?" asked Adilakshmi quickly.

Quickly, and with rising anguish, I told them both in graphic detail what had happened to him. I had assumed that as far as Meera was concerned, telling her the dreadful details was merely a courtesy. Repeatedly over the years Meera had told me that she "sees" the past of people who kneel before her "like a film."

But as I spoke of the horrors of Eryk's abuse I saw clearly that neither Adilakshmi nor Meera had any idea of what had happened to him. Meera gasped quietly twice, leaned forward, and looked at me, before she could compose herself, wide-eyed, like an actress in a silent film. Seeing my surprise at her ignorance, she too quickly reassumed her usual serenity.

I continued talking about Eryk, but inwardly I was reeling with rage. Who was this woman in front of me I thought I knew so well? Why did she lie that she knew everything about her disciples' pasts when clearly, in one very serious case at least, she knew nothing? By what right was she playing with Eryk's life when she had made no overt attempt to understand what had nearly shattered it? I wanted to scream with frustration and fury at myself also; was it to this woman that I had brought my Beloved to be healed?

"It is clear," I managed to say, and more icily than I intended, "that you do not know, Ma, anything about Eryk's past."

Meera looked studiedly blank.

Adilakshmi began chattering nervously, "Of course Mother knows. She knows everything. What could the Divine Mother on earth not know? She doesn't always *say* what she knows. She knows everything on—everything—in her own way."

Meera's look became blanker and blanker, as if an invisible hand were wiping out her features.

Adilakshmi started again, "I have been thinking. Mother and I were talking and talking about your problem. We love you so much. What we have to say to you today is this." Adilakshmi leaned forward. "There is no sex in Indian yoga, Andrew, none at all."

"Go on, Adilakshmi," I said, almost enjoying myself.

She warmed to her theme, "Sex and yoga are opposites. Sex blocks the Mother's Light. There is no sex in the Path to the Mother. Many people are saying to us: How can Andrew be doing serious yoga and having sex at the same time?"

I wanted to burst out laughing. No sex in Indian yoga? No sex in Hindu and Buddhist tantra? No sex in the temples of Madurai and Khajuraho? No sex in the Shakti cults with their veneration for the creative energies of the body?

"I am not having sex," I said calmly. "I am making love. There is a difference, Adilakshmi."

"No difference," she said fiercely. "Sex is sex is sex."

I breathed deeply and turned to Meera for the last time to try and explain my position.

"I am not on an ascetic path. I do not believe in one either for myself or for the majority of modern people. You know this. What I have been attempting, with the Mother's Grace, for years is to marry body and spirit, heart and mind, what we have called 'human' and what we have called 'Divine.' This is what I have been doing with your Grace and support ever since I met you. Being with Eryk and feeling in every dimension the beginning of a great healing has been a revelation of the truth of this adventure."

There was a long silence. Meera said softly and vaguely, "Of course, many people have very conventional ideas."

"Why listen to them?" I went on. "We cannot repeat the old denigration of the body; we have to consecrate the body, infuse its every movement and impulse with Divine Love. All true Love is sacred and Divine and so is any activity, physical or otherwise, that true Love enjoys. I know this as I know I am breathing and sitting here with you and no amount of ancient dead religious rhetoric is going to convince me otherwise."

There was another long silence. Meera spoke to Adilakshmi at length in Telugu. Adilakshmi translated with icy condescension. "Mother is saying that there is truth in what you are saying. However, she wants to make it clear that to do her work in the world we cannot simply follow our appetites and do as we want."

"My love for Eryk, Adilakshmi, is not an appetite."

"That is what you think, it is clear," said Adilakshmi. "Let us get back to what Mother is telling you. She is saying that it may be all right to have boyfriends or girlfriends or whatever when you are just a private citizen, but you are the Messenger of the Mother. You must be beyond everything and you must conform to society, to what the world wants in every way. In *every* way," Adilakshmi repeated. "Which does not mean that you cannot go on doing whatever you want, just as Mother does, but in her wise, *silent* way. You see what I mean?"

"I think I am beginning to," I said quietly.

I turned to Meera. "Do you agree with what Adilakshmi has been saying?"

Meera nodded emphatically, "Yes. It is the Way."

"So you are asking me to conform outwardly while doing whatever I want in a *silent* way. And this is why the film-star policy is so attractive."

"Yes," Meera smiled. "No need to confuse people. . . . The family must be protected."

I went on. "So, ideally, you are telling me, I should get rid of Eryk and stop having sex, but if I don't or can't, then I should *appear* to conform completely while keeping my *real* private life secret."

"Yes," said Meera. "This would be the wise way, no?"

I gazed from Adilakshmi to Meera and back again in horrified disbelief. How could the Divine Mother on earth be asking me to conform "in every way" to the habits and prejudices of a world her force was dedicated to transforming "in every way" before it destroyed itself? Didn't Meera know that to undertake the journey into the Mother I had had to go against *everything* and *everyone* in the world I had been born into—against my English Oxford education, my worldly friends, all the modern Western intellectual tradition? And here she was asking me to pursue a film-star policy so as not to "disturb" anyone. "I do not quite see the wisdom of such conformity yet," I said.

"Oh, Andrew," Adilakshmi laughed gaily. "The Mother's wisdom takes a long time to understand."

"I may never understand this part of it," I said.

"You will," Adilakshmi said taking my hand. "We have faith in you. You have always been obedient."

Immense grief swept over me and almost made me fall. I stood up and said unsteadily, "I have heard what I needed to hear. I must go now." I looked at Meera for the last time.

"Don't worry about anything," she said.

"No," I said, lying. "Be with me."

She nodded, yawned, and walked out.

Later Eryk and I walked in the dark snow-choked woods and I told him everything Meera had said. It was only an hour later, but already my "disciple" mind was trying to interpret what I had heard as a "teaching."

"Just as she has been confronting me all week with my latent homophobia, now she is making me see my terror of normality. She is only telling me to 'conform' because she wants me to face, once and for all, the fear that has motivated my whole search—the fear of being ordinary. But real wisdom is in the ordinary."

Eryk let me talk and then said quietly, "You do not see it now, but you will; the so-called Divine Mother is talking like the head of a corporation. Worse, she's talking like a pope. Clearly, she doesn't care what the other gays around her do, just as the pope doesn't care what a minor priest in Minnesota gets up to. But you, the Messenger, you have to put on a good image. It's disgusting. She's not telling you to 'conform' to heal you of anything; it is just a power move. She wants to control you and what you do. And she always says that she never tells anyone what to do and accepts all beings! What a charade! How can you possibly buy it?"

"I've been on a mystical journey for fifteen years—" I began angrily.

"And it has made you blind as hell. All Meera is thinking about is herself and what she imagines to be her power and her future. She couldn't care less about 'Andrew'; all she cares about is 'Harvey'— the writer and propagandist. Andrew can die or bleed to death, for all she cares. You can't and won't see this yet because it hurts too much. But you will. You will have to."

"I am too shattered and confused to see anything clearly at the moment," I said.

"I know," Eryk said. "But you must wake up soon. Ever since this madness began I have been praying to the Virgin: Wake him up, open his eyes, show him he doesn't need anyone between him and the Mother, him and you, release him from his long illusion. Thank God, we will be with Her tomorrow. I don't think I could stay here one more full day. Last night I dreamt that Meera was trying to kill me."

"Now you are going *too* far," I said.

"Anything at this point could be true. You have no idea what this woman is capable of, none at all." Suddenly, he looked completely broken and exhausted and started to cough.

"One thing we *can* be sure of," he whispered, "is that we are going to find out."

ACT II

Mary, Hold Us in Your Arms

✳

Surrender to the Mother.

BEDE GRIFFITHS

Every seeker who truly seeks authentic spiritual reality will sooner
or later meet the Virgin. This meeting signifies, apart from the illu-
mination and consolation that it comprises, protection against a
very serious spiritual danger. For he who advances in the sense of
depth and height in the "domain of the invisible" one day arrives
at the sphere known . . . as "the sphere of mirages" or the "zone of
illusion." One cannot pass by this zone without the protection
of the mantle of the Virgin.

MEDITATIONS ON THE TAROT

E ryk and I left Thalheim early Sunday morning before anyone was awake, in a dark and blinding snow storm that
grew more and more furious as we drove on into it, as if
whipped up by some hidden Force that wanted at all costs to keep
us in its power. "If we can leave Germany, if we can only leave Germany," Eryk kept saying, "we will be safe." Time and time again,
whirling snow would so whiten the front window of our rental car

that we could hardly see anything, only the dimmest imaginable blur of lights from the cars in front of us. Yet we drove on, even when the road became almost unnegotiably treacherous and the car started to skid and sway or tremble in the hissing storm wind as if it were made of balsa wood.

At the Belgian border, as if by Divine magic, the snowstorm suddenly stopped and a pale winter sun came out and lit up the lush green hills of the Ardennes.

And with the sun, a great curtain of sane calm seemed to descend on everything.

"I am the Virgin of the Poor," the Virgin had said to Mariette Beco, the twelve-year-old daughter of peasant parents to whom she appeared in Banneux in 1933.

"I am the Virgin of the Poor." As we drove through the sweet gray-green landscape of the Ardennes that phase kept returning to me.

The Virgin showed Mariette a sacred spring and asked her to plunge her hands into it. "This is reserved for me," she said. "And it is for all nations and the sick."

Over and over, I repeated Her words in my heart, laying the pain of these last days at Her feet.

We arrived at Banneux in a slight warm drizzle at about four in the afternoon. There is nothing glamorous or ostensibly holy or even interesting about Banneux; it could be any one of a thousand poor, tiny, faceless, gray and beige walled Belgian villages clustered round a church at the edge of one or other of the forests that stretch all over this region.

A few hundred yards from the main square, which doubles as a car-park you can still see the tiny one-story house where the Becot family lived. Near to it, to one side, there is a small humble-roofed chapel, open to the weather on three sides, with nothing in it but a statue of Mary as Mariette saw her, head bowed, grave, her hands slightly upraised in prayer, a rosary round her right wrist.

A little further on, there is a long trough with water running into it through slightly eroded lead pipes. This water comes from the spring that the Virgin revealed to Mariette when she appeared to her for the second time. All over Europe, all over the world, small bottles of this water go to anoint the newborn, heal the sick, comfort the dying. Sacred images are washed in it; houses that have known tragedy are purified by drops of it being sprinkled in corners. Through its power, the blind have come to see, the lame to walk, the desperate to find a hope beyond hope, the stricken strength to bear the unbearable.

At the end of the fifth apparition, the Virgin said to Mariette who was kneeling gazing up at her by the spring, "I come to comfort suffering."

Day after day, the water keeps pouring. It never runs dry.

I went first to the spring and bathed my hands and face in its freezing water.

"Mother," I prayed, "wash this suffering from me. Heal me in my heart, my soul, my body, my mind."

An old woman was standing by me, saying her rosary, and reciting in French the Litany of Loreto:

"Virgin most merciful
Pray for us

Virgin most faithful
Pray for us
Seat of Wisdom . . .
Cause of our joy . . .
Spiritual vessel . . .
Vessel of honor . . .
Singular vessel of devotion . . .
Mystical Rose . . ."

With each "Pray for us," a deeper peace enveloped me. When she had finished, the old woman turned to me, took my hand, squeezed it, and said, "You only have to speak to Her softly. She always hears." Then, she knelt in the dirt and I knelt with her. It is so simple, I thought suddenly, so simple to be with her, if you trust.

The woman studied my face intensely. "You are in pain," she said. "Something bad has happened."

"Yes," I said.

"The water of the Mother will heal you."

I went to the small chapel nearby and stood there with the others, praying silently and gazing up at the statue of Mary. Memories flooded me of other times I had come to Mary or tasted something of Her great love and power.

I remembered a night fifteen years before on the Greek island of Spetses when I had climbed to an old ruined Marian shrine on the top of a hill; I remembered the sun-baked face of the old Jesuit with whom I had spent three days in the shrine of Mary at Ephesus, talking of the Loving Mother, as he called Her; I remembered the hour of silent power I had spent kneeling in the shrine there, so lost in wonder that when I came out that I could not speak.

I have never been away from You, I said inwardly to Her, I have never been away from You.

I remembered how often in Thalheim—for months every day on my afternoon walk around the village and the woods—I had stopped at the tiny Marian shrines in the walls of the village and prayed to Her; I remembered the shrine to Mary near Dorndorf, which had been venerated for a thousand years, and where I had often prayed and taken flowers. I remembered a morning in Montreal during the year I wrote about in *Hidden Journey* when I was sitting in the kitchen of a friend reading the messages of Medjugorje and the room had filled with Divine Light and I had heard the words, "Now begins the Reign of Sweetness." Is the meaning of what has happened, I remember thinking, that I should return to You, You who have always been with me even when I did not recognize it?

A wonderful joy filled me and all the suffering of the last week for a moment seemed to belong to another life. I looked around at the people praying with me. Ordinary people, old and young, gazing up at Her with such simple devotion. They don't need any intermediaries with the Mother, I remember thinking, they don't need to kneel before a human being, they know the Mother is listening, they know Her Heart is always listening. The words came to me: "There is a direct Path to Me beyond all dogmas, all names, all forms. Just speak to Me and know that I am always present."

As we walked away from the chapel arm-in-arm, I turned to Eryk and told him of the memories of Mary that had returned to me.

We went into one of the gaudy and overlit souvenir shops that cluster round the Banneux car-park. Eryk bought me a simple wooden rosary, like the one I had seen the old woman praying with as she recited the Litany of Loreto.

"This will always protect you," he said. Then he smiled, "Remember our trip to Mahabalipuram last September? I had a Madonna and Child made for you by a local wood-carver. I had it made out of mango-wood: I knew how much you love mangos, and I wanted you to have a Virgin made out of the wood of your childhood. Do you remember what you said when I gave it to you? You said 'Now my Western and Eastern mothers are One Mother.'"

Just before we left the shop, Eryk took a postcard he had bought out of its paper bag, and handed it to me face down.

"This is yours," he said.

I turned it over, and gasped.

"You can't have known . . ." I began.

"Known what?"

"I've been looking for this image for years."

We gazed at each other in amazement.

Later, as we sat in an adjoining café, I told him the whole story. The postcard Eryk handed me was of Christ, standing, His hips slightly bent, His right hand raised in blessing and His left resting delicately on His heart. From his heart stream two beams of Light. The one to the right is pink; the one to the left white.

"This is so strange," I kept saying. "Years ago, in a New York thrift store, I found the head of this image in a larger reproduction. I was immediately moved by its beauty, its mixture of masculine power and feminine tenderness. I kept this Christ with me for

years, above my desk. One winter in upstate New York, I was gazing at it when suddenly Christ's eyes began to emanate a piercing
white Light. The experience went on for fifteen minutes and left
me certain that He had come to me and that I had been blessed
with His Presence. And now, today—on this day of all days—you
hand me the *whole* image."

"It isn't me who is handing you the whole image," Eryk said
softly. "It is the Mother." We looked silently at the two streams of
Light emanating from Christ's heart.

"Of course," I found myself saying. "Of course."

Eryk finished my thought for me: "The pink Light is the Light
of the Mother, the Light of Love for all creatures and for all Creation. The white Light is the Divine Light of the Father."

"Yes," I went on, "and they stream from Christ's heart because
the Christ-consciousness is the consciousness of the Sacred Androgyne, of the One who has merged male and female in the One,
who has married all opposites, who is Son of the Mother as well as
the Father."

"Today you have received not only the full Mother," Eryk said,
"but also the full Christ. You had the head before; now you have
the body."

As he spoke I heard an inner voice: "This image of the Androgyne
will guide you now. It is to find this Image that you came here. It will
accompany you now for the rest of your life. The meaning of your
life will be to turn yourself more and more completely into the
Being you see before you. Open, and go on opening forever, into
the fullness of your real love-nature, in whatever happens, whatever it costs. I will, I promise, rebirth you, body and soul, from the
dark waters . . ."

We spent the night in an old inn in Remouchamps, by a river that leaped and rushed and roared just a few yards from our window in spate from the rains and melting snow.

I was lying in our suite's vast Victorian bath soaking my back when Eryk came in, naked, except for a towel round his waist. The exhaustion and terror of the last week had left his face and he stood over me, smiling and fresh as a young god.

"Come into the bath with me," I said. He laughed, flinging back his head (I was so happy to hear him laugh again), stripped, and lowered himself beside me. I pushed myself right up against him, soaping his back and arms and armpits, breathing in his hair, the smell of his sweat mingled with aftershave, licking the curve of his neck, and his earlobes, lost in joy to be with him again.

"God, I've missed you so much," I kept saying. "I've missed this so much!"

"I love you with all I am or will be," Eryk said.

We both started to laugh and weep, and hug and kiss and tenderly caress each other. The sweetest and fiercest desire for him that I had ever known rose in a column of clear sweet heat from the core of my spine spread through my whole body and seemed to dissolve my body in its shimmering: I knew that he, too, was feeling this all-enveloping tender ecstasy because our mouths and hands and bodies moved in the rhythm of a completely shared harmony. There was only Love with a body, one body, made of our two bodies merged and fused together, moving with perfect knowledge to delight itself.

How could so much tenderness not be sacred? How could so much shared joy not be as sacred as anything on earth?

Our sperm ran together in the warm soapy water, and a fiery serenity, a Peace that is Fire as well, descended on us both and we clasped each other and held each other, letting the fire-streams that had been set free in both of our hearts stream toward each other in an almost palpable, almost physical heat.

That night I knew, beyond any doubt, that Eryk's and my love was a Divine human love; that he was my human Divine Beloved and that our union was holy and blessed by Her.

It was raining when we arrived at Beauraing, but that did not matter. The low calm gray of the day felt utterly peaceful as if we were enfolded in the wings of a vast bird that was sheltering us from everything.

If possible, Beauraing is an even less glamorous place than Banneux. The tree where the Virgin appeared was, when we arrived in mid-winter and in the rain, bare, even bleak. There were no flowers left by it, no worshipers in front of it. We were alone with it and its Sign in the rain, and that felt intimate and secret, the deepest kind of sharing between us and Her, for it was surrounded by no fuss, and it was totally ordinary, and wise as life and work and breathing are wise.

I walked in front of the tree with Eryk and then I saw her. I saw, I mean, the white statue of the Virgin that is in the tree stretching out its arms and revealing a great golden heart with eight flames. I had noticed the statue, but it was only when I was in front of it that its peaceful tenderness winded me, and the power that emanated from its majesty made me breathless.

"She is here," Eryk said.

We knelt in the rain and both prayed for Her protection, to be with us and with our love forever.

Then we went into the chapel across the yard. Eryk walked up to the alter, took two large open white roses from a vase on it, and walked toward me, his whole face alight with a joy I had never seen on it before.

"These are from Her to us," he whispered. "These are Her Gifts and Her Signs. This one is for you," and he handed me one. "Smell it, Andrew, breathe it in, breathe it in to every part of your heart and mind and spirit and know that our Lady of Beauraing is now everywhere in you, protecting and blessing you and your love and your life."

He spoke as if in a trance and I took the rose from him knowing that what was happening before Her altar was sealing us together forever, that She was now marrying us in Her Love.

Back in a bleak winter Paris, my back worse than it had ever been, sleepless and in terrible confusion, I fell again into deep panic. The marvelous days of Grace from the Virgin only split me further; how could I possibly square what I had known in them with what Meera had said to me and with the atmosphere of misery and depression I had experienced in Thalheim? And yet I could not yet face what Meera had revealed herself to be; I still had to believe I trusted her; I still had to wrestle repeatedly with my rage and doubt and bewilderment, to go on praying to her to be graced with the meaning of the teaching that she was trying to give me. My mind still raced with hysteria from one baroque, fantastic, and contradictory explanation of what she had said and done to another.

Two days after I returned, I rang my greatest spiritual friend, Astrid, who had lovingly accompanied me during the year of transformation I described in *Hidden Journey*. She had been with a south Indian Master for over thirty years; she, I felt sure, would be able to guide me now.

However, all Astrid could find to say was, "It looks very bad, terrible. What can I say? I don't pretend to understand what is going on, and I'm not going to give you any kind of pat explanation. I beg you to do one thing. Keep your heart always open to Mother Meera. Just keep your heart open in the agony and the darkness. It must be a test of some kind."

I told her that the day before my collaborator on *Dialogues with a Modern Mystic* had informed me that Meera wanted her name removed from the dedication page, and certain essential pages related to spirituality and gay sexuality removed. One cut in particular had agonized me—it had to do with Christ being the "Master" of all kinds of love, even homosexual, and about the blessing and dedication of desire being essential to the birth of Christ-consciousness.

Astrid's voice brightened. "Yes, it *must* be a test. If you show Mother Meera that you are willing to submit to even her most arbitrary seeming demands, to accept her doing anything, anything at all, even cutting out the most sacred parts of your book, even removing her own name from the text, then I am convinced she will *see* and *know* the depth of your surrender to her. She will know that you are willing to follow her into the finally absurd, and then you will see she will return to you everything you have abandoned to her. Everything you have surrendered will be given back to you a thousandfold. This is how *they* work, the illumined Ones. It seems like fascism, and is. But the Absolute is fascist."

The madness of Astrid's last phrase only broke on me later; at the moment, it seemed a terrible, but helpful, clue. I had to *submit,* to *submit* every claim to understand and judge to Mother Meera and then she would *see* my sincerity and a new part of my journey with and in her would inevitably unfold. Whether that journey would include Eryk and our love I didn't dare to speculate; my mind was already on the verge of breakdown from having to hold so many contradictions.

I followed Astrid's advice and made all the necessary cuts. I wept as I cut the paragraph on Christ and made a new bland transition in its place. Eryk said nothing and just watched me as I cut and repasted my book. Later, he told me, "It was like watching someone cut up a living child."

After two days, I told Eryk that I was going to ring Adilakshmi to report that I had done what I was told to do. Eryk said, "Ring her by all means, but I want to be here. I want there to be a witness to the conversation."

My need to believe in Meera's goodness reasserted itself. I sincerely believed that Adilakshmi and Meera would both welcome the news of my "surrender" and reveal to me the real meaning of the pain Eryk and I had lived through. I truly believed that in surrendering my work and my vision to her dictates I had "completed" my "disciple's" part of the drama she had engineered. Eryk would be sitting there beside me to receive her healing wisdom. A new life for both of us would begin.

I rang Adilakshmi.

"How are you, dear?" her bright, loud voice rang down the phone.

"Marvelous," I said. "So much is clearing, I can't describe how much."

"Oh I knew it would," Adilakshmi said. "I knew it. Mother is so powerful. Even the blindest of us she makes to see, even the most crippled to walk."

"I know, Adilakshmi, I have know her all these years. How could I not know? And I wanted you to know, Adilakshmi, that I have accepted nearly every single one of the cuts you suggested. Thank you so much—and thanks to Mother—for having spent all the time you did in what I know is a very busy and demanding life. I am so grateful."

Adilakshmi laughed and I heard her talk in Telugu to Mother

Meera, who must have been standing behind or beside her because I could clearly hear her slow voice.

I put my hand over the phone, thrilled afresh at the sound of Meera's voice, convinced that what she was saying to Adilakshmi would carry the vital clue for Eryk's and my healing.

Adilakshmi started to talk to me again, her voice singing with happiness.

"We are so happy you are seeing the truth, dearest Andrew. You are very blessed, you know."

"I know," I said, my voice filling with gratitude.

"Yes, you are very, very blessed. So many gays come to Mother."

"Yes, since the beginning many gay people have come to the Mother. So many of the people who first spread the word about her have been gay. Think of T. and P. in Montreal—her first disciples there—think of me."

I was babbling.

Adilakshmi waited.

"As I was saying, dear, so many gay people come to the Mother and for so many years, but it is only you who have heard the truth. It is only to you that the Mother has spoken her deepest truth. It is only to you, her Messenger and her beloved disciple, that she has decided to reveal her will."

It was my turn to wait. Adilakshmi's voice dropped to a stage whisper, "You are the only one of all the gays, Andrew, whom the Mother thinks evolved enough now to know . . . to know—" she paused again for maximum effect—"that there is no future of any kind for gays in the future of the Mother."

I gasped, and my mind went white.

Reassembling myself as if from a distance, I heard myself ask Adilakshmi to repeat herself.

"The connection isn't very clear this end," my voice said. "Could you repeat Mother's secret?"

Impatiently, Adilakshmi said loudly, "There is no future in the Mother's future for gays, none at all."

I repeated the words out loud.

Eryk gripped my hand and raised it to his lips. "I'm always with you," he mouthed. "Go on asking, get this clear once and for all."

"Forgive me if I'm being slow, Adilakshmi," I said. "What will happen to the gays in the future?"

"They will not exist, dear," she said brightly. "They will not exist. The Force of the Mother will make everyone normal."

"So gay love is not real love?" I said. "The Divine cannot be present in it?"

I almost heard Adilakshmi's smile. "Oh my dear, how could something that is not normal be Divine in any way? You are in delusion, dear. But this is the way of human beings. The Mother is not angry with you, you know."

I winced, "Is she there? Does she agree with everything you have said? Are you totally certain?"

"Of course she agrees. You heard her talking, didn't you? Do you think I would tell you such a great and holy secret without her being here with me?"

I started to feel overwhelmingly sick, as if someone had poured acid into my stomach.

"Are you there, Andrew, dear?" Adilakshmi's bright soaring voice returned.

"Yes, I'm here," I said, as calmly as I could.

"We have great faith in you, Andrew. Don't let your bad mistakes of last week make you ashamed. Everyone can get things wrong."

"Thank you, Adilakshmi."

Meera's voice said something.

"What is Ma saying?"

"That you are a good child," Adilakshmi said. "What higher praise could you have than that?"

I put down the phone after saying goodbye and ran to the bathroom to vomit.

When I came back into the room, Eryk had gone leaving a note: "Gone to pray."

To try to put some order in my seething thoughts and emotions I sat down and wrote: "How can I accept *this*? This is a nightmare. I keep expecting, hoping, praying to awake from this long nightmare, but it never ends, it only gets darker. How can Meera possibly be the Divine Mother and talk such murderous nonsense? And I can't pretend she didn't talk because I heard her, I heard her voice, and Adilakshmi confirmed that she had repeated exactly what Meera meant. Oh my God, my God. This isn't just prejudice (just!) or Hindu homophobia; it's far far worse. It seems to me Meera is speaking about homosexuals as Hitler spoke about the Jews. 'There is no future of any kind for gays in the future of the Mother.'"

I went on for pages of hurt, disbelief. At moments, the full bleakness of a hopeless clarity about Meera started, I can see now, to break through, but my ancient training as a disciple, my terror at giving up fifteen years of devotion and an entire way of life that went with it won in the end. I wrote:

"Astrid cannot be wrong. Meera is testing me to the limits of my ability to surrender to her. She is now driving me even further into her holy absurdity by confronting me with a statement that couldn't under any circumstances be true. If I just accept it, she will see I have understood and everything will clear."

As I wrote that, I broke down weeping, "Help me, help me." I cried out to Meera, "You have to help me see, you have to now."

Eryk came back quietly. He had been praying for us in Notre Dame.

"They are crazy," he said.

"It seems that way, I know."

"It is that way," he said softly. "I was sitting right here. I heard you repeat the 'great secret.' I made notes. You want to read them?"

"No," I said.

Eryk's face suddenly became white, exhausted.

"I'm always going to be with you, Andrew. I will never leave you. You are my Beloved. But you must awaken soon. You *must*. Not just for my sake, but for yours."

That night, after we had made love, we lay in each other's arms listening to the silence of the great starlit winter night. That night, too, for the first time, when Eryk turned to kiss me, I saw that his face was radiant with Divine Light. I told him, my voice breaking with wonder.

"You are shining, too," he whispered. "Love is shining."

Soft white radiance poured from his eyes, cheeks, shoulders. Suddenly a marvelous laughter possessed us.

"The world and Adilakshmi can say what they want," Eryk said. "But we know that our love is blessed by the Holy Spirit."

Slowly, the soft brilliance spread all over the bed and seemed to dissolve in its power the bed, the old Victorian sofa, my desk covered with icons and photographs.

One Love, One Energy, One Sea of Light.

Suddenly, Eryk began to cough violently, his face drawn and ashen; he disappeared for twenty minutes into the bathroom. When he came out, he looked terrified.

"What's the matter?" I said. "Why are you so frightened? What happened was wonderful, a new beginning; not frightening."

"I am not frightened," Eryk said calmly. "Just a little cough, that's all. It's been freezing since we came."

He got into bed and nestled close to me, his head in the curve of my neck. Within minutes, he was asleep. But I couldn't sleep. I prayed to the Virgin and Christ: Tonight, You opened a door to Love. Help us go through the door.

In the next three days, I learned from Adilakshmi that Meera now wanted me to withdraw an interview I had given to Mark Thompson for his book *Gay Soul*. In it I had explained how certain I was that one of the greatest gifts the Mother was now giving humanity was a healing of all sexual shame and all separation between soul and body. I had also explained at length how in ancient cultures dedicated to the Mother homosexuals had been accepted, even celebrated, as priests and shamans.

The night I heard the interview for *Gay Soul* could not be published I was unable to sleep. Back pain, panic, and a strange dread kept me awake. In the middle of the night, I saw Eryk sit up, stagger to the bath, and I listened as he was violently, prolongedly sick. I went to the bathroom and knocked on the door to see if I could help him, but he shouted "Don't come in! Don't you dare come in! I'm fine! Leave me alone!"

Ashen-faced, he stumbled back to bed and, shivering, drew the bedclothes up over his face.

"Don't speak," he said eventually. "There's nothing wrong, I swear. Please go to sleep."

I pretended to sleep but could not. All night the memory of a conversation we had had the previous September in Mahabali-puram, in South India, kept coming back to me. Eryk and I were walking back after dinner along the sands; he stopped, took my hands, and asked if we could sit down on the sand. "I think I can tell you now," he had said. "Three years ago, I had throat cancer. It went away after chemotherapy. I'm clear now. But the remission period is seven years and if it—or another kind of cancer—returns, well . . ." He shrugged his shoulders and did not finish the sentence.

In the morning, as calmly as I could, I asked Eryk to go immediately to the doctor, "Just for a checkup, just to see if you have a mineral deficiency or something."

Eryk played along with the charade, "Oh, there's nothing wrong, Andrew. Don't even think of being dramatic. I'm probably lacking zinc."

In the late afternoon, Eryk returned. He had been away for much longer than he had planned. He said nothing, sat on the sofa, and starred into space. Then he started to speak in a dull, emotionless voice, "Bad news. I have two lesions on my right lung. I had several tests just to make sure. That is why it all took so long."

"Oh God. Oh my God."

"There's more," Eryk's voice was grimmer. "The doctor—who knows me and my case and has been following me all these years—said to me: 'But everything was healing last time I saw you. You were looking strong. You were in love.'" Eryk paused. "You know what he asked me?"

I shook my head helplessly.

"He asked me if I had had any extreme emotional shock recently. In his judgment, he said, the lesions were fresh, perhaps five or six weeks old at the most."

FROM MY JOURNAL:

Last night after hearing Eryk's terrible news, I rang Astrid and explained everything to her as calmly as I could, trying not to scream or accuse Meera. Astrid said, "In all my thirty years of seeking, this is the worst and most confusing story I have ever heard. I withdraw what I said about keeping open to Mother Meera. I do not know what to say, or what you should do. I know nothing anymore. You have been brought into the darkness of total affliction and in that place only Direct Grace can be of any help. You must simply pray and pray all the time, because where you are now adoration is the only possible protection and help." She added quietly, "If I were where you are now, I think I would kill myself."

From Astrid, who always affronted all the many challenges of her life with stoicism and dignity, those words were not lightly spoken; hearing them was both shocking and a relief. Perhaps only someone who loved her Master as all-absorbingly as she loved her Master in South India could begin to comprehend the agony of what I was to face. "Every possible hope or foundation is being removed from my life," I said to her. "Yes," she said. "That is what is happening. And I have no idea why or how you are going to survive it."

And I have no idea, either. Sometimes the suffering is so horrible I would blow my brains out if I had a revolver. Early this morning I dreamt that Eryk and I flew to India, to Mahabalipram, and took poison together calmly on the beach. But it didn't work; we weren't allowed to die . . .

I have at last ceased totally to believe in Meera, let alone pray to her. Either she knew this would result from her actions and is responsible, or she didn't and is criminally ignorant.

Every time her face comes into my mind—and it comes a hundred times each minute, as it has for fifteen years—I thrust it away with disgust. Every time I find myself saying her mantra—and my heart goes on repeating it even when my mind has abandoned it—I unsay it consciously, beg the true Divine to free me from its thrall. For fifteen years I thrust the energy of my whole self into impregnating myself with her at every level and in every dimension; now, knowing what I now know, I feel as if invaded by her, possessed darkly by her, horrified that even when I have ceased to believe in her, she still goes on in me as if she has been seeded in my very cells. It is a disgusting feeling, this seeding, this possession, and every moment is so ferocious that I sometimes feel my brain will explode. Every moment I hold consciously to the feet of our Lady of Beauraing. All I know now is that in Mary is my hope and future and protection.

Eryk gets paler and paler all the time, and thinner, and goes on vomiting blood. How will we live? How will we survive?

Astrid said, "You are in the darkness of affliction." She was right. I know nothing. I know only that I believe the Mother, the real Mother, will never abandon us. I have no one and nothing to turn to but Her. Neither of us have. Eryk said this morning, "Now we can rely on nothing but the Mother's Grace."

I can't pray in sentences anymore. All I can pray is "Help us, Mary, help us."

From my Journal:
February 5th, Paris

Only twelve days before Eryk and I return to America. I
am going to tour and teach at the California Institute of
Integral Studies. My life, his life, my life's work, are in
ruins. Twelve days to reassemble some semblance of clarity
and purpose. Eryk jokes, "By the end of next week you will
have to be a completely new being." Both of us know that
this is not possible; both of us know this wound in our
hearts will not heal for a long time; both of us know that
the horrible dark suffering that emanates from what happened in Thalheim, that seems to have an almost palpable
occult *force*, will not dissipate any time soon. Neither Eryk
nor I can sleep, and when we do our dreams are full of
images of death and torture. Every day Eryk gets more
hollow-cheeked, and my back is so bad I cannot sit or
stand or lie down without extreme pain. Yesterday Eryk
said, "Everything has become suffering."

The only thing that survives the wreckage is our love.
Tragedy purifies and simplifies us both. Every hour, it
seems, my love for Eryk becomes more tender and absolute: if there is any blessing in all this torment it is this;
knowing we may lose each other, that we may be sepa-
rated by death, drives us both into Love's eternal present.
The ordinary rituals of the days become poignant; sipping
tea together or listening to music or walking silently arm-
in-arm to the shops or going to the cinema become sacred
rituals. Every moment with Eryk is precious to me; knowing that he is probably dying has broken my heart open
to him finally. Whatever shatterings lie ahead, my heart

cannot close now. And there is a strange mercy in that which we both acknowledge.

"Whatever happens," Eryk says often, "we know beyond any doubt that we love each other."

The morning after I heard the news about Eryk's cancer I was so devastated I could do nothing but sit at my desk and beg the Virgin to help and guide us both. I knew I could not go on for another day without Her Love supporting me; I knew I had no hope of surviving whatever lay ahead without direct naked experience of Her continual help; I knew that there was no hope of Eryk getting well or my life rediscovering its meaning and direction without being transformed by Her and in her Grace. "You have been brought into the darkness of affliction," Astrid had said. "Where you are now, adoration is the only possible protection."

"Help me, guide me," I prayed to Her. "Show me now, I cannot wait, the force and power of the direct Path, the direct connection with You." And, marvelously, almost immediately, words formed in my mind that had the clear and demanding force of true guidance, ,and I had my first initiation into how immediately the Mother can answer—and how wisely—if She is asked with total sincerity. "You must understand why you became Meera's slave," the quiet inner voice persisted. "You *must* understand everything as completely as you can. I will give you the courage to see and bear what you have to face. Face everything; use the agony you are in as a goad to drive yourself more and more completely into the Light of Reality. There is no time to waste; your whole future depends on how completely you can face what seduced you to worship the false Mother; any illusion you hide now will not only endanger you but also Eryk and the thousands of people who have followed and believed in your work."

There is no time to waste, I can see that. I can see that up to now I have been simply staggering from one suffering to another, simply reacting to a whirlwind succession of blows and betrayals. Now I must summon fiercely every power of reason and discrimination that I have, every possible insight and memory, to try to discover as soon as possible why I came to be sitting on that sofa on December 27th, putting my life—and the life of my Beloved—in the hands of a prejudiced, ignorant, manipulative, dangerous woman on a spiritual power trip. I will be in America in ten days beginning a tour that will carry me all over the States; I will be asked again and again why I have chosen to leave Meera, and I must be of real help in what I say and not simply react out of anger. If I can find the strength through the Mother's Grace to bare ruthlessly what drove my obsession with Meera, then I may be able to help thousands of other seekers trapped with abusive so-called Masters.

When I told Eryk about how fast the guidance from the Mother came and what it said, he smiled. "Of course, it comes if you ask. The millions of people who have prayed to Her over the centuries know She is listening and wants to help as quickly as possible; She is the Mother, for God's sake. As for what She said to you, you have no choice now but to subject your whole life and search to the most scathing kind of clarity. What other hope do you have of even beginning to be free of what bound you to Thalheim?

And if you are not free, how can you possibly begin to help others claim their freedom and the beauty of the direct relationship with Her? You have led thousands of people to the feet of the false Mother; you *have* to warn them and face whatever consequences that brings. I will be with you. Raging at Meera will not help; you will only look crazy. What you have to offer is a real analysis, and you can only offer that if you have suffered it. The more completely you allow the Mother to destroy your old false knowledge about yourself and Her, the more completely She can fill you with the awareness of what She is."

"What terrifies me most about this," I said to Eryk, "is that questioning my whole relationship with Meera will mean questioning all the experiences I imagined I had with her and from her."

"Of course," he replied, "but what else can you do? You have to question those experiences. You have to face that Meera cannot have transformed you as much as you wanted to believe, because she is not illumined, to put it mildly. If she is as ignorant and dangerous as she is, something in your belief in her must also have been ignorant, and because ignorant and unconscious, dangerous."

As Eryk spoke I realized I had to begin again in everything; I had to allow every structure I had built over so many years to be rubbled entirely. A part of me almost fainted with fear and desolation; and a part of me, the part, I suddenly realized, that had set me on the Quest in the first place, embraced this new, devastating challenge because it knew enough of the Glory of the Presence of the Mother to know that anything at all was worth it if it could help me arrive more authentically in its Grace and help others to do so.

Then Eryk said, "What we are living through *is* a teaching. Not Meera's teaching, but a teaching of the Divine Mother. The Mother is destroying the icon of the false Mother so as to take us both into the Love of the real One. Meera may imagine she *is* the Mother, but that only makes her mad; she is in fact, like us all, in the Game of the Mother. This horror in which we have been plunged is the real Mother's drastic way of waking you up to a new vision. Neither I nor you can know now what that is—but it will come: she will grace it. She is not going to put you—and me—through what we are enduring without giving something marvelous in return." He added, "Thank God you *do* know Meera cannot be the real Mother. Imagine if you had gone to America and talked about her everywhere. Imagine, too, if what has happened now happened in twenty years' time. You would have wasted an entire lifetime in the service of a dangerous illusion, and knowing you, if you woke up then, you would have no option but to kill yourself. This shattering of your relationship with Meera has come at exactly the time it was meant to come and at a time when you are still young and strong enough to learn and help others and go on. Be brave, be brave for our love; face everything, let everything you think you've understood go into her fire and be burnt away there. Above all, be *humble*."

"What would I do without your clarity," I said.

"What would I do without your hope?" he said. "You have what I need and I have what you need. That is why She put us together on this crazy adventure."

FROM MY JOURNAL:
February 9th

I have prayed all day for four days now, begging for clarity
and guidance. At first I was terrified that in "losing" Meera
I was losing the Mother, losing that mystical contact that
over years of meditation I have built up with Her Force.
This is not true; the intensity of the Presence, in Light, in a
softly explosive pulsing in the heart, is as strong and vivid
as ever; more so, in fact, now that I ascribe no name or
specific face to it.

In praying to the Virgin, I am not praying to a person
in a body but to a being with thousands of faces, the Love-
being that creates and sustains the universe and births Divine freedom and compassion in the soul. I am discovering
that what Grace gave me in the years of my adoration of
Meera cannot now be destroyed by whatever I feel about
Meera or by whatever Meera does; in the language of Sufi
mysticism, certain "stations"—kinds of inner awareness
which will not change and cannot—have been established
in my being and give me knowledge of the Divine and of
Divine Love. I cry with gratitude and relief every time my
soul sings in this gnosis because I know now that the adoration of the Mother that I have been practicing—however
"confused" or "deflected" it may have become because of
my fixation upon Meera—nevertheless has been authentic
and has remained with me as my deepest truth.

The only way to keep this certainty alive, I am discovering, is through adoration, through keeping up a perpetual
river of prayer to the Virgin in the heart.

For the last four afternoons I have gone to the large

baroque chapel of the Rue du Bac where the Virgin appeared to Catherine Labouré in the 1830s and gave her a miraculous medal. I kneel with the Koreans and Filipinos and the old women from Guadeloupe and the businessmen in Cerruti suits and the children sobbing quietly in wheelchairs and feel one with them, as stripped and bereft and naked before Her as they are. The Presence of a searing and holy compassion is overwhelming in this chapel; it isn't just desperation and hope for miracle that I see in the faces around me; there is also a certainty, a contagious and wonderful certainty that radiates from the tear-filled eyes and hands moving over the rosary beads that echoes in the prayers murmured from every corner—in Chinese, Armenian, Creole, Korean, Italian, all the languages of the world—a certainty that She is listening, feeling, suffering, grieving, hoping with us and in us, breath of our breath, salt of our tears.

Slowly, the recognition is building in me that whatever suffering lies ahead—and often my mind shuts down when I begin to contemplate it—I will not be bearing it alone. She will be bearing it in me and with me. However far I fall apart, I will—I see more and more clearly through Her Grace—fall further into Her, into the mysterious darkness of Her Love.

FROM MY JOURNAL:
February 11th, Paris

It is obvious: Meera's rejection of my sexuality and of my love for Eryk makes it clear that she never loved me for myself but only for what I could do for her or bring her. I had gone to her, I see now, because of the complexity of my own sometimes difficult relationship with my mother, out of my need for unconditional maternal love. Far from "healing" my wound with my mother, she had—whether consciously or unconsciously (and more and more I am forced by what has happened to believe that it was conscious)—perpetuated it at another level and manipulated for her own purposes the extraordinary energies it radiated in her direction.

None of this, I am seeing, had anything to do with what could be called love; it was a game of power, of control. It was this game whose hand she had shown me through the disastrous mistake of revealing her homophobia. If I were able to love Eryk and respond to his healing and transforming acceptance of me in every way, I would no longer be open to *her* manipulation, no longer be able to be kept at the kind of frozen distance at which she needed to keep me for me to go on being her willing accomplice. She had, I see now, to try to destroy the love between Eryk and me because her occult power must have revealed to her how it would in the end free me from her and free me from the need to project onto her my need for a Mother; in the experience of Divine human love I would discover the *real* Mother beyond form or concept and would discover that She was in me and around me at all times and in all circumstances.

Meera had to try and destroy my love for Eryk to keep me split and famished for her. Real Love—human Divine Love between two beings who are attuned in heart, soul, mind, and body—*cannot* be manipulated by any external power. This is why all the patriarchal systems—including the Guru system—try to split off their adherents from sexuality and the body and nearly always try to break up real relationships.

The system of projection and the manipulation of archetypes that patriarchy and the Guru game feed off can only be kept going by keeping the spirit split from the body, the soul from the genitals, so the real tantric union of the transcendent and immanent cannot occur and cannot initiate beings in the ground of their ordinary life, free from the need for any authority except that of the Mother's Love, and so free from control.

FROM MY JOURNAL:
February 12th, Paris

I haven't slept properly for over a week. I have asked the Mother for clarity, and it comes and burns away everything except its often excruciating precision. I know this is *direct* Grace and try to remain as open as I can, despite the terror it sometimes brings, and the continual exhaustion.

In the middle of last night I saw clearly, and with great pain, the extent of my own responsibility for keeping the farce of Meera's divinity going.

For years I believed that serving her with blind intensity was the best thing I could do. Now I see that just as Meera needed the kind of love-slave I was as a Messenger, so my early childhood wounds and the unconscious narcissism and need that they bred to endlessly prove myself made *me* need to be a Messenger. The pain of my childhood and the miseries of my adult search for love gave me a need for a role that would redeem my life. In Meera's world-film, I would be given one of the best parts—that of the angel-messenger. I see that I embraced this role with all my hunger to be loved and approved and celebrated.

This unconscious narcissism was fed by Meera. She needed someone to do what I could do—devote my trained Western intellect to her world "message"—and I needed to feel that I could be valuable, sacred, useful; I could never have been as sustainedly vulnerable to her manipulation had I not also unconsciously needed what it gave me; a role, a message, a kind of celebrity, a "star part," in fact, as unconsciously meretricious as the one Meera is playing.

I sat in the dark watching Eryk sleep and weeping for the pain I had caused us both. With those tears came another fiercer recognizing. I found myself stumbling over to my desk and writing down, as if receiving dictation:

"YOU HAVE KNOWN IN YOUR HEART—WITHOUT ADMITTING IT AND FOR YEARS—MEERA IS HOMOPHOBIC."

I had to stop for two hours at that last sentence. This awful peeling away that Mary's Grace is doing leaves me sometimes unable to move or breathe. Sometimes I feel I will have a heart attack. At other times I want to cease to be altogether. I went out into the dawn and walked up and down the Seine, and its gray winter flowing cooled my mind.

As I walked, so many insights, conversations, and incidents returned to me, perfectly strung together and interconnected for the first time. I realized that I have known for a long time that Meera is homophobic and simply could not bear to acknowledge it, because to acknowledge this would destroy that intricate and half-mad fantasy about her divinity that I needed to keep alive at all costs.

Five years before, I and some other devotees over one summer put together the question-and-answer book *Answers for Meera* in her former house in Thalheim. In the original draft—which I still have, thank God—Meera said, "Homosexuality is not a natural way of life." And she went on to extol, as usual, the glory of family life and "normality." I insisted to my colleagues that putting in such a passage would do the Mother irreparable harm; reluctantly, they eventually agreed and the passage was excised: *Answers* was printed without it. What is astonishing in retrospect is that I was not in any *personal* way affected by what Meera had said. I can't even say I "justified" it to myself; I hardly "heard" it at all. I realize now that I simply could not bear to believe that Meera was *really* homophobic because I could not bear to believe she did not bless my entire being.

When I explained everything I have been "seeing" to Eryk at breakfast he said, "You haven't been blind only about Meera's homophobia. You've been blind about everything to do with her. You refused to see her as she is, because you needed her desperately to be as you wanted her to be."

I was furious, although I knew he was right.

"Don't be angry at me," Eryk said fiercely. "I think I have already suffered enough in this farce."

A long silence. Then Eryk leaned forward, took my hands, and said:

"Go on. Find out everything, absolutely everything, you have been repressing. Make what you have refused to know *conscious*. This is your only way of getting out from what she was doing to you. You have to, to save your life."

———

That same night, another clue was given me. Eryk and I went to bed early. We lit candles round our bed and prayed to the Mother, consecrating our lovemaking to her, and then made love. That night, as it had before, the Fire descended. As I bent down to suck Eryk's cock, I saw that his body was radiant with a gold-green light. Startled, I looked up to see Eryk smiling down at me; his face, too, shone with an even more radiant gold-green Light. I heard the words: Love is looking at itself through both of your eyes.

I remembered how Hildegard of Bingen had talked of the "greening power" of the Holy Spirit, its "viriditas." I remembered that Khidr the Prophet—the Initiator in Sufi mysticism—was known as "the green one" because of his primal power and that the light of the heart is always green in Rumi. Had Rumi seen Shams' face stream with this splendor?

For a moment I was terrified. Was this some strange magic? Was this a test or a delusion of some kind? No sooner did those thoughts arise than I realized they were the last ruses of my ancient self-disgust trying to control the ecstasy that was now threatening to end its life forever. But nothing can control the blaze of authentic ecstasy, once it has been ignited by the spirit; no power in any dimension can prevent it bursting in the heart and spreading like a subtle bush fire along all the nerves and through and in every muscle.

"Suck me," Eryk whispered. "Do everything you have always wanted to do with me. I am yours."

And as Eryk said those words the gold-green Light around him grew fiercer, until his face was almost lost in the blaze that surrounded it. His beautiful athlete's body, naked and open on the sheets, glittered too, as if it had been rubbed with oil. All the men I had ever wanted, all the different types of male beauty I had ever desired, all seemed to be there before me in his one body. He was at once the soldier and the poet, the policeman and the artist, the innocent and wild young man and the masterly old sage, able to give and get exactly what he wants; he was angel and bike-boy, Krishna and wild, beautiful, half-drunken dancer. Everything could be done between us, everything given, without shame or fear; every wild desire could be expressed, because Love was expressing it and so transmuting immediately anything "perverse" into pure, deep, holy passion. In the Mother's Love that was burning in us and now around us (now the room, too, swam in golden light and everything grew soaked with its fire-water) there were no barriers, no forms, no guilt, no shame.

As I caressed him and rubbed his chest and legs with sandalwood oil and licked his cock and sucked it and dived again and again into ever-deeper, more explosive, pools of wild joy, I knew, with a knowledge that knew no possible doubt, that he and I were experiencing at the same moment exactly the same height of joy. I was with him experiencing my passion; I was his passion glowing with mine; I was my own desire fired through by the desire that swept him. When he gasped, my throat constricted. When he moaned, I found myself answering softly before my mind could intervene; when I touched the inside of his thigh, I felt I was touching myself—the inside of my palm and the slightly sweaty sweet-haired inside of his thigh were two sides of the same glowing skin.

Eryk and I came together in great laughing, rending cries that were like the cries of women giving birth. As I came, I was gazing at Eryk's chest, glowing in gold-green Divine Light; the Light coalesced as I looked at it and became a Sun.

I am birthing in you both My Son the Sun.

"You are shining," Eryk said, the only words either of us could speak as we sank deeper and deeper beyond thought or even feeling into a sea of calm, vast, pulsing soft flame that we saw, as we gazed in wonder around us, had ignited not only our room but the night of Paris outside our windows and the stars shining in it.

I rested in the great flame-silence. Then, I heard music. It was south Indian violin music, played quietly and rapidly. I was fully conscious and knew that my CD player was turned off, but the music was breathing from the walls around me. I smiled at this beautiful and tender Grace of Hers; this music is the one I have always associated most completely with Her rhythm of softly unfolding bliss in the universe; it is the music, too, of the country in which I was born, and I had often listened to it in the temples and along the seashore of the place I love most, Mahabalipuram.

As I remembered the sun-and-moon soaked seas and temples of Mahabalipuram, a dream-vision that I had had there on my first visit, when I was twenty-five and lonely, returned to me. I relived it—or it relived me.

I am in the inner sanctum of the shore-temple at twilight, the time when the small windowless room fills with red-gold light and the great Pallava sculpture of Siva and Parvati leaning on each other at the Feast of Life flames in the dying sun. Rapture fills me in the place in which I have always felt most whole and have always thought to be a kind of birth-chamber, in which, every time I have stepped into it, especially at this twilight hour, when the walls and stone themselves seem to become a sea of flickering red-gold light, I have felt blessed and reborn.

I am wearing white Indian clothes. There is a cool sea wind and a stick of incense before the altar surrounded by jasmine flowers. Incense and the scent of jasmine pervade the whole room. I start to sing—there is no one around—and I sing out loud, louder and louder, just the two names "Siva, Parvati," until they become one long ecstatic in-folding melisma, one single Name that flows in and out of itself, scented by sea wind and incense and jasmine. I close my eyes and pray in my heart to the One beyond names and forms and offer my whole being and life in adoration to It. Beloved, Beloved, Beloved is all my heart can say, over and over; all the joy of all the magnificent days and nights I had spent in that first astounded visit to the Eden that is Mahabalipuram fill me and spill over in praise and gratitude.

When I open my eyes, the sanctum is dark, the sun has set, and a large torch has been lit in a corner. Seated in front of me only about a foot away, his head in shadow, is the most beautiful young man I have seen. His perfect athletic body is naked except for a gold cloth that he wears around his middle. He holds out his hands to me and I take them. He raises them to his lips and kisses them and then lowers them between his legs, onto the large and gorgeous cock that was erect between them, tall in its small tower of gold cloth.

All shame or fear of blasphemy fall from me. I know the time and place supremely holy. I know too—I do not know how—that the man whose face I still cannot see is a priest, a yogi, and that the love he is offering me in this sanctum is one of the most sacred secrets of the Father-Mother.

Slowly and tenderly, the young priest opens the gold cloth round his waist, stands up, and sets it aside. His large, perfectly shaped, strong, erect cock moves slowly to my mouth as something in my chest explodes and the whole shrine catches fire. Safe in that

Divine Radiance, nothing is forbidden us. As our lovemaking becomes more and more purely abandoned, I see and know that what the young priest wants me to do is to drink him completely and that if I do drink him I will be drinking with his sperm the honey-milk of the Mother-Father, their Love-milk, which will strengthen and infuse with profound truth and sanity and health my whole body and being. His cock, I understand, is one of the nipples of the Mother through which I will be fed Her milk of rapture.

As I relive the dream just before the hot holy liquid, the honey-milk from his human Divine cock rushes down my throat, the beautiful yogi does what he did not do fifteen years before; he moves his head into the light suddenly so I can clearly see his face.

It is Eryk's face.

It is Eryk's cock.

It is Eryk's body.

The hot honey-milk fires my whole body and the words come:

"You dreamed of Eryk before you met him. He is my priest of Love sent to you in My Temple of Love. Adore him, cherish him, honor him. I made you for each other so your worship of me in each other could heal you both into birth. Be faithful now through everything to this extreme Grace."

The next morning I went to the Chapel of the Miraculous Medal to thank the Mother for the splendor of what She had given Eryk and myself and to pray for Eryk's health. As I was kneeling, the words rose in me:

"You are strong enough now to confront the memories of Meera you have never wanted to face."

I started to shake and tremble, for I was suddenly extremely frightened, for no reason I could understand.

"I will give you the clarity and the strength if you pray for them."

I left the chapel and walked in a slight, gray February drizzle to a café on the corner of the Rue du Bac and sat and waited. I did not have to wait long; something in my mind opened and a memory I had repressed for years returned to me.

I am in Montreal in autumn 1987. This was the year I wrote about in *Hidden Journey*. I went to Montreal to investigate the scandal that had blown up around Mr. Reddy (Meera's "uncle" who discovered her, who died in 1983) and Meera seven years before, when she had had to leave in a hurry, taking Mr. Reddy and Adilakshmi to Germany. I felt I owed it to the "integrity" of my book on her to listen to every side of the story; in fact, I was already so drunk on what I felt I was discovering about Meera that I had made up my mind that anything but Meera's own version would have to be lies or delusion. In the final manuscript of *Hidden Journey,* I took out every reference to my trip to Montreal—why even start to confuse people? I thought; they are already confused enough.

I am sitting in a dingy pizza place with one of Meera's oldest disciples—now ex-disciple—a poet, writer, and old friend in his sixties. He had left Meera during the time of the "scandal" and disavowed her violently. I asked Jean what had really happened in Montreal.

"You are trying to make me tell you the worst and saddest story of my life. Meera, Adilakshmi, and Mr. Reddy came to live in a house near ours. I saw them every day. You remember that big calm house don't you, always full of flowers? You came several times."

I nodded, tense.

"At first everything was idyllic. Until the disciples who were arranging everything discovered that all that Mr. Reddy and Meera seemed to be interested in was money. After a while, I started even to doubt what *kind* of power Meera has."

I froze. "What do you mean what *kind* of power? She has direct, extreme *divine* power. Hundreds have felt it. *You* have felt it."

Jean began again. "It is obvious that she has power. But there are many kinds of power. Occult power is not Divine power but can seem very like it. At a certain stage in the mystical journey powers—of clairvoyance, telepathy, ability to change or manipulate the minds of others—are born in the seeker's mind. If he or she uses them for personal fame or control or money, they are lost. All traditions speak of these powers, which to an untutored and experience-hungry seeker (which is *every* Western seeker I have ever met) can very easily look like—what did you say—direct, extreme *Divine* power."

"So what are you saying. Let's get to it."

"You don't want to hear, but I'll say it anyway. I and many others in that initial Montreal circle all came to believe that Meera was not in any way a Master but a kind of witch."

I jumped up and the restaurant fell silent.

"A witch? Meera?"

"Sit down and stop making yourself absurd. Meera is a witch, and that is why the group of us told her to get out and take Adilakshmi and Reddy with her. That is why none of us has ever been back to see her. That is why I will never have anything to do with her for the rest of my life. Look, Andrew, Meera isn't just any old witch. I believe she is a great black witch and extremely powerful. She can do many things, send experiences, appear in your dreams, give you what seem like awakenings, send you wave after wave of bliss. But this is not real Divine work; it is magic designed to entrap and ensnare. The Burmese have a word for it—I made quite a study of this kind of thing in the last years. They call it 'framing.' A black magician 'frames' a person by enchanting or hypnotizing them and then has them in his or her power to do with what he or she wants.

"Meera is a brilliant 'framer.' My guess is that she has had occult powers from childhood and has increasingly 'given in' to them. She knows that the vast majority of seekers can't tell black magic from Divine power and hardly even know such black magic exists and is real, and so she has, in the current desperate climate, a field day. By the way, I think the 'framing' actually happens in *darshan*. Most of the magic manuals I have studied stress how important it is to stare into people's eyes."

I sat stunned, unable to speak for what I imagined was rage and pity. Then I snarled, "Meera and Adilakshmi tell the story very differently."

"You don't surprise me," Jean smiled dryly.

"They say *you* were the money-hungry ones. *You* wanted to use Mother for your own ends and that is why you had to say she was a witch when she found you out. Adilakshmi told me personally that you in particular wanted to become a guru in Meera's place and use Meera's power to help you do so. But Mother said—I remember— 'I will always love him.'"

Jean laughed, "And you believed all that? My, you are a good little disciple! Didn't it occur to you for one moment that Meera and Adilakshmi were lying and improvising with the first things they could think of, that the kind of rubbish they fed you is what all false Masters feed their trapped victims? The best is 'I will always love him.' She may fool you, she obviously has, but that, old friend, is the oldest and worst line in the book. As for wanting to become a guru, look at me! I'm poor, for one thing; for another, all I want to do with the rest of my life is write one good book."

Jean paused. "I hear you are writing a book about her. I beg you not to."

"You're just jealous that I was chosen to write it," I said.

"My dear Andrew," he said, "I've been one of the chosen ones, too, remember. There are a lot of ex-chosen ones, around, let me tell you."

He got up sadly and tiredly. "You won't learn for years, and when you do your heart will break, as mine did. But there is life after Meera. One day you will know what I know now and you will also know that the great majority of the so-called Masters and gurus are also black magicians, just like old Meera. Did you know there are schools for black magicians in India? The majority are in Gujurat, if you're interested."

"I don't believe a word you are saying. You're just a sad, pathetic, defeated old man with no hope and no heart and no gratitude to the One who could have saved you."

"If I didn't know before you opened your mouth that you'd have to make a speech like that I would punch you in the jaw."

It was almost noon by now in the café on the corner of the Rue du Bac. Eryk would be waiting for me for lunch back at the apartment. But I knew I couldn't move from where I was. I got up to ring Eryk and say that I would be late and that he should lunch without me.

He heard the trembling in my voice. "Is anything wrong?"

I told him what was happening.

"Stay exactly where you are. Surround yourself with the Light of the Virgin. Go deeper and deeper into what you are remembering."

I remembered how, for years, Thalheim and the "scene" around Meera had saddened me. During the last four years I had, I realized, distanced myself more and more from Thalheim—from the

weird pervading atmosphere among the disciples of mutual dis-
trust, jealousy, and slow-boiling, stagnant hatred.

"No one is happy here," D. had said to me just last December.
"Everyone here is lonely and miserable."

For years now, I understood, I had not wanted to return to
Thalheim at all; I only did so to see Meera. For years I saw, too, I
had avoided asking myself the question: If everyone is so rancid
and desolate around her, how can she possibly be who she says she
is? Once, when I was writing *Hidden Journey*, Meera had said how she
sometimes deliberately fostered jealousy among the disciples to
make them more devoted to her; I had thought this strange at the
time but, as with so much else, believed that it was my own lack of
understanding of "Divine truth" that made me uneasy at what she
was saying.

What returned to me, then, in excruciating force, was my own repressed knowledge of Meera's limitations, a knowledge I had been
suppressing for over a decade but from which I now had nowhere
to hide. Without the heroin of adoration to blind and numb my
mind, memory supplied me with a whirlwind of Meera's blunders,
imprecise predictions, prejudices, and follies.

One day, knowing that I had some slight connections to the
Gandhi family in Delhi, Meera asked me to write a letter from her
to Rajiv Gandhi. She began it with a paean to Indira Gandhi's
"wonderful strength of will" and then said that it was the Divine
Mother's will that the Gandhi dynasty should rule India. She
ended by blessing Rajiv, telling him that he would be reelected, and
live to be a "great one." Two weeks after I sent the letter, Rajiv
Gandhi was assassinated.

Meera had also denied categorically to me and many others

that the Gulf War would take place in the months before it broke; she often told me with a smile that Saddam Hussein was nothing at all to worry about and I had believed her happily. Then, when war *was* raging, Meera claimed to be "monitoring" it from her television set; she sat glued to CNN all day and told Adilakshmi, who told me, "There is nothing I cannot do." Adilakshmi and other disciples spread the "rumor" that many of the allied victories were due to Meera's personal intervention in the field.

Now that suffering had begun to distance me from Meera, I could see clearly how ridiculous a great many of her pronouncements on world affairs had been. Meera often said in the early eighties that there was no environmental crisis to worry about, that concern for the environment was just "Western hysterics," and that social activism on behalf of the environment was just "theatrics"; it was only very gradually that she began to admit that something was wrong and even then she would repeat, smilingly again and again, "Human beings need not worry. God will look after everything."

In Madanapalli, in India, once, sitting at her kitchen table, she told me that evil simply did not exist, that everything I or anyone else thought of as evil was simply "ideas and thoughts"; I had been too stupefied to argue with her and for weeks had truly believed I had been given some sort of "ultimate" teaching about evil, some final perception of its "intrinsic unreality," which I had to adopt precisely because it came from her and went against everything I believed I knew. (But how could I, a mere human being, understand anything real?)

Again and again, Meera had made clear to me her rejection of feminism and anything to do with Women's Liberation, which both she and Adilakshmi thought of as "Western nonsense": Many times I heard Meera say that in most ways women were subservient to men, less intelligent, and far less reliable. Their place was with their husbands and in the home; careers for women were looked down upon as if they in some way detracted from women's true status. How could I have heard such rubbish with such serene equanimity?

Once more memories began, no power could stop them. Meera, I remembered, had not only made stupid comments on world affairs with great regularity; she had also given the disciples who asked her bad advice. She had encouraged disciples to move, or invest, or change jobs with sometimes catastrophic consequences. In my presence, she had told a French disciple, who was a friend of mine, to stay with his schizophrenic wife and to have another child with her to "balance her energies": The wife tried to murder the child several times, and the man's life became a hell that lasted for years. I heard her tell a Swiss female disciple (who later left her in outrage) that she had "no matter what happened" to stay with the horribly abusive man with whom she had been living; that was her duty as a woman. The man later tried to murder her and burned down the house in which they were living.

On many occasions, I realized, with fury and shame, I had asked her advice and followed it with destructive results. Even more extraordinarily, I had never confronted her with its failure. I had asked her "divine guidance" on whether or not I should invest in a restaurant on the coast in India; she said an enthusiastic "yes," affirmed that the man I would be investing in was "a true devotee of the Mother": He later turned out to be a shark, and I lost everything. Again, a year later, I rang her to ask her "divine guidance" on whether or not I should go ahead and found a television company with two new friends whom I did not completely trust; she assured me they were "fine religious people" and that the company would flourish: They, too, turned out to be crooks and the company went broke.

Some of Meera's close disciples even went so far as to claim that her frequent bad advice, false predictions, and astonishing denials of world crisis and environmental collapse were "tests" of our faith; she was, they would explain carefully, making what we, in our ignorance, interpreted as "mad moves" to sort out to which ones amongst us were really ready to follow her through everything and which of us were ruled only by our own minds and wills. "Everyone agrees after all," they would nearly always conclude, "that the Shakti runs through her."

Even at my most doubting and secretly troubled, I, too, had always had to agree that whatever the *human* Meera seemed to be doing or saying, "the Shakti runs through her." But what I had remembered in the café and what I was remembering now brought up a question that I could not avoid and which terrified me and made me tremble.

Who was to say that the powers Meera had were not being used sometimes for evil? Look at what had already happened to Eryk and myself . . .

What if Jean in Montreal was right and Meera was a witch, a dangerous and powerful witch, and not a divine being or avatar at all. What would that mean? Could it be that I had written a book about a woman who was in fact evil and had claimed her to be nothing less than the Divine Mother, and persuaded thousands of other sincere and innocent seekers to believe it also? Could it be that my blindness had put my and my Beloved's lives in danger? I knew, I realized, hardly anything about "black magic" or the occult; I had always believed myself to be protected from such powers by Meera herself.

Complete terror and grief swept my being. I felt utterly helpless. All I could do was pray to the Virgin: "Help us. Help us. Help us."

The next morning I told Eryk what I had remembered and understood, or begun to. He started to weep, "How could you ever have believed such obvious rubbish? How could you have allowed her to trample your mind? No wonder she used you as her Messenger; your need to be blind coupled with your gifts of expression, your connections, your impeccable 'intellectual' credentials made you the perfect tool."

I could say nothing. As Eryk went on speaking, I remembered a sentence that a friend of mine who had known Sartre had once told me; when she asked Sartre how someone as shrewd and brilliant as he was could have gone on believing in communism so long, Sartre had laughed wryly and said, "I have noticed that some intellectuals have a wild unconscious need for simplification to save themselves from their own minds." I had, I realized now, adored Meera's "simplicity," embraced its fervors uncritically, to "save myself from my own mind" and its doubts, probings, and ambiguities. I had believed that in doing so I was "going beyond" the mind; in fact, I had been committing mental, spiritual, and ethical suicide without knowing it or even beginning to suspect it.

Precisely because my mind was so secretly riddled with anxieties and an overwhelming sense of the complexity of the issues facing myself and the world, I was driven to love a mindless, mind-free simplicity that would drug and reassure me, a simplicity that was as absolute and restful as my own true sense of things was shifting, mysterious, and painful. It was from this unconscious tension between what my heart and intellect really knew about life and the world-situation and what I desperately wanted to believe was true that arose the hunger to be blinded, which made me so useful to Meera, so willing to explain all her follies as sublime, unsearchable wisdom: I had been as useful to her in fact as Sartre and de Beauvoir had been to all the communist dictators who needed someone prestigious to justify them in public. In an only marginally subtler way, I had done for my generation what the Sartres and Beauvoirs had done for theirs—purvey in the name of Evolutionary Progress a simplified "exalting" illusion that actually blocked rather than inspired real progress.

Like them and like many other intellectuals and artists in the "New Age," I had, half-consciously, abetted manipulation and lies and used the power of my mind to defend and justify evil in the name of what I imagined to be an overwhelming Good.

IN MY JOURNAL I WROTE LATER THAT DAY:

When I finished explaining to Eryk what I was discovering, he said, "You've indulged in the masochism of blindness; now don't indulge in the masochism of self-hatred. Everything you are saying about yourself and what you remembered and what you did is true; what is also true is that you did whatever you did and wrote what you did out of real love. You were a fool for some good reasons, don't forget them, otherwise you'll forget the best of what you are and still have to give."

What Eryk said to me was merciful and healing, but for now I am not taking his advice. I have to if not to hate myself then to allow myself to be thoroughly and completely shamed: I have to face each twist and perversion of my blindness and vanity if I am ever to get free of her and help others caught in these "guru" movements.

Even now, even after everything Eryk and I have discovered, a part of me still yearns to be convinced that all
this nightmare is a "teaching," longs for Meera to ring and
say that I have passed some high and baffling test and
can now "rest." There are even crazy minutes in which I
want to believe—and almost do—that everything I am re-
thinking and remembering is not real; that I am being
"tested" by such "memories" to see if I will finally have the
courage to abandon all reason for her and so prove my eternal Love.

It is the passionate hunger in these moments to believe
the completely impossible that makes me aware of just how
profound and complete her manipulation of me has been,
and how indiscriminately abandoned my surrender to her.
It is very hard to write this, but a part of me *still* wants to
commit emotional and intellectual suicide at her feet, and
so save myself the terrible suffering of "waking up." There
is a struggle going on in my psyche between the person
"waking up" and the one who does not want to see, and between the one who wants now to do without any kind of
spiritual opium and the one who has been hooked so long
on guru adoration that he cannot bear to give up so potent
a drug up and is terrified of life without it.

The effort to believe in Meera was so vast, I see now,
and so incessant that the thought of unlearning it makes
me reel inwardly with exhaustion. I see now that the idol-
ater has to die along with the Idol, and that idolatry has
such violent and convincing joys that it is hard to give them
up or even, sometimes, to want to. So much of what I have
believed myself to be is bound up so intricately with my

love for Meera and who I believed her to be that letting that die or be exposed to truth is like letting myself die. Some lines from the Portugese poet Pessoa haunt me: "When you peel off the mask you did not know you were wearing, the skin of your face comes too."

The accusing memories go on. I seem to have opened some internal Pandora's box; nothing I do can shut it. This time the memories focus on me, on the exact nature of my responsibility for the creation of the Meera cult.

I see myself in 1980 in my stark medieval room in All Souls College at Oxford writing in two hours of "in-spiration" all the *Questions and Answers* that were put into Adilakshmi's book on Meera (which I also edited). I worked from bare scraps of what Meera had said, fragments of sentences and hints, which my devotion expanded into paragraphs. I truly believed that my love for Meera and the experiences I felt I had received gave me the right to express in words what her Silence was saying, to take everything I knew and felt about the Divine Mother and condense it into Answers in her name. And nothing of what I wrote and elaborated was corrected or changed in any way: that confirmed for me that I really was "receiving" Meera accurately.

I remembered, too, how when I came to write *Hidden Journey* I would take small things Meera had said and ex-pand them into larger, clearer statements, which again were accepted without question. I felt that by doing this I was offering her my mind and gifts to do with what she wanted, and so was purifying myself of all artistic or spiritual vanity. In fact, I now realized that I had allowed myself to be manipulated and exploited. I now believed that Meera took the full intensity of my projection onto her and used it for her own ends; of course if I hadn't been in some sense a willing participant in this charade it could not have taken place. My unexamined vanity made me thrilled to be Meera's voice. I believed with my whole heart that my "adoration" of her made me able to speak *for* her, or at least to elaborate greatly on what she had said. Clearly I was not wrong—because neither Meera or Adilakshmi ever corrected anything.

What in bald terms did what I am describing mean? That in the name of service and surrender I had in fact allowed my vision and experiences to be appropriated by Meera and used in her own game. Wanting with all my heart to serve and surrender to the Divine Mother, I had in fact lent my name, words, and vision to the creation and worldwide distribution of what is increasingly seeming to be a dangerous cult.

From my Journal:
That Evening

Another question I can no longer avoid keeps returning to savage me. If Meera is a false Master, a wolf (or worse) in sheep's clothing, then what does that make of the thousands of experiences, the long journey into the Light that I thought I took with her and in her?

Which of the experiences were real and which were the phosphorescence of projection or the result of some kind of occult manipulation? And if the whole journey was "unreal," then how could I now be seeing the Divine Light normally, hearing the Sound of the Presence and enjoying the initial glories of tantra? Was it Meera who "awoke" me or did I project onto her an awakening that had already begun before I met her, and which she used for her own purposes? How could I tell the difference between what I had experienced "through" her and "without" her?

As these questions twist in my brain I remember with increasing clarity a conversation I had with a Frenchman I met in Mahabalipuram in 1992, a conversation that had scared and repulsed me at the time but which now seems to contain many clues to what Eryk and I are discovering.

I had met Jean-Louis walking on the beach. He was a thin, caustic, thinning-haired Frenchman from Marseilles in his early fifties; he wore a saffron robe and had, he said, been a *sannyasin,* a traveling monk, in India for ten years.

During the first hour of our meeting, I rhapsodized to him about Meera. He had listened with increasing impatience, then burst out with, "The problem with the Indian tradition is its absurd, even pathological, overestimation of the power of the guru." I spluttered and ranted and quoted the Scriptures, which claimed that without the guru there could be no enlightenment.

"Good," he laughed, "very good! I can see you have done your homework. Every system has to have plausible apologists and the Guru system has some of the best. But one day you will have to grow up and see that God is inside you and within you at all moments and you can live in God and for God without the need of any intermediary. If you have the guts, that is."

I said, "To reveal the Inner Guru and give the devotee the 'guts' to live in direct contact with the Inner Guru is what the external guru is meant to do."

He laughed unpleasantly. "That's what they all say they are doing, of course. But in practice of what they are doing is creating a system of projection which, together with the occult powers they use and manipulate, keeps you captive."

I listened in horror as he warmed to his theme. "The guru claims that it is he or she who 'wakes up' the disciple. In fact, it is your adoration of the guru that wakes you up. The gurus know this. They know that everyone is writing with their lives and thoughts a letter to God; what the guru does is intercept that letter and readdress it to himself and take all the beauty of your devotion and all its power for himself. Instead of allowing you to flower naturally in a direct relationship with God, the guru claims to *be* God and so claims all the devotion that should flow to God for Himself or, in your case, Herself. This is vampirism of the soul and not liberation. And the rewards are fantastic. With the energies of thousands or even millions of hypnotized disciples in the occult bank, the guru has immense power and can have whatever he or she wants on this plane all the money, power, sex, influence imaginable. But none of this has anything to do with anything holy or Divine."

I had never heard anyone say anything like this and listened with fascinated horror.

"So there are no real gurus, then?" I asked.

"Very few. And they are hidden. There have, of course, been great adepts whose level of realization and love made them able to transmit something—think of Kabir, or Ramakrishna, or Rumi—but the modern gurus are fakes, and the system they are trying to keep alive is corrupt.

With Westerners as gullible, ignorant, and sensation-crazy as they are, anyone can set up shop and make a good living gulling others. I'm thinking of doing it soon to pay for the education of my grandchildren back home."

"So how would you explain the experiences I have had and still have with Meera?

"Mon cher," he began. "If the Divine wants to initiate you, He or She will do it through and by anything—that dog over there lying on the sand or that straggly wind-swept tree. So why shouldn't God use, in your case, a young Indian girl who is deluded or wily enough to say she is God? *Your* love was genuine, after all, and it was through your love for Meera and *your* wonder and joy that the Real Mother woke you up. Meera is not sending you the experiences; the real Mother is. Meera is just *using* your experiences to bind you to her."

I laughed disbelievingly.

"You can laugh," Jean-Louis said testily, "but I've been all around the guru circus on several continents and am telling you the truth.

"Let me just say it baldly. After fifty, smoothing over the truth becomes a major sin. What I want to tell you is that a false Master can have a real disciple. Don't faint! What matters is the adoration of the disciple. The Tibetans are clever foxes about these matters and they say that if you worship the Master as a Buddha you will get the blessing of the Buddha and if you worship the Master as a human being you will get the blessings of a human being. The Master can be a black magician and a debauchee (in my experience many of the younger Tibetans are both), but if you, the disciple, worship even that fraud as a Buddha, the Buddha

Nature in you will respond to you and try and instruct you through and in your devotion.

"From everything you tell me, I can tell that you sincerely believe Meera to be the Divine Mother on earth; the Divine Mother is liberal, She takes what you are directing to Meera for Herself; the Mother *is* being worshiped through your adoration of Meera and would be even if Meera was in reality a schizophrenic on a binge of occult power. What matters is the sincerity of *your* motivation and the passion of *your* adoration; these are the forces the Divine uses. So, if you worship Meera as the Divine Mother with your whole being—as you seem to do—then you *will* receive the blessings of the Divine Mother, because the Mother respects any love offered to Her, through whomever it is offered. One of the blessings She might be preparing for you however is *seeing* through Meera and so turning directly to Her."

He watched the fury and amazement fighting in my face with wry amusement.

"Ah," he said. "It is all a bit more complicated than you imagined, eh?"

"Let me try to make precise what you are saying," I said, ignoring his dig. "Technically, Meera need not be a Master or Divine or enlightened, but I could still be awakened by the intensity of my love for her?"

"Of course, my little Oxfordian. Who knows what Dante's Beatrice was really like? She could have been a pert, vain, dull-minded slut for all we know. The truth of what Beatrice was like in some daily, ordinary sense is not nearly as important as what Dante *believed* Beatrice to be. It was that *belief,* after all, that fueled the *Divina Commedia.* Beatrice must have had something to awaken Dante's imagination, something in which his psyche could delight and onto which it could be projected—but it was that ecstatic imagination itself which, inspired by and infused with Divine Grace, went to work on him and dragged him up all the stairs of God.

Do you know the story about the Buddha's tooth? An old woman gave her wastrel son everything she had to go and buy a tooth of the Buddha. She was pious and wanted to spend her last years worshiping a holy relic of the Enlightened One. Her son was a cynical womanizer and spent every penny of what she had given him on wine, women, and song. He then picked up a dog's tooth that was lying in a gutter and washed it and took it back to his mother, claiming that it was the holy relic she wanted. The old woman was overwhelmed with wonder and joy and began praying to the tooth immediately. Her son pitied her gullibility but said nothing. Three weeks later, he happened to enter the room where his mother was praying; there on the table before his mother, who was praying raptly with her eyes closed, the dog's tooth was blazing with Divine Light."

Here in my room in Paris, as I remember talking to him on the beach, he seems almost to materialize in the air before me. Everything he said returns with acid clarity.

"It is simple," Eryk smiled when I repeated the Frenchman's conversation. "Your projection onto Meera did arouse in you certain Divine energies that led to a partial awakening. The visions and dreams and insights you had in *Hidden Journey* into yourself, the soul, and its relation to the Mother are all real. But what the Frenchman didn't say and what I have come to believe in these weeks—no, not to believe, to know—is that the awakening you had had to have been partial because you were in love with a pseudo-Mother, not the real one. You could be taken by the real Mother only so far as long as you remained hooked on Meera and the drug of the blisses that seemed to stream from her."

"So that is why the Mother destroyed my relationship with the false Mother."

"Yes. She is setting you free from all the illusions and fantasies that made you need an intermediary, an Idol, so you can see and be with Her directly. This is her terrible Grace."

FROM MY JOURNAL:
Next day

As I think about what Eryk said about the Mother's "terrible Grace" I suddenly begin to see the meaning of an experience I had exactly a year ago, a few weeks before I met Eryk.

This time last year—February 1993—I was about to leave Paris to go to London to make a film about my life. I was scared and full of doubts of every kind about the project, and so, just before I was scheduled to leave to begin filming, I fell ill with a severe bout of flu that left me prostrate for days.

On the third or fourth day of illness, at about six in the evening, I passed into another reality. I had never experienced anything like what then happened. I had read about shamanic visions and how they were not dreamlike at all, but astonishingly, overpoweringly real. Just before the "vision" began, I remember looking at my watch; it was nearly six P.M. When it was over, it was about two in the morning.

I left Paris and my body behind and found myself flying above a sun-drenched river delta. Beneath me, a large rich jungle steamed; the air rang with the clanking and whirring noises of animals; it was late afternoon there, too, and a red-gold light drenched and saturated everything. I was really flying and with tremendous joy at being free and weightless.

Gazing down at the delta, I saw that it was, in fact, full of people—people of all ages, races, sexual combinations—all naked and all in the water, holding hands or embracing. Two old men were laughing in each other's arms by the side of two teenage lovers, an old married couple rested on each other's shoulders while, near them, two beautiful young women combed out each other's hair. No one had any shame or prurience; I had never seen anything so holy or beautiful as that throng of happy naked human beings in the red-gold waters. In each being, all kinds of joy—spiritual, emotional, physical—seemed fused into one flame of happiness. I knew I was witnessing some Spring Feast of the Mother, some vast celebration in the glowing waters of life, of Life itself, of fertility and passion and loving exaltation. I knew, too, that the vision I was seeing was at once ancient and futuristic, at once a glimpse into the lost past and a glimpse forward into the possible future of a humanity liberated from body-hatred and shame, free at last to anoint each other with rapture. As I gazed down in increasing wonder and joy, other flying beings joined me in the air and we swam along its invisible currents together, soaring up and down and crying out "Sanctus, Sanctus, Sanctus, Holy, Holy, Holy," like angels. All I wanted to do was to go on soaring and singing endlessly.

Then a soft but stern voice said, "Now stop flying and enter the earth." At first I had no idea what this could mean. The voice repeated itself, more fiercely this time, "Enough flying around! Have the courage to enter the earth." I looked down; the red-gold light had vanished, the delta was empty. Suddenly, I felt a large dark Force seize hold of me and drag me down to the ground. I felt fear and panic, but just before I hit the ground I found the courage to say out loud to the Mother, "Whatever happens now, I accept it. I am in You; do with me what You want." No sooner had I said that prayer than I began to merge with the earth, to seep into it and feel it seeping into me, darkly, softly, inexorably, through my skin into my blood cells, into the marrow of my bones. Everything became earth, dark soft earth; waves of terror swept me as, again and again, I thought I would pass out or be choked by this descent into the Unknown. But the Force held me and I could feel its power feeding me strength; I had no choice but to give into it and to what was happening.

Slowly I became nothing but blind dark trust and sank and sank deeper into a dark where I could see, hear, or feel nothing. Only the thinnest imaginable veil seemed to separate me from total unconsciousness. All I knew was that I would only survive if I gave in completely to the grave, dark, infinitely still Force that was holding me in its arms; only It knew how to preserve me as I sank and sank. And so I surrendered more and more to It until at last I gave up completely, gave up all hope of ever returning to the "world" or of ever stopping to sink, deeper and deeper, into the darkness of the earth.

At that moment, I entered—or was "birthed" into—a large dark empty room lit by one light bulb. The walls were dank with filthy, dark green moss; the room was vast, and windowless. Slowly, as I walked around, I realized with horror that I was in a vast underground warren of some kind (the first vast room led into others just as vast and dank)—in a warren that could also be some kind of underground concentration camp. It was when that insight pierced me that I noticed I was not alone. In the shadows by the walls were sitting, separate and silent, hundreds of dirty, naked children whose eyes started up at me in despair. All I could see in any of them was a longing to die, or to be killed. I had seen that look once before, in India, in the eyes of a dog lying with a broken back in a ditch.

My first instinct was to run. The same voice that had told me to enter the earth now sounded again in the air around me and mocked me, "You have no right to turn away. You must see and feel everything to be complete."

"Who are these people?" I asked, and the voice mimicked my English accent: "Who are these people? Who are these people?" Then the voice said with infinite slow sadness, "These people, as you call them, these ruined children are the souls of everyone you know, of all those beings trapped in the concentration camp the world has become." I sank to my knees in grief, because suddenly I saw, with no illusion or possible consolation, how lethal the life of the modern world was to everyone who lived it, and how trapped in lies and illusions everyone was. What an infinite, unbridgeable distance there seemed between these trapped children and the beings at peace in the red-gold waters somewhere a million miles above!

A door opened and a ray of thin bleak light lit up a child in a far corner. I could not tell if the child was male or female; all I knew was that it had just been beaten; its clothes were bloody and in shreds. As I looked closer at it, I saw with horror that a disease like leprosy had eaten away half of its face; where it should have had a chin, it had only a dark bloody hole. Deeper even than the shock I felt at seeing it was a repulsion so great I could hardly repress it, a repulsion that I saw had something murderous in it. I remember thinking that if the child had been a fly, I would have crushed it with my foot. Yet, despite myself, I kept on gazing at it, and the voice, calm and loving this time, said, "This child is you, is yours. Walk toward him and pick him up and give him love." I froze; denial shook me; how could I be *that,* I who had only an hour ago been flying with other human seraphim above the New Eden? The voice said, "Denial will not help you now. Everything you have ever experienced has only been to give you the courage to take the next step and pick up the child. If you do not find the courage, nothing you have ever done has any meaning."

Nothing I have ever done was as difficult as starting to walk across the room toward that child, who kept gazing at me without expression. I knelt down, picked him up, and put him on my shoulder. His hands, gentle as silk, as surreally delicate as the hands of a lemur, started to fondle and caress my face, and with each caress I sank deeper and deeper into a fire of tenderness. My whole being became pure love for the wounded and beautiful creature I was holding and who was touching me with such pure love.

As we stood together, half dazed by the brightness of the love between us, all the other children started to come out of the shadows and stand around us. Eyes that had been despairing now shone with something like joy; a few small faces even began slowly, uncertainly, to smile.

"We cannot stay here," I said. "We must get out. We must get out above or we will all die."

"There is no way out," the children said in a weary whisper. "No one has ever found a way out."

"But there has to be," I said, "and together we must find it. We must believe there is and then we will find it."

With my child on my shoulder, I started to walk from room to room followed by the children looking for something that might be an exit. We wandered in the half-dark for a long time. At last, we came to a large chamber with a staircase leading up from it to a bolted door. I knew—I did not know how—that through that door lay freedom. Without saying anything, the children and I linked hands and started to pray with our entire strength. We went on climbing the staircase and finally reached the large back door. First I tried to open it, throwing myself against it, and banging against it with all my remaining power. Nothing happened. Then the voice said, "Only together can you open the door." Huddled together, into one body, it seemed, I and the children started to push against the door. It swung open, into blinding sunlight.

Immediately, I and the children were standing outside, in the open air but surrounded by snarling soldiers and television cameras and reporters with faces like weasels. One of them thrust a large black microphone into my face.

"What do you believe?" he screamed mockingly.

I knew that everything would depend on what I answered. I summoned up all my courage and cried out, "I believe in the power of the unconditional Love of the Father-Mother."

Then something terrible and amazing happened. There was a horizon-to-horizon explosion, the loudest sound I have ever heard, like the sound of a thousand summer thunderclaps shouting together. A sheet of red-gold flame— the color of the light that had burned on the river delta— unfurled blazing and crackling across the entire sky.

The fire vanished. The children and I found ourselves alone; the cameras and soldiers and reporters had disappeared. We were on a calm, featureless plain. Then, from the right, we saw an army of black tanks coming across what looked like a desert toward us. Instead of being afraid, we sat down in a circle. The tanks turned to clay toys. Masked soldiers in black clambered out of them, running toward us screaming obscenities; but they, too, quickly froze and turned into replicas of the clay soldiers discovered in Chinese imperial tombs. Then, as we gazed quietly, both the clay tanks and the clay soldiers crumbled, a sweet bright white light started to seep toward us from the horizon. It grew greater and greater until it filled the sky and the desert and surrounded us with its calm fire.

As the first waves from this sea of radiance started to rush toward us, the experiences ended, and I found myself back in my bed in Paris.

I knew then that what I had experienced was one of the most important events of my life, but I had only the dimmest insight into its meaning.

Now, a year later, after all that had unfolded in Thalheim and after, I begin to understand something, and what I understand deepens my insight into the "terrible Grace" Eryk spoke of. Meera's betrayal has compelled my "descent" into darkness, into the concentration camp of the tortured and abandoned, with whom prolonged suffering and humiliation is gradually making me one.

And yet this "descent" is accompanied at every step by Grace—by the vision of tantric ecstasy that preceded it, by the love that radiates from my refound "child" to myself (and from Eryk to me and back), and by the certainty of eventual escape and transformation, if I can believe and trust enough in the unconditional Love of the Father-Mother.

I know now that I am in the camp, in the dark, just beginning to climb the staircase toward the door; I know that ordeals of every kind must lie ahead; I know that Eryk and I will have to face many, and extreme, dangers, whose scope and scale I know, too, that I don't yet—and cannot—know; I also know that whatever happens release is possible. The Father-Mother will not desert us, if we cling to their Love and believe in its Divine power to overcome any obstacle and heal any wound; how can I ever forget how the whole sky lit up when I cried out my faith in Love? And I know too now, reinspired by the vision I had a year ago, that what Eryk and I are suffering is not simply for and as ourselves. Something new is trying to be born through our agony that will help free many others as well as ourselves. That is why we must now be strong whatever happens, hold to the truth and *believe*.

Ten minutes after I wrote that, Gabriela rang. Gabriela is a great Rumanian psychic and healer in her early fifties. Famous throughout Europe and America, she is asked to help by hospitals and police forces all over the world. Eryk had met her in extraordinary circumstances in a train after his brother committed suicide, and the two had become friends. Her many accurate predictions and gifts of healing had convinced him of her authenticity, as had her refusal to accept any money for her services. "Gabriela," Eryk often told me, "lives like a medieval fool of God. No one ever knows where she is. She goes where she is led." In her youth, Gabriela was trained by a great European saint, himself famous for his powers of clairvoyance and healing.

I took the phone: "Gabriela, I don't have to describe to you in what an agony we are. Please advise us."

"Don't trust anyone and tell everyone as little as possible about what is going on, especially about the revelations you are receiving when you make love."

Neither Eryk nor I had told her anything about our tantric experiences.

"When your manager Mr. Long rings (how could she know his name?), be very careful what you say. Write a statement that you are withdrawing from Meera and going on your Path alone. Do not say why yet. The moment for announcing what has happened has not yet come. It will come within the next seven or eight weeks and you will know when it has arrived, but any move now would be premature. You both need to be stronger, and you in particular, Andrew, need to be clearer. I know that you are being helped every day, given many dreams and memories and visions to help you—but inevitably you are still recovering and confused. That will get better."

"Gabriela, there is something I must ask you."

"You can always ask me anything. I don't promise you I can always reply. I don't know everything, you know. I'm not an avatar! I'm just Gabriela! Don't project anything onto me, I'm your friend in the Virgin, that is all!"

"In many of the memories and recognitions I am receiving, one theme comes up again and again—that Meera is, or may be, an occult magician and not a Master, that she has for a long time perhaps always been using her vast powers not for Divine ends . . ." I was stammering.

"Are you asking me if Meera is a black magician?" Gabriela demanded with her usual directness. "I'll tell you frankly; I'm still not sure. It is possible. Time will tell. I know that may be a frightening answer, but I want to be completely honest with you. I'll be with you whatever happens; I'll try and ring every day: Over the years I've had a lot of experience with evil powers. Eryk will tell you. With adoration as your protection you will be safe whatever happens; you are in the real Mother's hands now."

"You're still not sure, but you are suspicious?" I pressed Gabriela.

"I never trust these so-called 'Masters,'" Gabriela said, "mostly because I know from my own training just how easy it is to send experiences and blisses to appear in other people's dreams after a certain stage. And reaching that stage is not particularly difficult and certainly does not mean you are Divine or anything like it. If I wanted to I could appear in your dreams tonight and tell you all sorts of rubbish. I'm not boasting. I'm just telling you it's not that hard. But hardly anyone knows these things any more, so everyone is prey to occult cheats who want power."

That night, Eryk woke screaming. His face was black with terror. He clung to me for ten minutes, sobbing, unable to speak. Then he told me, "All night I have been having the same dream. I woke up several times, trying to end it, but the dream went on and on, as if it were real."

"What was in the dream?"

"I don't want to say."

"I have to know. We are in this madness together."

"Remember what Gabriela said about the 'power to appear in dreams?' Well, tonight . . ."

He looked around the room as if still terrified at something. "You must think I'm going crazy," he said, "but it was so real."

"For God's sake, tell me!"

"I was in a dark empty room with Meera and Adilakshmi. They were both dressed as they usually are but the expressions on their faces were horrible, they looked like rabid animals. They took me—they were so strong suddenly I could not escape—and then they strapped me to a chair and hit me again and again. Then, slowly—I can see it now—Meera got out a long knife. At this point I woke up several times, but the dream always returned to that moment with Meera looming savagely above me holding the knife to my throat. Each time she told me what she was going to do to me; 'I'm going to flay you alive and then burn all the evidence.' And she would laugh, a horrible wild laugh."

Eryk couldn't go on. He had started to shake all over.

"It was *real,* Andrew, not a dream. Not like a dream. Real, as real as you and I on this bed."

I was terrified, too, but had to pretend to be calm to have any chance of calming him.

"After what you have suffered," I told Eryk, "it is not surprising that you should experience a dream like this. It puts into one terrible scene everything you have undergone."

"Shut up," Eryk shouted. "I don't need your psychological platitudes! Can't you see, Andrew, can't you see? Meera and Adilakshmi want me dead, not sick, but *dead*."

"It isn't helpful to speak like that," I began, but Eryk put his hand over my mouth.

"I am telling you that they want me dead. The dream I have just had was not an 'anxiety dream.' Don't you think I can tell the difference by now? It was something like possession and it terrifies me."

"What can we do but try and stay calm and pray?" I said ridiculously.

"I'm already sick with cancer and may be dying. What more could they want? Who would believe any of this? Oh God, oh God, what madness this all is."

Next morning, we tried to ring Gabriela, but she had already gone out on one of her "missions."

"We must do something to put ourselves under the Virgin's protection," Eryk said. "Something concrete. We have to leave in two days . . ."

Suddenly, his haggard face brightened, "We'll go to Chartres; it is only two hours away. We will go to Chartres and put ourselves entirely into the hands of the Black Madonna there."

We dressed hurriedly. Just before we were about to leave, the telephone rang, and I picked it up.

"My name is Carol," a calm woman's voice said. "I got your number from Louise [a friend of Eryk's in Brussels]. I have heard something of what happened at Thalheim and want to tell you what I, too, have experienced so you will know you are not wrong or alone. In the middle of January I rang Mother Meera—I have been to see her twice and asked her to bless my lesbian lover. Adilakshmi spoke for Meera, but I could hear Meera's voice in the background—and she said, 'Mother does not believe in homosexuality. It is not a right or normal path. She cannot bless either you or your lover if you continue in your love.' At first I could not believe what I was hearing and thought it must be some kind of test. I asked again, and again heard Meera's voice in the background: 'Mother says again that she will not bless you.' I put down the phone, my faith in Meera shattered. Then, through Louise and others, I heard a little of what had happened to you. I want you to know that if you ever need a witness, I will be that witness. If you ever need anyone to confirm your story, I promise to do so."

I was stunned and grateful and felt that Carol's call was a direct proof that, however dark events seemed, Eryk and I were being protected.

We arrived at Chartres toward noon. It was a gray, grizzly, mist-wreathed late morning; the town seemed deserted. We had the cathedral to ourselves, except for two old women who knelt silently before the High Altar.

Our Lady of the Pillar stands halfway up the cathedral to the left; she is gleaming jet-black, crowned, surrounded by a cloak of rich gold brocade, and she holds a scepter in her right hand and Jesus in her left. She is far smaller than she seems in reproduction— no larger than a five-year-old child. Ringed by a vault studded with votive sacred hearts, Her stark eyes stare out across a sea of flickering candles. You can miss Her if you are not looking for Her, but as soon as you do look at Her, the ancient and mysterious power that emanates from Her, that seems far older than the cathedral itself, draws you to listen to itself and will not let you go. Eryk said, as we approached Her: "She looks burnt, as if She has been through a fire of agony."

We knelt before Her.

As I gazed at the statue and saw the Virgin's face, I remembered the face of a Kali statue I had seen in a temple near Calcutta in Bengal, at the temple of Dakshineswar where Ramakrishna, the great Indian saint and lover of the Mother, had spent much of his life. I remembered, too, all that Bede Griffiths had told me about the Black Madonna, and about how he had turned to Her in his dark night. I understood for the first time why I had been drawn so deeply to *this* image of the Virgin; because it is one that reconciles and fuses East and West, the Eastern cosmic vision of the Mother as destroyer as well as creator, terror-bringer as well as birth-giver, with the light-filled tender Western vision of Mary, the Mother and Queen of Mercy. The Black Madonna is Kali-Mary, the complete Mother, the Mother of anguish as well as bliss, of time as well as eternity, of nature as well as light, the dark womb of the universe, the one in whom life and death, terror and bliss, are one, the mysterious One beyond all dogmas, all forms, all names, all possible description or comprehension.

As that understanding flamed in my mind, I looked at the face of the Black Virgin again; this time, for one terrifying moment, I saw in my mind's eye Meera's face. At once I understood that all these years I had been projecting onto Meera my need for the complete image of the Divine Mother now before me, that I had been investing Meera with all the powers, grandeur, and mysteries of the Dark One in whom my Eastern childhood and Western Christian upbringing could meet and mingle, that I had been worshiping not the real Dark Mother, that now shone before me again, but an idol of her, a dangerous substitute. None of that mattered now; that delusion belonged to a life that was now dying; I was at last really before Her, before the Black One, stripped by pain to face Her at last.

Knowing that I was now before Her, the One for whom I had always been looking, the One in whom all paradoxes, cultures, worlds, and powers are united, shattered me. I started to sob. Eryk had by now left to walk on his own around the cathedral, so I did not have to hold myself together. Even if he had not been there I doubt if I could have restrained myself; the tears that I was weeping had been held back for a lifetime, perhaps many lifetimes. I wept for all the mistakes I had made, for all the suffering Eryk and I had already been through, for Meera and her fraudulence and the danger to which it exposed her and others. I wept in fear, in longing, in abject loneliness, in rage and despair. The grief that possessed me more and more completely was not simply my own or Eryk's or Meera's but belonged to all beings and all things. In it, all the animals and plants trapped in burning forests seemed to be grieving with me; in it, all the horror of this moment when Nature is on the brink of total destruction seemed to be concentrated. In a way I cannot describe and knew as Her direct Grace, I found I wept—and could weep—not only for but as the poor, not only for but as the animals trapped in a dying world, not only for but as the whales and dolphins and vanishing birds. I knew the horror I was living to be one with all forms of horror everywhere, with the horror of every lost, betrayed, tortured, abused being in every camp or prison or perverted family, with every animal, fish, and plant trapped in a holocaust of greed. Some small piece of the measureless immensity of suffering in every part of the world pierced me and exploded within me and wept through me to Her.

And then I knew that the Dark One was weeping also. I did not have to look up and see tears on Her face; I felt Her tears running down the walls of my soul. I knew that what I had felt for these terrible and privileged moments before Her was what She always felt, that the pain I could not contain but had to give to Her was only a tiny fraction of the immense agony She, as the Mother and essence of all things, was always enduring. And to whom could She turn to assuage Her suffering? She died in every animal, suffered in every blazing tree, screamed with every abused child, lay awake night after night with every abandoned lover; her heart could never close or grow cold or simply not notice because everything that happened had happened in Her to Her. I saw, gazing up at Her through my tears, that She was at once burned by an anguish greater than anything the human imagination can conceive and also simultaneously, by a paradox reason cannot understand, beyond all anguish precisely because She had embraced it so completely and so defenselessly. What could evil do to one so totally burned already? What could destruction wreak on someone already so devastated? I saw that in the raw majesty of Her anguish and in the fathomless love and dignity with which She was at once showing and bearing it, She was giving me, and all beings, the highest and least flattering or consoling teaching about pain—that it was inevitable, mysteriously necessary, and could only be transformed through the acceptance of final surrender into Wisdom.

As the full sternness and majesty of what the Dark Mother was representing started to bear down upon me, I started to shake. I realized that I had come to the moment in my life in which I would have to open myself totally to a suffering whose range and extent I knew I still had not glimpsed.

The suffering I had borne up to now was only the beginning. There were horrors and ordeals ahead, about which I had no possible idea now. I realized, too, gazing up at Her austere and unflinching face, that there would be no question of surviving such suffering; it was not meant to be "survived." Neither Eryk nor I, I understood then, would "survive" what was about to unfold; we would either die or be reborn.

As I saw and understood this, I read again the prayer of Our Lady of Chartres and this time saw a smaller prayer added at the end. I read it in wonder and gratitude:

"O Immaculate Virgin, who births to grace and to glory all the beloved of God, deign now to gather me deep into your Mother's breast and so to form me in You that at last I may become like Jesus!"

Only continual adoration and ever-deepening trust could help either Eryk or myself now. For only they could keep us always open to Her, always alert to Her Grace, always reliant on Her protection, and always willing to accept whatever anguish Her transformation demanded. There was no escape possible. Our work was clear.

ACT III

Into the Storm

✳

It seemed at this time that God had given permission both
to human beings and demons to torment the servitor.

HEINRICH SUSO

You placed your face against mine and whispered
"Why has the king made you so pale and thin?"
He has set your barn of straw on fire
To grace you the alms of his own wheat . . .
From every direction, agonies have crowded you
To drag you at last towards the directionless.

RUMI

A s we landed in New York to begin months of teaching in
America, Eryk turned to me, gray and exhausted, with
large black rings under his eyes, and said, "Now the real
madness begins."

Eryk and I both knew we were entering a dark whirlwind in
which anything, anything at all, could happen. In the months to
come we would often joke dryly that had we known when we arrived what was awaiting us, we would both have died.

From my Journal:
February 18th

In New York, staying with Leila L., my oldest and best friend. Thank God, we don't have to explain anything to her. Eryk had rung Leila in December on the night after my first interview with Meera; the two of them had wept together on the phone.

"I never liked the Indian girl," Leila keeps saying. "I wanted to warn you so often but you were so obsessed. And that Adilakshmi! Eyes like Vegas dollar signs! Terrible, terrible woman!"

Leila came into my room while Eryk was taking his bath. "Darling," she said, taking my hands, "I know you well. You will want to speak out about everything soon. You will want to tell the whole world. Please don't. Please keep as quiet as you can as long as you can. I wish you could go away now to India with Eryk and just sit by the sea."

"You know I can't run away."

"I know how naive you are. I know how many of the people you have called friends for years say terrible things about you behind your back. I know how many of them would jump at the opportunity to jump up and down on your corpse. I love you like my son; I do not want to see you massacred. Your whole career, your whole life— and Eryk's—are at stake. I know a lot about sects and cults; people in them are capable of anything. I don't think you have any idea yet of what rage any announcement about what has happened would arouse."

"But what choice do I have?" I told her. "I helped start the whole Meera circus. I announced her to the world as the Divine Mother. I have a responsibility to say what I now know and help others get free of her and others like her, just as I am beginning to be."

"All very noble," Leila said. "Why don't you just cut your throat now? Do you seriously believe people will want to hear the truth about her or the others? All people want is fantasy, and to talk about their so-called experiences; they don't want anything so embarrassing as 'facts.'"

We sat silently and sadly.

Leila kissed me. "I know perfectly well you are not going to follow my advice."

"Of course I'm not."

"Well, my darling," she said, "I've always loved fools, being one myself. I will always help you, you know that; but don't expect that many others will. You'll be 'unfashionable' for quite a while."

February 26th. Night:

Eryk and I arrived in San Francisco three afternoons ago. Teaching will begin soon. What a joy and relief to be here! It is the beginning of spring and the whole world is bathed in translucent blue spring light, the great California light of God's perpetual presence. This afternoon I lay on the bare wooden floor of our front room and let my agonized back soak up the warmth of the sun; Eryk lay alongside me and for a few moments we felt serene. Then anxiety at how I would deal with everything in the months ahead—what I would say, what questions would be asked?—returned, and my head and back started to blaze with pain.

The apartment that the California Institute of Integral Studies has found for us is austerely beautiful. It adjoins the Zen Center and was created in its present form by Richard Baker when he was abbot. High, vast, empty, light-filled rooms—a wonderful front room, cut into two, with ancient wooden shutters and a long Japanese wood table. Nothing on the walls except light, no chairs except in the kitchen, matting everywhere, and great square windows that stare wide onto Page Street. From just below the front window a huge magnolia tree extends, curling and dancing its limbs into the light.

I said that the walls were empty: that is, with one exception, in the front room. On the left wall there is a Japanese scroll which reads, "The blossom of the Mind-Heart is opening! May it never close!"

Both Eryk and I relish every detail of our new home; the old cooker in the kitchen with its exposed zinc tubes, the different dark deep stains on the Victorian shutters, the immense silver-tapped bath like something out of Isak Dinesen, our bedroom at the back with its worn, light-brown mat walls, and its small balcony outside where in the mornings all the sparrows of the neighborhood jig and chatter to wake us up.

"Whatever happens now," Eryk said yesterday, "we will have this empty barn of light to weather in it."

I found myself answering, "Yes. It is a place beyond the past, beyond any past, where we can begin again."

When I can't sleep—which is every night because my back is in agony and my mind a pit of swirling knives—I walk up and down the moon-filled apartment, opening the windows to the cool night air, drinking in the calm geometry of the shutters and table and lying in the great Victorian bath without any water imagining myself back in a house in the hills of my Indian childhood which had a bath like this and great, empty high-ceilinged rooms full of the smell of lavender.

I am grateful, too, that the area in which we are is one of the most depressed of the city; too much beauty could be narcotic, and while I long for refuge, I want to remain as ice-clear as I can. The great front window with its magnolia tree opens out onto one of the dirtiest streets of San Francisco, always noisy with traffic and thronged with drug addicts and prostitutes, some—the really young ones—often so high that they totter as they try to thread the traffic. Just down the street past the Zen Center there is a clinic, outside whose doors mentally sick patients sit or stand and smoke for hours, looking harrowed or staring into space and muttering to themselves. Eryk has already befriended one of the homeless men who lives out on the street corners near us—Larry, a sweet-faced, gap-toothed derelict in his fifties who claims to be an ex-millionaire and to have won the Pulitzer Prize for literature. He is always happy to see us, and courteous in a turn-of-the-century way, with eyes so open and sky-blue that it hurts to look into them. The small amounts of money we offer him and the food Eryk cooks for him delight him; when we approach, he opens his arms and cries, "Hello, my boys," and dances, shaking out all his layers of rags.

I have known poverty all my life, having been born in India. But now I feel stripped and defenseless myself, and a wholly different compassion possesses me, far deeper and more transparent than any I have ever felt.

From my Journal:
March 4th

I hoped, crazily, that the California sun and the beauty of our apartment would slow down the progress of Eryk's cancer; but he is visibly paler, thinner, sicker every day. Whenever I ask him how he is he says, "Fine!" but I know he is only protecting me. His eyes have two permanent black rings under them. Last night, I heard him being prolongedly sick in the bathroom. It takes every effort of concentration I possess not to think all the time about his cancer; everything in me reels from the possibility of losing him, or of watching him suffering over a long period. And when the money for the next few months' teaching runs out we will have nothing left. If, as is certain, his cancer gets worse—how will we pay for treatment? Where will we live? All either of us can do is pray continually to Her.

Although I have not yet spoken out publicly about what happened in Thalheim—Gabriela in her daily calls to us from Belgium insists that the time is not yet ripe—rumors are rife both among the California devotees and the spiritual community at large. During this last week I have been secretly contacted by many devotees of different Masters who have also been abused; I realize that what Eryk and I are going through is part of a large epidemic of abuse that no one is taking seriously.

Five days ago, at lunch, a leading American Buddhist teacher told me in detail that sexual and physical abuse had now reached devastating proportions in Buddhist ranks; just last week, he said, a young man had come to him in tears saying that his Lama had anally raped him to "open his chakras" and "purify his karma." Another Tibetan Master had seduced a young married woman, promised her marriage, betrayed her with as many as twenty other women, and then started to beat her, claiming that "every blow was a direct grace" since he was an enlightened Master. I had heard these appalling stories and asked the American if they were true.

"I have met the woman," he said sadly. "I know it is true." The pain Eryk and I were going through was horrible enough. What must she be feeling?

The next day—almost as if scripted by the Mother—I met for coffee an ex-pupil of mine who had heard from close friends who had been with us in Thalheim. She told me her dreadful story, sobbing and furious. Several years before, she had met one of the most famous young American "Masters" who claims to have a consciousness "higher than the Buddha and Christ." Even though she was suspicious of him, his ferocity and charisma thrilled her and she became convinced of his power. He had sexually harassed her, insulted her in front of others as a "fat, middle-aged bourgeois cow," extracted most of her savings from her. "I realized after several years of this," she said, "that all he was interested in was sex, fame, money, and power, that there was nothing at all Divine in his enterprise." When she at last brought herself to leave him, he had his "minions" harass her, ring her up, and scream obscenities down the phone, wait for her outside her house and throw stones at her.

"For over a year my life was a nightmare. None of the so-called spiritual journals wanted to hear my story. I was dismissed as a paranoid hysteric while he was invited to every conference and given the ultimate 'star' treatment. I often thought I was going mad. Not only did none of the spiritual journals want to listen; I went to most of the so-called leading Masters of the New Age and none of them would defend or help me: I discovered what I am sure you will discover—that they are a bunch of canny politicians, unwilling to defend any victim until they have proved their case 'definitely,' far more concerned about their spiritual careers than about risking anything to help anyone else."

I asked her if she felt she had recovered. She laughed harshly, "How do you recover from rape of the soul?"

The same night at dinner Eryk and I went with one of the friends who had been at Thalheim with us to meet a man from El So-brante, who had been in a Hindu religious movement and who had left it because of its homophobia.

Although Jim had left the movement several years before, he seemed still profoundly shaken by what had happened and tears filled his eyes frequently as he spoke. "I knew, of course, early on that the movement despised and condemned homosexuals. Since I partly despised and condemned myself, I accepted this. I tried for years to suppress my gayness—successfully in many ways because no one suspected—and I rose high in the ranks to a responsible po-sition in which I had a lot of power and respect. Then, I couldn't bear denying my nature anymore. I was found out, hounded by the very people who had looked to me for years for spiritual direction, vilified throughout the Movement for every kind of moral de-generation, and thrown out of the house I was renting from the

Movement and from my job. After fifteen years of devoted loving service, I had no friends, no job, no money, no life. I had a nervous breakdown. It has taken me years to begin to believe again in love."

"Did anyone help?"

He laughed harshly, "You'd think you'd find someone to help in California—after all, the place is crawling with smiling therapists with soft voices. What these therapists told me was that I had an unconscious father complex and hadn't yet come to terms with my 'rage.' None of them—not even the gay ones—wanted to confront in any way the reality of what had happened. No one in the spiritual community wanted to hear anything either. No one wants their fantasy of India and the exotic East destroyed. But if you look into it—as I was forced to do—you discover that the whole Indian thing is riddled with homophobia, and sex and body hatred in general. Look at the ways P. [a famous female guru] is treating the gays and lesbians in her ashram: She is allegedly telling them to break up with their partners, give up their sexuality, and live celibate. Many, I am told, have been removed from their positions in her movement. Is anyone complaining publicly? Do any of the large spiritual journals have articles about what is happening? Of course not! No one wants to pierce the New Age bubble or get sued by some jet-setting guru's Harvard-trained lawyers. And no one can blame them. I didn't speak out publicly against the Movement when I left it. I was warned that if I did my life would be in danger. I knew enough by then to know that no one would protect me."

And he told me exactly the same thing as the women at lunch had done. "None of the New Age Masters will do anything to help you. All they are concerned about is their reputations and the money it brings them. They are not going to put out for some hysterical abused women or queer. Let the show go on! They might be cautiously sympathetic in private but ask for their *public* support. . . .

Forget it. Most of them know just what an inferno of abuse is going on, but they don't have the guts to speak out about it. I don't think they care. So long as they are on the cover of *Yoga Journal* regularly, why should they?"

I was profoundly shaken by what he was saying. As he slammed the Indian tradition he had so loved, I felt irrational anger rising in me against him. Slowly, I understood why; I was still agonizedly attached, somewhere, to the same tradition, and unwilling, even after all I and Eryk had been through, to see its limitations. I told him what I had been feeling. "How could you not be angry somewhere?" he said. "You have been duped as I was. It hurts."

He smiled sadly. "And you have been duped by a woman, a Mother. I, after all, was in a consciously patriarchal set-up. You thought you were in the bosom of the Mother, safe and protected. Do you know what I think about all the so-called modern Mothers from India? That they are Jehovahs in drag. For all their mouthing of 'universal love' and 'universal compassion' and all their hugs and smiles and *darshans,* they are the same old patriarchal, sex-hating, life-denying, power-drunk wine in curvy new bottles. I've heard stories about every single one of them that for me disqualifies any of them from being anything like a Master or even a responsible teacher."

He looked at me with a grim amusement. "It is a terrible thing looking behind the swinging crystal-studded gold curtain of the New Age fantasy and seeing the cruelty, charlatanry, and manipulation behind. It almost ruined my mind. Why I'm telling you all this is to *warn* you. You are far more of a public figure than I am, so you will get it far worse."

"What advice do you have for me?"

He laughed, "Trust hardly anyone. Dare to see just how corrupt the situation actually is. And hope that if they shoot at you, they miss."

Eryk asked me what I thought of him when we drove back.

"I felt that suffering had made him cynical and a little paranoid."

"I was afraid you might say that," Eryk laughed.

"Afraid?"

"Yes. You see, I believed every word. Everything he said had for me the ring of miserable truth."

Eryk looked at my face and laughed dryly again. "Last year we believed that California was the Beginning of the New. This year we might find something very different. If even a twelfth of what he said is accurate, we are in a very scary situation indeed. What with false Masters, crazy disciples, lazy spiritual journals, and corrupt, cowardly, local teachers who will not stand up for anyone or anything and who are conniving with the silence about abuse . . ." Eryks's voice trailed off. Then he smiled acidly, "Well, it won't be dull."

Eryk and I had been telling many friends and devotees of Meera in California what had happened. Fortunately, we had witnesses— especially L., who had been with us in Thalheim and had seen our anguish and subsequently left Meera. Letters from these friends now started pouring into Thalheim—furious, hurt, bewildered letters praising Eryk's and my move, demanding explanations, and asking some very fierce and pointed questions. Copies of these were sent to Eryk and myself and brought us some relief.

When Gabriela rang on the morning of March 15th, I told her everything that had been happening: Gabriela laughed dryly: "Meera will have to lie now and say that she never told you to leave Eryk. Otherwise she 'might as well fold up shop and start a restaurant.'"

"Meera will not lie," I said.

"Snap out of your dream. You are dealing with very ruthless

people. Anything is possible. The madness is only just beginning. Pray constantly."

On March 17th the madness began. That morning I was recording an interview on Rumi with Michael Thoms of New Directions. Thank God, he was too tactful to ask me any questions about Meera. I came back to find Eryk silent and white-faced.

"Are you sick?" I said, trying to keep the panic out of my voice.

Eryk said nothing.

"For God's sake tell me," I said. "What on earth is going on?"

Eryk took me by the hand and pulled me softly into the front room where we had put the phone. He leaned down and turned on the answering machine. After a few crackles, a male voice said in a bad, horribly accented French, "If you do not shut up and shut up now you will be killed."

At first my mind did not register what I was hearing. The French accent was so bad, so comic opera, I felt like laughing. Then, suddenly, the horror of it struck me.

"Oh my God," I said.

"Oh my God," Eryk echoed ironically. "So now the disciples of the Divine Mother on earth are delivering death threats."

"She can't know this is happening," I said. "Meera wouldn't allow this if she knew, I'm certain of it."

Eryk laughed, "Three months ago you told me she was all-tolerance and all-compassion and never ever interfered in anyone's life. What will you be saying in three months' time? What will you know?"

Over the next ten days, four more death threats followed, all announced in the same crazed voice and bad French. The "messages" varied; the last one said, "You think you are so clever, both of you. But wherever you go, you are watched. You can be killed any-where. Remember that."

The whole atmosphere of Eryk's and my life together sickened; each time I left the house I prayed for protection. The threats, we found out, had been made from a call box near C.I.I.S. in the heart of San Francisco; the police warned us to take them very seriously and to keep them continually informed.

On the phone, Gabriela gave us the name of the person who was making the threats. She couldn't possibly have known the name; it was "given" to her.

"But don't say anything," Gabriela said. "You will not be be-lieved. He will deny everything and you will be made to seem mad."

"You are telling me to say nothing and just let this man go on harassing us?"

"You have no choice. People will want to believe you are crazy, Andrew, rather than accept your version. Now you start talking of death threats, they'll know you're crazy. Tell the police and as few other people as possible. Only those you can really trust."

"I'm terrified, Gabriela."

"I know. But you are protected."

FROM MY JOURNAL:
That night—March 27th

Gabriela says Eryk and I are protected. I have to believe that or I would go mad. My real terror is not that I would die; sometimes I find myself almost longing for that. It would be one solution, after all. What I am really afraid of is that "they" will maim or kill Eryk. Last night I dreamed we were coming out of the grocery store and a car drove past and a man in a black hood leant out and gunned Eryk down. Only he did not die. He was paralyzed from the waist down and could not speak. I woke up sweating and again dreamt of Eryk getting hurt. This time we were coming out of the CD shop on Hayes Street; a man shouting "Meera is divine! Meera is divine" came up behind us and stabbed Eryk again and again in the back. I heard the words, "He will live but he will be brain-damaged. He will be a vegetable."

This morning I asked Eryk, as casually as I could, if he was frightened. "Every time I go shopping," he said, "I look at you and think, 'This may be the last time I ever see Andrew.'" He put his head in his hands. "I used to watch the T.V. and see Beirut on the screen and think—whatever's wrong with my life, at least I'm not in those streets. But now I am."

"Do you really think they would do anything?"

"I talked to the police yesterday. They stressed that anything is possible, especially in what the man called 'matters of cults.'"

Obsessively, I keep asking myself: "Does Meera know? Could she possibly know?" The thought that she might know—or even be orchestrating this madness in some way—is too terrifying to sustain, and I constantly block it out whenever it appears. What scares me most about this childish hunger in me to find Meera "innocent" is that I know she is not, and cannot be. And if a part of me is still in denial, how strong will that denial be in others?

At the end of March, calls from other devotees who had by now heard the news, started to come in. J.P., a gay Ivy League lawyer whom I had introduced to Meera, rang me on March 28th and demanded to "know" the real truth.

His voice grew nasty, "It is only *your* truth anyhow. Who else was in the room with you and Meera and Adilakshmi?"

"No one, obviously."

"So why should I trust your version?"

"Meera has everything to gain by lying, and I have everything to lose by telling the truth."

His voice grew nastier. "Even if what you are saying were true, Andrew, I could not care less."

"You are gay and you say you do not care that she tried to separate myself and Eryk and also told me later that there was no place for gays in the world of the Mother? Are you mad?"

I was furious with him because I was scared; his replies showed me how powerful denial could be. If J.P. had to choose between his imaginary Mother-projection onto Meera and a truth about her that annihilated that projection, I had no doubt but that he would choose the fantasy.

J.P. continued blithely, in his high-pitched wasp voice, telling me what to do. "You must ring Thalheim immediately and clear all this up. Mother and Adilakshmi have been trying to contact you for weeks."

I cut him short. "That is a lie."

He started to almost scream. "That is not helpful! That is not helpful! You must get more balanced!"

At his last phrase, it took all my self-control not to burst out laughing. Here was an Ivy League lawyer, brilliant and forensically minded, so blinded by adoration of Meera that he literally couldn't hear anything I was saying—and he was telling me to be balanced.

Then he started to scream, "You're lying! You must be lying! Everyone knows you're lying! You've been lying all your life!"

And J.P. hung up.

Later, he was to tell everyone who would listen that I was lying and mad. He even rang up C.I.I.S. and offered to help find a lawyer who could get them out of their obligations to me. "I've known him for years," he said to the president. "He's a mad megalomaniac!"

Another gay friend (also a friend of J.P.'s) rang a day later, L.M.

He was more nakedly aggressive: "Look, Andrew, we all know you are lying. Everyone knows."

I listened as he spilled out years of jealousy and vitriol. When he had finished, I said as calmly as I could, "Last November in England a film of my life was shown on Channel 4; it had Meera all over it and was dedicated to Meera. This year I have two books yet to come out with Meera on almost every page. Last year I spent months organizing a tour for Meera in California. Why on earth would I be saying what I am saying if it wasn't the truth? Why as a gay man can't you hear me?"

L.M. went on obsessively, ignoring anything I said. "You just want to be a guru yourself. You've just decided to get rid of her, as you get rid of everybody in the end. You use people, suck them up, and then spit them out. Now it is Meera's turn."

Then he started to laugh eerily, "You know how I know you are lying? Ma herself told me. She is telling everyone who rings Thalheim that you are lying, that you invented the whole thing. There were no conversations; she never asked you to leave Eryk—how could she? She loves and accepts everyone. Everything you are saying is a wicked lie. She does not say that of course. She is the All-Compassionate. She says, 'Andrew still has the keys to my house and he is welcome any time. I forgive him completely.' You don't deserve such a wonderful Mother. I'm telling you the whole thing, Andrew, so you know that your stupid little game is up. You're finished now. Who will believe you against her? A mere Oxford poseur beside the Avatar of the Age? You haven't got a prayer."

The hatred and violence in his voice made me reel.

"Are you listening," he screamed. "I hope you fucking well are listening."

Slowly, in a daze, I hung up on him. So, Meera's "official position" was that everything I was saying was a lie. I went into the dining room and lay on the floor, dissolved in anguish and terror.

Eryk was out shopping. I walked through our sun-filled flat like a zombie, picking up cups and putting them down, trying to read a days-old newspaper. It took me at least an hour before I dared to register what L.M. had told me.

Eryk knew as soon as he came back that something dreadful had happened.

"Andrew," he almost shouted. "Andrew! What is it! Your face is white!"

I told him.

Gabriela rang two hours later. "Meera panicked. She realized that you were not to be stopped. I believe that she will do anything at all to preserve her wealth and power. She knows perfectly well that J.P. and L.M. are jealous of you and have been for a long time; I think she is manipulating them too. And she knows that her followers will be famished for any scrap of reassurance she can throw them."

"I must speak out soon. I cannot bear being silent."

"The moment will come within the next two weeks. You'll know when it comes. Say nothing until then. Nothing, do you hear? You must be calm and sober and do and say nothing."

"Because we are in danger?"

"Yes—but you are protected. Remember that. Do you trust me?"

"Yes."

"I will ring, I promise, every single morning for the next months and tell you what I am receiving. The Mother will help us both."

"Sometimes, Gabriela, I can't help doubting . . ."

"How could you not? You're human, aren't you? And you are dying to one whole life. But very soon you will receive a sign."

"What kind of sign?"

"I am not sure. But it will be a big and very definite sign that the Mother is looking after you and that you are being protected. It will come soon."

"Gabriela," I began.

She cut me short. "Have I ever lied to you? Do I have anything to gain by encouraging you falsely? Don't I know how dangerous everything is? Why do you think I'm ringing you so often? Pray and believe."

Only two days later, the sign from the Virgin that Gabriela had predicted was given.

Eryk and I were in the habit in those early weeks of our return to California of going almost every other day to worship in the old Mission church in Dolores. The vast, shadowy, cool church and the sun-washed cemetery full of weathered, soft-faced statues, wild roses, and their mingling scents brought us some peace.

That day Eryk and I were particularly despairing. Sleep continued to elude me; often I felt I would never sleep calmly again. Walking down to the Mission on a perfect, cloudless spring afternoon, we both admitted to each other that without the other we would have nothing left to live for.

We prayed a long time that afternoon in the empty church. Our lives, in fact, had become almost continued prayer. I never stopped repeating under my breath, "Mother save us," and whenever I looked at Eryk his lips were also moving in prayer.

After praying, we went, as we usually did, to walk slowly round the cemetery. It was strangely empty that day—strangely, because the weather was wonderful and usually the Mission cemetery is full of lovers of history and old roses. We sat near a small battered statue of the Virgin and went on praying to Her, our eyes closed in the sun and fragrance streaming to us from all directions. There, in that garden of the dead that was also a rose garden, we sat, utterly wrung out but open to the warm calm that was trying to reach us, in the sun on our faces, in the sun-washed slight wind, in the heat of the stone bench, in all the brilliant reds and yellows and purples of the roses.

Just before leaving, I bought a small, gaudy plastic picture of the Virgin that I found in the shop. In it, the Virgin (whose pale, wasp-blue eyes and flaxen hair made me smile) was opening the front of her tunic to reveal a flaming red heart.

A more "refined" or artistically rich an image would have moved me less. The more I looked at Her, the more intensely and mysteriously I felt that She had sent us exactly *that* image to assure us that She was suffering with us.

Almost immediately after I had bought it I felt a fierce sharp pain in the middle of my chest—as if I had been stabbed there. I had to stand and breathe for a few minutes before it subsided.

When Eryk and I returned home I placed the card on my desk, leaning it against the photograph of Ramakrishna in ecstasy that I have carried everywhere with me since I first bought it ten years ago in India.

After a quiet tea with Eryk, I went back into my study to pray and saw that my desk was covered with what looked like water.

"Eryk," I called out loudly. "Why did you spill water on my desk?"

He came in, a little angry. "I didn't do anything."

He went toward the desk, put his hand into the "water," and then put it to his nose. Slowly, he turned round. His face was transformed; tears were shining in his eyes.

"What is it?"

He couldn't speak. Very slowly, he stretched out his hand for me to smell. The sweetest and most pungent perfume of rose that I had ever smelled filled my nostrils.

I still did not understand.

"How did rosewater get here?"

Tears were now streaming from Eryk's eyes.

He came toward me and folded me in his arms. "It is a miracle," he said softly and slowly, as if speaking to a child. "It is a miracle. The rosewater is Divine. It comes from Her. It is streaming to us from the heart in the picture."

I held him a few moments, doubt and wonder fighting for possession of my mind. Then I went to the desk and picked up the picture. It was covered with rosewater, and the place where Her heart was exposed smelled intensely sweet. Eryk was right: The "rosewater" was streaming from Her Sacred Heart. I turned slowly round in the room, as if seeing it for the first time. It was now about five in the afternoon and the whole study was drenched in rich gold sunlight.

Eryk and I knelt on the ground and bowed our heads to Her. Then, still in silence, I went to the desk and put my hand in the rosewater, opened Eryk's shirt, and rubbed his whole chest with it praying out loud, "Take the cancer away from my Beloved, my Mother. Let my Beloved live."

And Eryk opened my shirt and trousers and put his warm wet hands all over my back.

"Heal my Beloved's back, my Mother. Let him walk straight and tall again."

Although it was in the middle of her night in Europe, Eryk and I rang Gabriela.

Her wild gypsy laughter made the phone rattle.

"Aha! Aha! I told you! Your Mother will not abandon you! Listen to Gabriela!"

Again I asked Gabriela if she thought Meera was a black magician.

"I am still not sure. But we will know one way or the other soon."

"That sounds terrifying."

"The Virgin has just manifested Herself in rosewater for you and you are terrified! Don't you know the Virgin is Queen of Hell? Don't you know that there is no greater power than Hers against evil of all kinds?"

Suddenly I remembered the image I had seen in the Rue du Bac of the Virgin standing on the snake of evil; I remembered, too, that the night before I had fallen asleep at last at about five only to wake a quarter of an hour later after a nightmare of an immense black snake racing toward me. I told Gabriela.

"Don't worry!" she laughed. "The Mother will tread down the snake! You'll see! You'll see!!"

She was so happy she began to sing in Rumanian so wildly off-key that we all burst out laughing.

———

Later that night, Eryk turned to me in bed and asked me to marry him. We had been talking about marriage since our journey to India the previous September. Before I met Eryk I had never imagined myself married to a man; I had accepted the prevailing view of society that marriage was for heterosexuals without even thinking about it; no one in my circle of gay friends had married their lover.

When Eryk first began talking about marriage, I had been amazed; here was a young man, fifteen years younger than myself, who believed passionately in the religious power and significance of an union declared before God, who wanted, above all things, a relationship of complete fidelity and mutual surrender. Initially (back in September) I had been doubtful: I could still hardly believe that I deserved a full and holy love. Now I was not doubtful but scared: I was scared that marrying Eryk would open my heart to him so finally and irrevocably and that if he died I would not be able to survive it.

"I'm frightened," I said.

"I know," Eryk whispered, ruffling my hair.

"But I know, too, we may not have much time, either of us."

"No."

Eryk waited, with his eyes closed.

"Let us marry as soon as we can," I said.

As soon as I said it, I was flooded with joy and relief. I hadn't realized how much I wanted to be bound in God to Eryk.

Next day, we began to make preparations feverishly. We set the date for April 16th; we asked our friend Lauren Artress, a minister of Grace Cathedral, to marry us and she accepted; we went down to a printer on Market Street and ordered the invitations. They were extremely simple; on the top we wrote "Amor Omnia Vincit": Love Conquers All Things.

FROM MY JOURNAL:
Late that afternoon

Eryk is sleeping beside me, so calmly and so fresh-faced it is impossible to believe he is as sick as he is. He has been as happy as a schoolboy all day, singing and laughing and giddy.

What is marriage for me? Above all, it is a saying yes to love, a final yes at last, and a final yes to Eryk, whose love for me is the greatest Divine gift I have been given in this life. I know our love is holy and transformatory: I know that the Mother has brought us both together into Her great crucible of Tantra. I know that choosing to marry at this exposed and frightful moment of both of our lives will take us both more and more profoundly into a commitment that can only open us further to suffering as well as joy. I am already entwined with Eryk; when we make love I am feeling his feelings, sighing his sighs. Many, many times, I finish his sentences, hear his thoughts, know from a small glint in his eye or down-turn of his mouth exactly what he is experiencing or desiring. I know that marriage will be an immeasurable deepening, before Her, of this already searing and uncanny intimacy and a part of me is terrified—as terrified, I realize, of the Oneness with him and love I have always believed I wanted as of the exterior ordeals that are just threatening us.

I also realize that there simply *is no time* for the luxury of fear, and so again and again I pray to her, "Dissolve and destroy my fear of love. With one hand, I see, You are giving me the initiation of tantric love; with another, you are holding out to me infinite grief. I know I cannot have the first gift without having the courage to embrace the other, that the two are related in a mystery I will only gradually understand, that only so extreme a situation such as the one You have brought us into could open our hearts so absolutely to the revelation after revelation you make our lovemaking radiant with. What is Tantra but a continual dying-into-Love, into You—and how could such a dying not be, at times and even for long stretches, terrible and painful as well as glorious? I see Your terms, my Mother, my Black Mother; give me the courage to accept them, and to suffer without self-pity. Give me the strength and Grace to be for my husband what he needs me to be."

Almost as if in occult response to the new level of trust in Her and in each other that Eryk and I had reached, the external nightmare of threats and denunciations deepened. In the next three days that followed our decision to marry (which we confided only to our closest friends), Eryk and I were besieged by insulting and terrifying phone calls from all over the States and Europe.

Gabriela said when I spoke to her about what was happening, "This is just the beginning. You will have to develop a sense of humor."

I exploded: "A sense of humor? What the hell do you mean?"

Gabriela chuckled. "I realize that I am asking you to laugh in hell, but you must remember that the one thing the devil doesn't have is a sense of humor. The people who are ringing you are half-mad and are being manipulated; try to listen to what they are saying with complete detachment as if it did not apply to you. It doesn't. They are merely demonizing a projected version of you so as not to face the truth. In fact, they are projecting onto you their own inner craziness and disarray because they can't stand them."

"And you call that funny."

"Yes. Delusion is funny. If you keep your ears open you will learn more than you ever wanted to know about almost everything. Which is the point of the Mother's exercise. To do the work you will have to do in the future, you will have to know as much as you can stand about illusion, the craziness of fake or garbled spirituality, and the evil that can use it."

At first I was resentful of Gabriela's uncharacteristically dry tone. Then I understood that she was being so matter-of-fact because the clarity she was attempting to give me was the only possible way of surviving the suffering and fear so devastating an onslaught caused Eryk and myself.

"Surround yourself at every moment," Gabriela whispered, "with the Light of the Mother and try and listen as if you were listening to the radio."

Gabriela's advice calmed me slightly. After every horrible call I would note what had been said and study it, as if I were a scientist studying lepidoptera.

Slowly, I realized, too, that there was something ghoulishly humorous about the situation. For one thing, not one of the callers who felt they had the right to ring and insult me or Eryk ever bothered—or dared—to ask what had really happened; as soon as either of us started patiently to explain our position, the caller would invariably start shouting or hissing rage and venom. Although I knew by now that such "deafness" to truth could turn lethal, there was a grim amusement in it too. For another thing, not one of the callers who rang *knew* Meera; all of them had been to Thalheim and counted themselves her disciples but none had actually spoken for more than a moment or two to the Idol they worshipped in the silence of *darshan*. And yet they felt complete confidence in telling me exactly what I had experienced and "misunderstood" and not for one moment did they stop to reflect that I, after all, knew Meera far better, far more intimately, and for far longer than they did. In the weeks in Paris that followed what happened in Thalheim I had undergone my own inner purgation of my projection onto her of everything I wanted and needed; now I heard all the different versions of this projection spat at me with eerie and frightful force through the telephone. All the voices of need and hunger and overassertion to cover up secret doubt that I had heard in myself now shouted in different tones at me from "without."

"At least you know now," Eryk said grimly, "that your understanding of the way Meera uses and encourages projection is accurate. Here are all these devotees of the supposed Divine Mother who is supposedly preparing a revolution of Love spewing violent hatred down the phone, refusing to listen to anything either of us can say, and in the name of Love crucifying two human beings whose only crime is to tell the truth."

Sometimes as the tirades went on and on ("You are a traitor to the New Age." "You have betrayed the holiest Being on the earth, the hope of the world." "You will die for what you are doing and you will kill Eryk." "You are a pathetic and evil liar trying to gain attention for yourself."), I would try and say as gently as I could, "Believe me I understand your rage: I know the need and passion that moves you to have to condemn me and Eryk. Four months ago, I shared that need and that passion and might have reacted as you are now to anyone who was telling you what I am telling you." Saying that, however, just made things worse. "Don't try and fuck me with your evil cleverness," one caller (a Harvard doctor) screamed. "Cleverness is easy; I worship the silence of the Mother." Another said, "I know you, Andrew. You can justify anything. You always have the answers. But this time I am not going to be fooled by you. Adilakshmi is warning everyone about your perverse mind and its ability to twist anything."

After the first day of threats and insults I stopped trying to explain anything; I realized it was useless. The inherent madness of the Meera cult, the madness I had done so much unconsciously to script and encourage, was now turned towards me and Eryk. The devotees' hysterical defense of Meera was as crazy as their belief in her as a Divine omniscient avatar; one lunacy birthed the other. Both had their own fierce weird life, which had nothing to do with "reason" or "justice" or even minimum respect and decency. I remembered the words of Christ about false Masters in the Gospel of St. Matthew: "By their fruits shall you know them." With one half of myself, I felt an increasingly profound fear; with another, an almost infinite sadness that I had helped create a cult which was dragging so many beings into real moral and spiritual danger. Clearly, none of the callers could hear themselves, hear the vicious cruelty of what they were saying; clearly none of them could begin to imagine what spiritual disaster they were preparing for themselves. Supposing Eryk and I were killed, wouldn't the truth of what happened in Thalheim have to come out in the end? And then what? Not only would the devotees have the madness of their false faith to live with but also our blood on their hands. How would they survive the guilt that would inevitably ensue? How would they preserve a shred of faith in themselves or in the real Mother? I could do nothing, I knew, but my heart ached and I prayed for Meera's devotees, even as I prayed to be protected from them.

Over the course of those first weeks in California, my relationship with Jake Long had become increasingly surreal and strained. I had had to retain him as my manager and as the organizer of the tour that would begin in April: I had neither the time to organize it myself nor the money to cancel it. Besides, I needed desperately whatever money I could make; I had no way of knowing when or how quickly Eryk's cancer would deepen and what medical expenses would cost. Jake had, I knew, decided, as he put it, to "stick with the Mother"; I knew, too, that everything I said to him was reported back. I kept a careful record of every conversation I had with him and told him in detail everything that was happening—about the death threats, the terrifying phone calls, Eryk's decline. This was partly tactical; I wanted to be certain that when all the facts came out Meera could not hide behind "not knowing anything about what disciples are doing in my name."

As Jake told me, also, in several different calls, so-called "old friends" of mine had rung him and told him "terrible stories" about me—about how I was a mythomaniac, a sex fiend, an alcoholic, someone incapable of even imagining let alone telling the truth. Whenever he repeated one of his stories, I would say, "But you told them, of course, that I am telling the truth. You were there, after all, and you are representing me." He would pause, cough, and change the subject. I also used to tell him: "If all these devotees say I am a liar—then why do they believe *Hidden Journey*? Why did so many of them change their whole lives for something a 'liar' wrote? I hope this is what you are telling them, too, as my representative."

At the end of the three days of insulting telephone calls and two more chilling death threats (one traced to New York and the other from Southern California), I had had enough. I decided to ring Jake and confront him.

"You have to do something," I began.

"Do something?" he said bewilderedly.

"You know perfectly what I mean. For weeks now I have been telling you that Eryk and I are in danger. For three days I have received cruel and threatening telephone calls, and anything at all could now happen. It is time for you to tell the truth."

Jake breathed heavily and said nothing.

I went on. "You know that Meera is now saying that I am lying, don't you? You know that she is denying completely that any confrontation or conversation between us took place. You know she is saying she never told me to leave Eryk."

Jake continued to breathe heavily and say nothing.

I raised my voice, "You know she is saying these things, don't you?"

Jake mumbled a quick, "Yes. I heard."

I took a deep breath, "So, as my manager, as the man supposedly in charge of my interests and legally bound to defend them, I must now insist that you make a public statement saying that you know that what I am saying is true. You were there, Jake. You saw me and Eryk in despair. I told you day after day what Meera was saying; you yourself had repeated detailed conversations with Adilakshmi and Meera and knew what happened as it happened. Eryk reported to you everything he saw and experienced. You have no choice but to tell the truth now, and tell it fast."

There was a long silence, and then Jake's voice came back, "But Andrew," he said in a singsong lilt. "Andrew, my friend, I wasn't in the room on December 27th. You were the only one in the room with Meera and Adilakshmi."

"What the hell are you talking about?"

"You saw me about fifteen minutes afterwards."

"Yes," he admitted. "But I wasn't there. How can I be sure what really happened? How can I be certain that you aren't inventing . . ."

I screamed with fury, "You bastard. You fucking bastard! Don't you understand, you madman, what a hell Eryk and I are going through? Have you no heart?"

Jake paused and said again, "I wasn't in the room. I didn't see or hear anything. I don't remember what happened at *darshan*. I simply do not remember. My memory is faulty at the best of times. I don't remember anything."

I stood frozen with fear.

"Do you understand?" Jake said slowly, "I don't remember anything."

"Yes you do," I spat. "Yes you fucking well do. You remember it all, all the suffering, all the agony, every nuance of the negotiations. You remember the film-star policy."

"No I don't."

"Yes you do," I said desperately. "Look, Jake, I'm begging you. Eryk's life and mine are threatened. My whole career is threatened, Eryk may be dying. You have to . . ."

His voice became nasty. "I don't have to do anything."

I realized that nothing would move him.

"You know what happened and that we are telling the truth. And yet you are prepared to do and say nothing as Eryk and I are torn apart and perhaps even killed. What you are doing is a crime and in the end its consequences are bound to return to you in one way or another. I believe you are conspiring with evil, and evil will use you and discard you. The net you are helping Meera weave around us will in the end close around you, because we are telling the truth and I swear to you that the Divine will not let us be destroyed."

And I put down the phone on him.

Eryk came in at the end of the conversation. I told him what had happened.

We sat on the floor, our heads in our hands.

"I didn't want to tell you this," Eryk said finally, "but yesterday I spoke with L., who knows John and Jim, our friends in Washington state who were with us in Thalheim, our great gay friends." Eryk said the last words with mocking irony.

"Don't tell me their memory is now faulty?" I said trembling. "Surely they wouldn't . . ."

"Yes, they would. L. rang them to testify on our behalf. They said that nothing happened in Thalheim. They don't remember anything."

"But they saw us in anguish for days. They were the first to know. Their whole work and lives have been dedicated to gay liberation."

"Nothing happened," Eryk said. "Nothing at all happened."

"Oh my God."

"We have been abandoned. And if we are killed, they will claim we brought it upon ourselves by our posturing and 'dangerous lies.' She will get away with everything and anything."

"No she won't. She cannot. The Mother will not allow it."

But my voice sounded more confident than I felt.

Eryk said, "Now you must speak out and in public, before their lies destroy us."

"There is one other thing we can do too," I said. "We can write a complete account of what really happened, and I can add to it everything I know about Meera's earlier career and everything I know about her finances in Germany, India, and America. We will send the dossier to my banks here and in France, and to friends who will keep it in their safes. At least if anything happens to us, the truth will have a chance to come out."

I worked most of the night writing in a calm, logical fury every detail of what I now knew about Meera and about what had happened. I sent the ten-page document Federal Express next morning to carefully chosen friends around the world who could be relied upon to keep it safe and not to read it unless, as I instructed them, "Eryk and I are harmed."

Then I rang Jake and left a message on his answering machine. I told him that unless Thalheim stopped lying immediately I would speak out publicly and reveal everything I knew about Meera and her affairs. I told him about the dossier I had compiled and sent out. I told him that if anything at all happened to Eryk and myself, the dossier would be revealed to the press.

I told him very carefully that I had no intention of ruining Meera or anyone else, and that the friends I had sent the dossier to had been given instructions not to read its contents under any circumstances apart from Eryk's or my injury. I said that its contents would never be revealed, whatever happened, unless either Eryk or I were harmed. I knew enough about Jake by now to know that he would use any opportunity he could to make me out "crazy" or an "abusive menace"; I wanted my message to make clear that I was in every way conscious of the law.

"Do you seriously think any of this will do any good?" Eryk asked me. "Jake thinks you are finished. He thinks you are already destroyed. He won't take your 'dossier' seriously."

"But Meera will know that it exists, and that may tie her hands a little."

Eryk looked doubtful.

"I had to do something," I said lamely. "I can't just wait scared out of my wits that the next time you or I go shopping there will be . . ."

"Stop it. Stop it now." Eryk said putting a hand over my mouth.

ACT IV

Speaking Out

*

I have seen the wicked in great power,
and spreading himself like a green bay tree.

PSALM 37

Who shall separate us from the love of Christ? Shall tribulation,
or distress, or persecution, or nakedness, or peril, or sword?

ROMANS 8:35

The moment that Gabriela had prophesied when I would be compelled to speak out in public about what had happened came sooner than I thought.

The retreat on the Divine Mother that I had arranged to do for C.I.I.S. that year was held on the weekend beginning Friday, April 1st, in a retreat center in Santa Rosa, with about a hundred and forty people. I began the weekend in a state of almost paralytic anxiety; just before we left for Santa Rosa, Eryk and I had received another death threat. A voice had screamed onto our answering machine, "Shut your fucking queer mouths or else."

The moment came on the second day of the retreat, on Saturday, halfway through the afternoon. I had been speaking all Friday evening and Saturday morning about a path to the Mother that would be simple, immediate, and direct and need no priests or gurus; the tension and anger in the room were palpable. Then, on Saturday afternoon, a beautiful slim blonde women rose at the back of the large room and said, "Andrew, you have repeatedly been making disparaging remarks about gurus. Can you explain why?"

The room—and it seemed, the entire universe—went silent. My knees started to shake and I could hear my heart thumping hard against my rib cage. I took a deep breath and prayed. Then for an hour, as calmly and lucidly and honestly as I could, I told the story of what had happened in Thalheim.

The result was pandemonium, a vehement boiling over of energy of every kind. Several close friends of Eryk's and mine were present in the audience; they immediately came to me with tears in their eyes. "We know you must be telling the truth and our hearts ache for you and what you are going through." Others angrily dismissed what I was saying as "disgusting paranoia." The room broke up into factions; several people stormed out. Next day thirty people left the retreat altogether saying I was clearly crazy and out of control.

The story was out. When Gabriela telephoned us the next day back in San Francisco, she said, "Expect the worst." Letters poured into the office of the president of C.I.I.S. Many were extremely insulting and hostile.

The reaction to the news about my marriage to Eryk was also vehement. Lauren Artress, the minister at Grace Cathedral who was to marry us, much later told us how she was bombarded with calls at her office, denouncing us. The death threats continued. One said, "Don't think you'll live through your wedding day; we'll throw a bomb through the window."

I heard from reliable informants that C.I.I.S., too, was in a turmoil of controversy. Certain of my colleagues had already pronounced me a "fraud" and a hysteric (not one of my colleagues in the months that followed ever publicly defended me). Many of the students who had "loved" me the year before when I was giving classes on Rumi (some of whom had also gone to visit Meera on the strength of my advocacy of her) now began to claim that I was "seriously unhinged." Rumors were already circulating that a considerable body of students wanted me to be thrown out; there was talk of meetings and signed petitions.

"Do nothing," Gabriela would say over and over again. "Do not react. Stay as calm as you can. Anything you now do or say will be scrutinized for signs of imbalance. Your hope is to stay stone-cold sober."

I began my classes at C.I.I.S. on the "Divine Feminine in World Religions" on the Thursday after the Santa Rosa retreat. I had hardly slept, it seemed, for weeks; my back was so painful I could walk only with difficulty and had to be heavily medicated to be able to sit down to lecture; Eryk was growing weaker every day. I was so scared and desperate to follow Gabriela's advice to appear calm that I did not dare at the beginning to talk as I normally do, from notes and spontaneously; I read everything in as uninflected and

"English" a monotone as I could manage. I was having to work out my new vision in public, exactly as the events that were so brutally shaping it were occurring. This was almost intolerably stressful, and had it not been for the encouragement of old friends in the audience who knew I could not be lying and who had no stake in the "guru business" but loved my work, I do not think I could have gone on.

A week after the "announcement" at Santa Rosa, Jake Long wrote me a long rambling letter terminating our arrangement. He accused me of filling his life with "unparalleled psychic anxiety," of causing him sleepless nights and stomach trouble. ("We return the compliment," Eryk laughed dryly), and of "threatening" him by "visions of punishment." It was a masterpiece of Southern Californian hypocrisy. Clearly the message I had left on his answering machine ten days before had scared him.

Fortunately, just when Eryk and I both believed that I would have to cancel everything, one of the friends who had been with us in Thalheim and who had also left Meera in disgust offered to be my manager. I accepted her offer and she, with patience and courage, picked up what Jake had dropped and helped Eryk and me get through the tour.

FROM MY JOURNAL:
Saturday, April 9th

Just a week now to our wedding. The fiercer and more cruel the threats and insinuations against us grow, the more fervently Eryk and I believe in the truth of what we are doing.

All the details are now prepared—the order of the readings from various mystical traditions, the order of the music, the nature of the service itself (the old Anglican wedding service, the one in which my parents and their parents were married). Our beloved friend, Sandra S., has offered flowers and champagne.

Now all we have to do, as Eryk said dryly at lunch, is to survive the week.

In fact, Eryk and I had two weddings. We asked Tara, a Buddhist nun and teacher, to bless us formally before the great ancient gold Buddha in her living room. She agreed, and her brother and sisters insisted on inviting us after the ceremony to a feast. Her brother K.P. said, "We are your brothers and sisters now—how can I not celebrate the marriage of my brothers?"

Our dear friend Catherine flew in from Paris to be with us; the ceremony that Tara prepared for us, on the evening of Thursday, April 14th, was piercing in its simplicity and loveliness. We all wept together as Tara held us in her arms and offered our love to the Buddha. "You have come across an ocean of suffering to this sacred moment," Tara said. "You have fought many monsters and suffered over many lifetimes to be able now to join your hearts and hands together. Now, no power in heaven or hell can separate you. May all the Buddhas and Bodhisattvas protect you forever!"

The whole of Tara's family waited for us on the other side of town. Her sisters had prepared for Eryk and myself two marriage garlands, the most beautiful and fragrant and magical that I have ever seen—of all kinds of pink and white carnations woven together. K.P., smiling, with tears in his eyes, caressed our heads and necks and blessed us over and over again and himself placed the perfumed and still-moist garlands around our heads. He had been sick with heart trouble for over a year and looked drained and exhausted, but he was almost incoherent with joy for us, prouder and fonder than any father could have been.

"May you be eternally happy! May all your enemies be enlightened and come to love you as I love you! May all the forces ranged against you dissolve like smoke!"

This great old Burmese gentleman did not refer to what we were doing as a "blessing"; he quite unconcernedly, it seemed, called it a "marriage." I thanked him just before we left for being so forthright.

He looked at me as if I were mad. "My dear Andrew," he said. "Love has no categories. If every married couple has as much passion, loyalty, and truth as you and Eryk do, the whole world would be a happier place."

"Have you ever been at a marriage of two men before?"

"No, but what does that matter? Marriage is marriage, isn't it? If two people of whatever sex want to dedicate themselves to each other for life in the eyes of God, that is a holy and wonderful thing and I am honored to be your host tonight."

I embraced him and kissed him in tears. Then, with his arms around me, leaning his head sweetly against mine like a little boy, K.P. steered me into the family shrine. "I am not one to give advice," he said softly, "because I have lived long enough to know that hardly anyone listens to anyone else. But I want you very much to listen to me now.

"Promise me that whatever anyone says or does, you will not give up standing for your truth and vision and for the truth of your love. Never deny anything that you are being taught by the Spirit, even if acknowledging it risks death. Honor is more important even than life. All real advances begin in one man or woman's decision to acknowledge the truth whatever it costs them. And one day you will see, your and Eryk's suffering will grow a great tree of blessing and freedom for others. I will not be alive, I know, to see that tree, but I will be in the wind shaking its branches so the blossoms can fall everywhere."

He embraced me and held me against his chest.

"My family will always protect you and believe in you and pray for your protection and enlightenment."

Eryk came in and stood in the door to announce that the meal was ready.

K.P. went up to Eryk and stroked his cheek. Then he turned to me. "Who could have a braver and sweeter husband than you, Andrew? In the dung of suffering you have found the diamond. Guard it well."

Eryk and I awoke on the morning of our wedding—Saturday, April 16, 1994—awash in a strange serene joy that expanded continually during the day. As if by a miracle of the Mother, all fear and anxiety had left us; Thalheim and the letters and calls and betrayals seemed to belong to another dimension, another life. We both felt we were moving in the atmosphere of Her blessing, and every detail of the day that unfolded had the rightness and dreamlike perfection that blessing gives.

Whenever I ask Eryk what he remembers about our wedding day, he says "our joy." It seemed to us both that the joy we knew that day was too vast to be ours alone; it was Nature's also, the Spring's; it was the joy of the Christ and the Virgin at the consummation of real Love; it was the joy of all lovers everywhere. The waves of tragedy and horror that had repeatedly threatened to engulf us in the months before suddenly, marvelously, receded, as if they had never been there at all—to reveal Her world of Love glittering and laughing in everything.

Sandra came in the early afternoon with two vans full of fresh white flowers and crates of Veuve Clicquot, and supervised the transformation of our austere Zen spaces into a temple of flowers foaming and spiraling everywhere and sending their perfume round every corner and into every room.

"I want today to be perfect for you," Sandra said. "My prayer for you is that today is so beautiful it gives you strength for everything that might lie ahead."

Out of a large bag she fetched, laughing, croissants for our first married breakfast, small delicious soaps, and bath oils in a pink basket. Taking us both by the hand, she pulled us into our bedroom and arranged each object tenderly around our bed. And then as Eryk and I stood amazed and delighted, she left the room in a Chaplin shuffle to scrub the toilet. Ten minutes later, I met her in the hallway.

She kissed me and said, "Your and Eryk's joy should be bottled and given to everyone. Are you nervous?"

I nodded.

She took my hands in hers. "When I first met you, you were so lonely. You told me once you believed you would never find love. Well not only did you find love, but you chose love above everything. And now love is choosing you." She looked me up and down, "Now go and shave again! Brush your teeth ten times! Comb your hair!"

Our ceremony began with Leonytne Price singing Schubert's "Ave Maria"; from the first we wanted everything that was done or said at our wedding to be dedicated to the Virgin. As that sun-washed exalted voice filled the room in praise to the One who had saved us and protected us and brought us across so much suffering to the splendor and peace of this day, I stood with Eryk at the back of our drawing room and gazed around in wonder at him, at the flowers, at all our friends gathered there gazing with joy at us. I remembered the day three months before in early January when at the chapel in Beauraing Eryk had reached and fetched a white rose for me from the altar. I thanked the Virgin with every cell of my being for everything She had given us, and for the Beloved She had sent me.

The ceremony we chose was, as I have said, the Anglican marriage ceremony; both Eryk and I wanted to take our vows in the Christian tradition, in which we had been brought up, in honor of our families and in gratitude to Christ and the Virgin. But we had readings also from other mystical traditions, because for both of us the Virgin is the Universal Mother, the Source of All Wisdom and All Splendor, whose grace underlies and sustains all revelation. So, after the "Ave Maria" had finished and filled our front rooms with its alpine and fragrant peace, I read from the Brihad-Aranyaka Upanishad, invoking as I did so inwardly all the faces of the Mother in India—Durga and Kali and Saraswati and Lakshmi—and all the beauty and healing wonder that India had given me from the beginning of my life:

> "In truth it is not for the love of a husband that a husband is
>   dear; but for he love of the soul in the husband that a
>   husband is dear . . .
> Power will abandon the man who thinks that religion is apart
>   from the soul.
> The gods will abandon the man who thinks that the gods are
>   apart from the soul.

And all will abandon the man who thinks that the all is apart
from the soul.
Because religion, power, heavens, beings, gods, and all rest on
the soul."

Music flowed throughout; we wanted to honor the Mother in
sound also and to have the whole ceremony inspired by the rapture
and beauty of the women whose voices had meant most to us, and
who had most powerfully moved us to the truths of love. So Leon-
tyne Price was followed by Barbra Streisand who sang "People,"
and Streisand was followed by Maria Callas, who, after we took our
vows, sang "Depuis le jour"; and Marlene Dietrich reduced the
room to tears with her poignant version of "I Wish You Love" at
the end. And all the while our stuffed tiger Balthazar sat in regal
joy on the futon, in the front room, bestowing on the proceeding
his magical wise smile.

A Jewish rabbi, to honor Eryk's Jewish heritage, held a canopy
over our heads; a Zen abbot stood next to him; Burmese Buddhists
stood in resplendent feast-day saris near the door; a Christian
woman, strongly and beautifully, took us through our vows; an ag-
nostic psychoanalyst read, in French, and with passion, a long passage from the Song of Songs; photographs of Ramakrishna and
Bede Griffiths and a lithograph of the Curé of Ars, the great
French saint and healer, gazed on all of us from a table by the window, ringed by flowers. As many of the Mother's religious paths as
possible were represented: All the beauty of the spirit seemed to be
dancing around us and in us.

As we said our vows together, Eryk began to weep. The tears
streamed down his face and kept streaming. Sandra stood by him,
his witness, and, for that day, his mother, holding him up. I knew
why he was weeping—from relief, from amazement, from grati-

tude that at last, he, who had suffered so much in his life and been deprived of so much, should be graced by so much holy delight on the day he had wanted to see come more than any other—the day when he and I would be joined together forever in Her. I knew, too, that he was weeping because he had not believed that we would ever see this day; he had not told me, but I knew he had thought that we would be killed or that he would die before we could be united before and in Her; the fact that we hadn't been struck him at last as he stood, so young and beautiful with a gardenia in his buttonhole, gazing round at the smiling faces of people who love him, as a miracle, Her miracle. And so his tears were tears of bliss, birthing-tears, tears of praise.

I did not weep, because from the moment the "Ave Maria" began a vast peace descended on me and claimed me for its own. Everything that happened—in the ceremony and throughout the beautiful and gentle feast that followed—happened in a Divine calm. Each word, each gesture, each note of music had, in that calm, an inevitable justice and beauty; the whole event seemed like a carpet that She was unrolling before me, slowly, and with infinite love so I could inwardly savor each subtle miracle of design.

All the guests had gone. Eryk was in the front room, gazing round for one last time at all the flowers and drinking in the evening air. I walked into our bedroom. All round our bed, small candles had been placed that made the room float in flickering light. Our garlands had been placed on our pillows; boxes and pots of white flowers smiled from every corner. The room was filled with the perfume of fresh lilies, Her flowers.

Next day I rang Sandra to pour out our thanks to her for all she had done to make our marriage so marvelous. She said, "I want you to know something. Your wedding yesterday was the most beautiful wedding I have ever been to in my life, the most true and the most naturally holy. Love herself came. Everyone felt it! May every conceivable blessing accompany you now."

We needed all the blessings we could receive in the days and weeks that followed, for our marriage unleashed a torrent of malice and abuse, which threatened to overwhelm us with even greater force than anything we had up to then experienced.

On the Monday after our wedding, Eryk opened a large brown package to find a dead snake in it. On Tuesday, the first of many obscene packages arrived addressed to us both—dildos and "sex-aids" and cut-out advertisements for porn films. On Wednesday, we heard that an anonymous letter condemning our union and my position on Meera and giving Thalheim's phone number ("Where the truth can be known") was circulating C.I.I.S.; a copy of it was anonymously mailed to us with "Frauds!" scrawled across it in large red writing. The death threats continued on our answering machine. Certain of our friends had not been able to attend our wedding, they had said, because they were "away": We found out that they had been in San Francisco all the time, and that they had been ringing everyone they knew (including those who were present and who told us) saying that we were marrying "to provoke a scandal" and that we deserved whatever happened.

Such an explosion of malice wounded and terrified us. The beauty of our marriage had been so holy that we had believed the Blessing that had descended would keep us from harm. Now we understood that precisely because the Blessing had been so great, those forces that wanted to see us humiliated would redouble their attack.

Gabriela said with tears in her voice: "What was born on Saturday was a Holy Union. What took place in such joy was not only a great step forward for you and Eryk but for all gay lovers and all lovers everywhere: It was a beginning of the Triumph of the Mother. Everything that does not want this Triumph and the freedom it offers to everyone will try to destroy it. This is inevitable. There is an occult law which makes difficulty and disaster test every advance. There is nothing you can do about this, Andrew. Just make your every moment a prayer for protection."

"How much more of this madness can we bear, Gabriela? There is never a moment's breathing space, never a moment's peace."

"I would be lying if I told you I knew. You are going through a terrible ordeal because a tremendous Secret is being revealed for everyone through your and Eryk's love. You and Eryk are not special; the Secret is for everyone and She is giving it through your love to everyone who can reach for it. But you and Eryk are among the pioneers, so you will have to suffer the most. This is how it is. But you will always be protected and blessed by Her. This I know as I know my own name."

"Even if we both die," I said sarcastically.

Gabriela said nothing and then whispered, "Never ever say those words again. This is a time when you need every hope and faith you possess."

On Friday, April 22nd, Eryk and I flew to Fairfield, Iowa, where I was to give a weekend workshop, and the most horrible weeks of our lives began.

On Saturday, Eryk and I were taken to a hotel outside town, surrounded by dry sunlit fields. After lunch, we decided to go for a walk, just to be alone together. I was extremely worried about Eryk;

he had coughed all night and, not sleeping at all, he seemed more nervous and distracted than I had ever known him.

We walked in exhausted silence until I asked him, "Darling, you must tell me what you are going through. It is the only way I can help you. I have to know, whatever it is. Don't shut me out."

"Swear that you believe me if I tell you."

"Of course I will believe you. When have you ever lied to me?"

"I know you know I have never lied to you. But what is happening is so strange and terrifying."

I felt a chill run through my body. Did he feel he was now definitely dying? Had he received a sign—from a dream or from signals in his own body—that the process of decay we both so feared had now started?

We walked on through the flat, empty, sunlit fields under the vast Iowa wash-blue sky, stretching cloudlessly from horizon to horizon.

"I don't know how to say it . . ."

"Eryk, please, just say it. Whatever it is."

He walked on and turned, his pale face suffused with a fear so great I couldn't bear looking at it and lowered my eyes.

"Do you think I'm mad?" he whispered. "Do you think I'm crazy?"

"Of course not," I almost shouted. "Of course you're not mad. I don't know how you have stayed as calm and sane as you have through everything we have suffered. But I know you are in your right mind."

"Are you sure? Are you absolutely certain?" he asked me fiercely, coming up to me and holding my face in his hands so hard I flinched.

"Of course I'm sure. If I wasn't sure I'd probably be dead," I said.

"Oh God, don't say that," Eryk shouted. "Don't say that word!" Then he started to sob.

"Darling, you must tell me now. What is going on? What are you so afraid of?"

"I'll tell you. You remember about a half-hour ago, when we were having lunch, I left the table?"

"Yes."

"There was a voice that had started in my mind, a quiet, soft, feminine voice that was speaking. Nothing like this has ever happened to me before. At first I thought, everyone must hear it. It is so loud."

"And what was it saying?"

"It was saying, 'You are useless. You must die. You are useless. It is time you left. Without you, everything would go easily. You are the obstruction; remove yourself.' And it—she—was saying it so calmly, even sweetly and seductively, I was for a moment tempted to believe it. After all, I have brought so much trouble and torment into your life."

I started to protest, but he put his hand over my mouth—"If I don't tell you now I will never tell you. I left the table and went upstairs. I stood in one of the upstairs windows and the voice went on, louder this time: 'Jump, you useless idiot. You must jump now. Just jump and kill yourself and all will be well and the suffering you are causing everyone will be over. You do not deserve to live.' Believe me if you can, Andrew, but I am not mad; it was not me speaking; I have never wanted to live as much as I want to live now, with you and for us. But the voice grew very insistent. 'Open the window, now. Jump! Jump! Jump!'"

He started to sob uncontrollably.

"We must ring Gabriela immediately," I said. "I know you are shattered but not suicidal. God knows you are exhausted and sick, but I know you have never wanted to survive as much as you do now. I do not know what is happening but Gabriela will, I'm certain. Let us go back into the house and ring her now and face whatever she has to say together."

As I steered Eryk slowly back to the house, I prayed, "Mother, please let Gabriela be in. Please let her see and know exactly what is happening. I am in the dark; I know nothing; help me, help us."

Gabriela picked up the phone immediately, sobbing.

"I know," she said before I could say anything. "I know. The voice is attacking Eryk, trying to get him to kill himself. Oh God! I'm doing everything I can. But it is very powerful. . . ." Her voice trailed off. I had never heard her so fragile and uncertain.

"Gabriela," I said as calmly as I could manage. "What is this voice? What is happening? You have to tell me however terrifying it is."

"I have to now. The moment has come," Gabriela said, calmer now, her voice a low sad monotone. "For months you have been asking me now. Is Meera a black magician? And for months I have been giving you the reply: 'I do not know yet.' That was the only lie I have ever told you."

I waited in terror.

"I didn't tell you then because you couldn't have been strong enough to stand it. Not only do I believe that Meera is a black magician, but she has immense power. I sense a force of evil behind her more vast than any I have ever encountered."

My mind went white and I could say nothing.

Then I said, fighting for my words, "So Eryk's illness . . ."

"Yes."

"And the waves of horror and malice . . ."

"Yes."

"And now this voice. . . . Could it be hers, trying to destroy Eryk at this most vulnerable moment?"

"Because you married last week, the force has to redouble its attack, so as to try to destroy the Blessing before its truth can spread. Do you see?"

Gabriela's voice was frail and exhausted. Suddenly I realized how passionately she loved us and, with wonder, how closely her heart and soul and mind had followed ours.

Eryk was listening in the phone, too, struck dumb, his hands trembling.

"What is this black force she is using?" I asked, putting my hand over my heart and saying the Hail Mary silently over and over again.

"It is simply the force of evil that is available to anyone who wants to surrender to it," Gabriela said. "To me, Meera is not a Divine Master; she is a witch. Others have told you this and you did not listen. As you grow in the mystical Path, powers come to you. This is known in every mystical tradition. Powers of clairvoyance, telepathy, mind control. These powers are great temptations; Jesus Himself was tempted by them by the Dark One in the desert; most of the so-called Masters of today have embraced these powers and are using them in the dark way to dominate and exploit others. I see Meera as one of the worst and most powerful of these 'black' magicians. I have known this for three months now, but I couldn't tell you sooner. You were not ready to hear it and telling you would have driven you both to despair."

There was a long silence.

"What are we going to do, Gabriela? What in heaven's name are we going to do?"

Gabriela started to weep. "All I know is that I am not powerful enough to help you as well as I would want. This force is worse and larger than I thought. But above all, do not despair. Tomorrow or the next day I am going to leave for Greece, to visit in a monastery

I know there an old man who is the greatest exorcist of the Greek Orthodox Church. You must believe me when I tell you that this man is the greatest and holiest I have ever met of all those who work with these forces. I will go to him and we will have a ceremony in the monastery with all the monks and all of us together, with the Grace of the Holy Virgin, will, I swear to you, save Eryk and you. I promise this to you on my life."

Suddenly the madness of what we were all living together struck me and I felt like laughing out loud. Here I was, in Fairfield, gazing out at flat placid fields in Iowa, talking to a Rumanian mystic healer who, to save us from the force of evil of my ex-guru, was going to go to a monastery in Greece . . .

"Oh God, Gabriela, will anyone ever believe this story of ours?"

"One day you will be able to tell it all. One day. But I beg you on the Virgin, do not say anything about what is going on to anyone. No one will believe you now. Half of California already thinks you are crazy; talking of Meera as a black witch will convince everyone you have gone insane. You will have to keep this information to yourself for a long time and suffer it in silence. Are you listening to me? Don't expose yourself to even greater danger by talking about what you do not yet understand. You will be given every chance to understand, and then, when the moment is ripe, what you say will have the authority of the truth."

"When will that time come?"

"I do not know," Gabriela said sadly. "I do not know. All I know now is that whatever happens, you have to go on appearing as lucid and sober as possible. It is your one hope."

I stared at Eryk who had his face in his hands and a great wave of terror and despair swept me.

"I do not know," I said, "how either Eryk or I will bear this."

"I will not give you false hope," she said. "I am not a miracle-worker or a guru; I don't deal in illusions. What I will say is that I will see to it that everything possible is done. Meanwhile, you have to deepen your practice of adoration of the Virgin. With blind, wild faith, you must dive into Her and cling to Her with all your being and hold Eryk in Her Light at every moment. That is the only advice that I or anyone can give you now."

She paused and said, "I am going to be fierce with you now, Andrew. For many years you have had stupid illusions about evil and been naive about its presence in the world. Now you must pray to be given the guidance to see, and without fear of hysteria, just how powerful it is, especially at this dreadful time, and especially in the so-called "spiritual" world. You must pray for guidance because you have been blind and ignorant and vain and imagined that your own level of awareness was 'above such things.' This was madness; now you have to see. Beg for the strength to bear what you will come to know and the faith to work Her will. What you and Eryk and I are in, you now know, is an occult war, a real, terrible occult war on whose outcome far more than any of us can know depends. Knowing this should not make you vain; it should make you humble. A desperate humility that prays at each second for wisdom and clarity is what you now need. Your responsibility is to allow your every illusion—especially about evil—to be finally shattered so that She Herself can lead you forward."

I started to shake with sobs.

"Don't cry," Gabriela said fiercely. "You don't have time. Pray. I will ring you from Greece."

Eryk and I went out into the light, shattered and silent.

"Is the voice still there?" I asked.

"Yes," he said, "calmer and louder than ever."

I seized him and held him to me. "She will not win, I swear. She will not. The Mother will win. The Mother will protect us."

We knelt in the field.

"Mother, forgive my ignorance and vanity," I said. "Save your children who have no other hope but You."

LATE THAT NIGHT, I WROTE IN MY JOURNAL:

The voice in Eryk's mind goes on . . . All I can do now, apart from praying for Eryk's and my protection, is to pray for guidance on how to understand the black forces Meera is using. I pray all the time, "Please Mother, open my eyes; let me see Meera without illusion; let me see whatever forces she is manipulating as clearly as possible, so I do not make myself or Eryk their victim." Everything in me is trembling in fear and desolation; I have no experience at all in fighting the occult; like so many other seekers, I have hardly ever thought about it. And never imagined that I would need to.

However much a part of me still does not want to believe that Meera could be capable of something so evil, I know Gabriela could not be lying. What would be her motive? Where else could the voice tormenting Eryk come from? Then I remembered how—coincidentally—other people who had left Meera, or tried to, had undergone terrible ordeals which I had explained at the time as the necessary consequences of their treachery against the Great One. A couple who had lived in Meera's house decided they did not believe in her anymore. They then left and for three years disaster after disaster rained down upon them.

I remembered a conversation I had had with a now ex-disciple very early on when I returned to Meera in 1987. We were walking together in the hills above Thalheim, and he was explaining to me why he was leaving her. "There is too much darkness and mental misery around her," he said. "Sometimes I think she is a vampire, sucking our psychic lives, feeding off our devotion to increase her own power. I cannot shake these thoughts; I know they sound crazy; I am going away to clear my mind." He never returned and two years later left a message on my machine in Paris, "Remember our conversation; I'm more than ever convinced that it is true."

So many warnings and signs. . . . Oh my God, how stupid I have been! If I have any excuse at all, it is that my whole generation of seekers is absurdly naive about "occult" powers. We live in an age of so-called Reason, after all, where these things "cannot" be real. We believe in the mystical, the Good—but we have forgotten the Evil. And if there are "good" powers capable of every kind of healing, why shouldn't there be powers capable of being used for every kind of destruction? What is worse, in my case, was that I had, in fact, read in all the mystical traditions about "occult" powers—in St. John of the Cross's "The Ascent of Mount Carmel," for instance, where the saint distinguished between visions that are sent by God, which cause humility and the desire to serve, and visions that are sent by the "devil," which reinforce spiritual pride. I had read in Ramakrishna about how occult powers come to everyone who progresses on the Path as a temptation and potential destruction; I had read in Rumi how many of the Masters of his day he believed were nothing more than "black magicians like Pharaohs," not mystic guides at all, but beings who wanted only temporal power and fame.

I was so convinced by Meera's holiness that I never for a moment consciously imagined that she could be manipulating such powers. As I write that, yet another memory returns that could have warned me, had I been able to listen. I was sitting with a famous Tibetan Master in a garden in northern California; we had been laughing and talking. He turned to me and said, casually, "Would you like to learn some yogic exercises to get disciples? There are certain exercises adapted from Saivism which are very powerful." He said it so casually I hardly registered what he was saying until the night afterwards. At the time I simply laughed and said, "No. I have enough problems as it is." The night after, however, I woke up in bed in a cold sweat. What on earth had P. meant? Was he himself using such exercises? Wouldn't that be black magic? At that moment, all sorts of conversations I had had in Ladakh and Nepal came back to me about how certain sects of the Tibetans were Masters of black magic, and how tantric Buddhism had as profound a mastery of the "black" arts as of the "white." But there again my "devotee's mind" simply could not stand to pursue what might have instructed it. I didn't dismiss what T. had said; I conveniently forgot it.

Gabriela said that nearly all of the contemporary so-called Masters are in this black occult game. I remember that Bede Griffiths had said the same thing. If Meera is a witch, then anything could be true. And what then? Are hundreds of thousands of sincere seekers being used and manipulated? Does this occult manipulation on such an evidently vast scale ensure that no real spiritual revolution can take place? Is it part of what could only be called a "demonic" scheme to thwart and abort the Great Birth into Divine human independence that the Mother is preparing for humankind? Just entertaining such thoughts is terrifying. Everything depends now on whether humankind can go through a spiritual change of heart; what can happen if most of the so-called guides to this change are themselves in the hands of the dark? Has the vision at the end of the Book of Revelation—a vision I have always smiled at patronizingly—of a worldwide "demonic" Pentecost of false prophets now become reality? Is this the time which exemplifies most clearly and frighteningly Christ's warnings against "wolves in sheep's clothing"?

FROM MY JOURNAL:
Wednesday evening. San Francisco

We came back to find that Meera's publishing firm wants to sue me for thirty thousand dollars for quoting my own recreations of Rumi without permission in *The Way of Passion*. They know very well what a horrible situation I and Eryk are in; they know I have no money and that Eryk has cancer.

"Don't panic!" Eryk said. "They will never be able to get away with it in a court of law. All they want is for you to swear to be a good boy and do everything you can to sell the books on your tour."

I hope Eryk is right. I'll do almost anything to avoid

having to pay. If I have to give what little money I have, how will I pay for Eryk's medical expenses? And how can he not get sicker in the horrible turmoil we are living?

All morning I have been praying, "Please, Mother, do not let me hate Meera. Please do not let me hate K." I find that I can stand much more than I imagined I could even a week ago—how else would I be able to function at all? But what I cannot and could not stand is to have my soul raped by hatred. I pray to the Mother constantly to save me from becoming deformed by cruelty. I cannot pretend to feel love for Meera and her cohorts, but I have sworn to myself that I will not feel hate, whatever happens. Sometimes I can't help it; my whole being erupts in a wild anger, but I know that way madness lies. I feel the madness waiting to devour me at the fire-edge of that anger, and there are times when it seems almost voluptuous to yield to it, to drown in it. But to do that would be to lose everything now and to fail forever the task She has given me, that of trying to stay lucid and controlled in this hell.

Eryk said, "You can't go mad. For one thing, it would give K. and the others too much satisfaction. Can't you see that is exactly what they want you to do? She either wants me to die so you get terminally depressed and return to her, or she wants you to go crazy and so kill the truth of what is happening and so probably kill us both. Either way, Meera wins."

Meanwhile, the death threats continue. This morning, a female voice laughed crazily and screamed, "You will die! You will die!" down the phone. Eryk and I tried to laugh it off—"very Nosferatu, don't you think?"—but neither of us could manage a smile. Two callers in succession rang yesterday to tell me (not without some strange perverse pleasure) that a letter was circulating, supposedly from Thalheim, which claims that I am jealous of the Mother; I do not want to remain a humble and loving child of the Mother; I want to be a guru myself. I may say I am against gurus of every kind, but that is only a way of becoming a guru in secret; and that I have, in fact, gone mad and am very dangerous.

Letters are pouring in. I am tempted to collect them all and publish them one day as revealing completely the "shadow" of this great New Age we are supposed to be living in, but Eryk makes me burn most of them. What is almost as frightening as the garbage streaming through the letter box is the *silence* each of the letters and callers keeps about Eryk. It is as if he doesn't exist, as if his suffering, his agony are not important, as if his role in all this is entirely negligible. For a while I have been suspecting that this wounds Eryk deeply; after all, as an abused child, he knows far better than I ever can the tyranny of silence. Now he has to face that no one cares about what he knows, has seen, heard, lived, and witnessed; that everyone is so swept up in the melodrama of Andrew versus the Divine Mother that they ignore Eryk completely, partly because his evidence could only support my—our—position, and partly because all insight and compassion seem to have left those who now hate us. Yesterday we were walking quietly in the street when he turned to me and said, "I can't stand being ignored any more. I can't stand not being able to speak." His face twisted in suffering. "If you and I are killed or if I die, I will simply be the 'young man' in the story. No doubt it is spiritually 'unevolved' of me, but I cannot bear to be wiped out yet again, and when there may be so little time left for me to witness anything. Can you understand?"

I held him and kissed him. "I understand." But I knew that I did not. How could I completely fathom the suffering he must be going through now being "gagged" as he was, and ignored?

K.P., our Burmese friend, Tara's brother, died three days ago, while we were in Iowa. Eryk and I have been in deep mourning since. We were with K.P.'s family tonight; Tara said over and over, "I want to die." The other sister wandered helplessly around the house, pale as smoke. We all feel as if the removal of so good and supportive a man as K.P. is an ominous sign; we know that it is irrational to feel like this, but the atmosphere of pain and fear is so pervading.

Tara was able, even in her grief, to ask me about what was happening with Meera. I told her everything and asked her what she believed about black magic.

"Of course it exists," she said sadly. "The Westerners are very naive. Any fraud can ensnare them. There are schools for black magicians in India, you know; many gurus have been trained there. This is common knowledge in the East. In Burma, there were many, many black magicians and my teacher used to fight against them." She held my scared and exhausted face in her hands and we wept together.

"Dear Andrew, whatever you do, do not be afraid. Some fear is inevitable. But keep your heart always centered on the Good. I will pray for you and send you all the protection I can. I cannot believe that the Mother has put you through so much suffering for nothing." Her voice trailed off. "Forgive me," she added on a whisper. "I'm too much in pain to say any more now. You know what I learnt on the day K.P. died? That fifty years of practicing meditation mean nothing. Nothing works."

We stared together out of the window at the gray rain.

On Friday the 29th, Eryk and I flew to Washington. We were both so exhausted we could hardly walk on the plane—but there could be no question of canceling: I had to give the central address at a conference in the Smithsonian on the Divine Feminine. Sympathetic friends had warned me that rumors that I had gone crazy and had "broken down" were being circulated by Meera's disciples all over the country; in public I had to appear calm and judicious or be discredited. The lecture went well; I said nothing about my break with Meera but made it clear that I no longer believed in the Guru system, and now was taking the direct Path into the Mother. I was surprised and heartened by how many people in the audience came up to me in the book-signings afterwards and said things like, "I am so happy someone is at last speaking out about how corrupt the Guru system has become." I felt like embracing an older woman who said, "I went to Thalheim on your recommendation. Who didn't? What I found was a mini-fascist state. I hated it and thought there was something wrong with me. I am so relieved you have left her and are now on your own Path."

I was scheduled to be interviewed for *Common Boundary Magazine* on Monday morning, and I dreaded it. All my self-preservatory instincts told me to be as bland and noncommittal as possible. Besides, *Common Boundary* had a Meera disciple working for it who had already made it plain where he stood; had this person already convinced the editor that I was lying and was the interview itself a "frame-up"? By now, anything was possible. Besides, I had no idea about the woman who was going to interview me, Rose Solari; was she a guru-worshipper? Even if she had not already been "talked to," would she be ready to hear the insights Eryk's and my suffering were birthing in me? I lay awake most of Sunday night praying to the Mother that I would be given the chance, if it was Her will, to tell our story to the spiritual world at large, and asking Her to warn if there was danger.

"You'll know as soon as you see Rose Solari," Eryk said. "I'm certain of it."

When Rose Solari walked through the door of the flat where I was staying, I immediately knew I could trust her. I have rarely liked anyone more at first sight; Rose exuded clear, rich warmth, and the kind of razor-sharp skeptical intelligence that is rare in the "spiritual" world. I loved her wild, mischievous beauty, her no-nonsense eyes, her frizzy and abundant blond hair, and her wit; she had me laughing almost immediately about a marriage she had attended where the bride and groom had "plighted their troth" in swimsuits on a beach and with a bona fide white witch. Even more refreshingly, she had none of the soft-voiced, sandalwood-scented piety characteristic of the "spiritual" journalist; this was a woman who could pilot a plane or be a scathing lawyer.

So I plunged, and told her everything. As soon as we sat down with the tape recorder, I began. Four months of anguish had, I found, crystallized my perceptions more profoundly than I had imagined; given a chance at last to make as lucid an analysis as possible, I found the words and phrases and formulations came with an almost eerie effortlessness.

During the interview, Rose said little. She let me talk, but she listened with her whole being, her body completely calm; sometimes, rarely, she would look up at me directly, her eyes full of compassion and concern, as if to say, "Go on. Don't stop. I'm with you." Her solidarity with me gave me the courage to be as frank as I could.

At the end of the interview, Rose and I hugged each other.

"Do you believe me?" I asked immediately.

"I know you are telling the truth. I feel it. Why would you lie? You have everything to lose. What you are saying reverses your whole life."

"God bless you, Solar Rose," I said, and then started to laugh.

"Why are you laughing?"

"Rose Solari, Solar Rose. The Virgin puts her stamp on everything."

I held her hand and smiled at her. "Thank you for the gift you have given me of being able to speak nakedly. I cannot begin to tell you how precious that is. I will always bless you for it, as long as I live."

"I need all the prayers and blessings that I can get."

"One thing scares me," I said. "I have given you the whole story. There has been a lot of craziness already. Are you sure that you can handle the responsibility of steering these truths through? It will not be easy. Eryk and I have had death threats. Meera herself is lying now and saying nothing happened. The Meera disciples are crazy with rage and prepared to say and do anything, it seems, to defend their Idol. You yourself could be in danger."

"Look, Andrew," Rose said quietly. "I'm not easily frightened. I'm stubborn and I hate being bullied. Get the picture?"

She sat quietly looking at her hands.

"I was never attracted to gurus; I've seen friends suffer too much at their hands. I don't like giving my mind away either—and nearly all the gurus I've ever heard of demand a kind of surrender of intelligence I have always found crazy. I admire that you are not merely slamming the Guru system but also offering a caustic analysis of your own responsibility in what happened; that won't make you any friends, but it is the only way to help others. I also agree with your call to an end of the dreary spiritual narcissism of the not-at-all New Age. Human beings have to move forward now into a claiming of a direct relationship with God and into a real critique of the world that leads to direct social and political action along every front. Or we are finished. I believe that you've come out and said it, and I will fight for your right to say exactly what you want as you want."

Eryk came in.

"Are you finished?"

"Yes. I said everything."

"Oh my God."

"It's fine. Rose believes us and is going to see that the interview goes through, whatever the opposition."

After Rose had left, Eryk turned to me. "When I first heard you talk I shook with terror. But after a minute of being with Rose I knew that you had been wisely guided. She is a very surprising person, very clear and very brave. I didn't think people like her existed anymore."

"I feel that the Virgin sent her. It is grace."

"Yes," Eryk smiled. "And just in time. When will the bomb drop then?"

"In four months, the interview will be printed in the September issue."

"Perhaps we should arrange to be in Alaska. What's the climate that time of year?"

FROM MY JOURNAL:
Wednesday, May 4th. San Francisco

Throughout the weekend in Washington and the last two days back here in California, Eryk and I have avoided mentioning Gabriela's visit to Greece to each other; we knew that any talk of "black magic" would make us even more scared than we were. Besides, not being able to talk to Gabriela—she did not know where we were and we had no idea where she might be—made us both nervous; her wild Rumanian laughter and guidance had become the food of hope to us . . .

This morning, thank God, Gabriela rang from Belgium.

"O my God," I shouted. "You're back! You're alive!"

It wasn't until I said, "You're alive!" that I realized that for the last week I had been secretly fearing that an "accident" would happen to her.

"Of course I'm alive, you fool! It will take more than an Indian witch to stop Gabriela!"

We both laughed wildly, releasing days of tension.

I summoned up my courage and asked, "So what happened?"

Immediately, Gabriela's voice changed and became calm and solemn . . .

"I flew to Athens a day later than I had planned—last Wednesday. Then I had to get to Meteora, the place where the monastery is, where the great old monk-exorcist lives. That took a day and a half. When I arrived, he saw me immediately. I explained the situation, and I told him that I believed that only he had the power and experience to deal with forces of evil on such a scale. 'It must be bad, Gabriela,' he said, 'if you don't feel you can deal with it.' 'It is the worst I have ever seen,' I said. The old monk called all the other monks from their cells and went to work immediately in the main chapel where there is a very holy icon of the Virgin."

She paused, as if gathering her strength. "I don't know how to tell you what happened next. I have never seen anything like it. Promise me that you will believe me. It is very, very important that you believe."

"I believe," I said. "I do not understand—how could I?—but I believe."

"The old monk began his ceremony of Invocation and Exorcism. The monks surrounded him and prayed and chanted passionately. It was powerful and holy and beautiful—the chapel lit up with candles and full of incense, the saints and the Virgin glowing in glory on the walls and gazing down on all of us and blessing us. You and Eryk were so close to me, so deeply in my heart, as I stood there and prayed with the old man. Then, it happened, the moment I had been wanting and dreading." Gabriela paused, "I'm still shaking a little."

"What happened. What *exactly* happened?"

"The Force materialized in front of all of us, in a horrible, writhing, smoky black mass. There was a terrible smell that filled the whole chapel, a smell of dung and corpses, I can't describe it. This black, writhing mass was immense; it went almost to the top of the ceiling. I have seen many appalling things in the course of my work, but never anything like that. I believed in the protection of the Virgin, but for one or two moments even I, even after all these years, felt terrified that what we had invoked would be too powerful to control."

She paused and coughed loudly, nervously. "The old monk went on chanting calmly and then as the Force whirled faster and faster, making horrible smacking and hissing sounds, my friend said in a loud voice, 'In the name of the most holy Virgin and Jesus Christ, the Son of God, return to where you came.' Immediately, and with a terrible scream, the Force ran to the door of the chapel, ran out, and slammed the door behind it so hard that the walls of the chapel rang."

I could say nothing. Gabriela's description completely winded me. I looked out at the afternoon sunlight falling calmly on Page Street, and started to say the Hail Mary under my breath.

"Are you all right?" Gabriela asked anxiously. "Speak up! Don't frighten me! Are you all right!"

"Give me a few moments to recover, Gabriela. What you are telling me is, let us say, a little extreme."

She laughed her wild Rumanian laugh.

"Thank God you weren't with us in the chapel. You would have fainted. The old man himself told me afterwards that the Force was the worst and most powerful he had ever had to deal with. And for him, that is something."

"What will happen now?"

"Wait. I have something truly wonderful to tell you, something that you should always remember from now on whatever happens. As soon as the Force had left, screaming and slamming the door behind it, a peace descended on all of us. And as we stood in its atmosphere, the icon of the Virgin began to blaze with Divine Light. It began calmly at first, but soon the blaze of Light filled the whole room. All the monks saw it. We all knelt and prayed to Her. The Light streamed and streamed from the icon; it was as if She Herself was there, in Her Glory."

The awe and rapture in Gabriela's voice reduced me to tears.

"She came!" I wept, "She came! She showed Herself to help us and bless us!"

Gabriela was weeping too.

"She is fighting with you and for you. She will guide you through the whirlwind of evil. What we all saw that evening was a miracle, Andrew, a great miracle. No one in the monastery will ever forget it. I will never, ever forget it."

My heart filled with joy and indescribable relief.

"Forgive me asking you this, Gabriela."

"You can always ask anything."

"What do you think will now happen?"

"The Force has been sent back to those who sent it. It will work on them the evil they wanted it to work on you. Sooner or later, Thalheim and the Meera cult—at least in its present form—will be destroyed. There is still a great deal to be gone through and endured for all of us—but the worst is past and what happened in the monastery will ensure, I swear to you, that the Evil will not and cannot win. It can still damage but it cannot win."

FROM MY JOURNAL:
Saturday, May 7th

Gabriela has been ringing several times a day, warning us of various "plots" being made up against us, giving names and addresses of people she cannot possibly know. Her gift is hair-raising. Two nights ago an acquaintance rang and invited us to a "gay" dinner party. Gabriela rang about twenty minutes later. "On no account go to the party," she began.

"S. is trying to trap you. She is feeding information to the group in New York and is extremely jealous of your love for Eryk."

"How do you know all this?" I asked in wonder.

"My guide tells me. I'm nothing but a loudspeaker," she laughed. "And I certainly speak loud!"

Then she said, "In the next period all sorts of people will try to 'reconcile' you with Meera for their own ends. Some will be doing it maliciously; some will be doing it out of what they imagine to be goodwill. You will also be meeting people who will give you different 'explanations' of what has happened. Say as little as possible; remain calm; listen to the madness as if you were a scientist. What is, in fact, happening is that you are being given a complete picture of the ignorance, corruption, and empty thinking of the spiritual world. Try not to hate anyone; remember you, too, have been in denial and illusion. But listen with all of your powers of discrimination and you will learn everything that you need to protect the vision that is being given to you."

On Monday, May 9th, I rang Meera's publishing firm to try and dissuade them from suing me for quoting my own Rumi recreations in *The Way of Passion*. I told them that I had not thought of asking permission, because I had truly believed that my work on Rumi would only make the translations Meerama had published better known. I summoned up all my courage and begged them not to sue—or at least to give me a seven months' waiting period (until the end of the year) to see if the Rumi collections they had published sold as well as I hoped they would. They agreed, but not before telling me to "reconsider my wild ways."

I spoke with someone at the publishing firm: "Don't you think, dear Andrew, you've gone a bit far recently."

Me: "Too far?"

"What I mean is—it's rather touching actually—how can I put it? Let's see. You so overidealized Meera that when she showed you her small feet of clay, you just went crazy and overreacted. I understand. We all understand. We have been afraid for you for years. You are always so enthusiastic, so extreme in whatever you do. No half-measures for you! You see, the rest of us always knew that Meera was not omniscient, not perfect. That there are whole sides of her that are very limited indeed. She is limited by her culture, her lack of exposure to the real world, by her overprotection by Adilakshmi. Oh the list goes on and on. I don't mind telling you that I have been disappointed many times by predictions that didn't come true."

I couldn't believe what I was hearing. Here was someone who was a head of Meera's publishing firm, telling me that Meera was limited. I didn't, but I wanted to say, "Then how do you justify your earning money off books of Meera's in which she claims to be all the things you say you know she isn't—omniscient, limitless, boundlessly accurate, and just?"

At the time, I remembered Gabriela's warnings and kept calm and waited.

"I wanted you to know that I know that many of the things you are saying are not untrue. But the fact remains that God comes through Meera, flawed though she obviously is."

Me: "How are you certain that it is God that is coming through Meera? After all, if she is as flawed as I think we both agree, perhaps this 'flawed' being may be using the energy at her command for her own 'flawed' purposes."

Another silvery laugh. "You mean you think Meera is some

kind of black magician? Really, Andrew, how ridiculous! She's just a simple Indian girl with immense Divine power after all."

Me: "You are certain of that?"

"Of course. We're not going to talk any more about *that,* I hope. What I am trying to tell you can be summed up in one phrase. Don't throw the baby out with the bath water."

Me: "I don't believe anymore that there is any baby in the bath water."

"I know you don't mean that."

Me: "Yes I do."

"Well, there is nothing more to say."

I hung up the phone, and I sat with my face in my hands. Eryk came in. I told him everything that had been said. He sat on the floor and put his arms around me and leaned his head against mine.

"Gabriela is astounding, isn't she? I thought we had heard everything. If Rose Solari—I mean *when* Rose Solari rings her— S. is bound to tell her that you are a well-known liar and madman. And there she was saying to you that she knows Meera is limited and maybe, possibly, perhaps, even homophobic. So she knows— she must know—you are telling the truth. Believe me that when our story comes out in all of its detail, she and her husband will have left Meera and be telling everyone, 'I wonder why Andrew doesn't ring us? We used to be such close friends.' Promise me that you will never have anything to do with any of them."

"Don't worry," I smiled thinly. "I think I'm getting the picture, at last."

Eryk and I prayed together.

"Isn't it strange," I said, "how we can trust no one? All my life I believed . . ."

Eryk cut me short, "All your life you believed that people were as passionate and sincere as you were in the spiritual search. That was vanity and ignorance. Now you have to see how perverse much of the New Age really is. I saw it the first time I came to California, but I didn't want to say it to you because you were so elated. Besides I thought it was just me; that I was European and cynical. I told myself, 'Stay open!' "

"And look what happened! How can you forgive my blindness?" Eryk smiled and kissed me.

"I love you and know you are a good person. You are my baby, that is all."

"I don't deserve your loyalty."

"If you didn't, I wouldn't give it to you. I have no time to waste on anyone or anything I don't love and choose. I love and choose you."

Eryk kissed me lightly and left the room.

Suddenly, I felt my heart explode in pain and joy and gratitude. Eryk has every reason to leave me. He has been tortured, ignored, humiliated, under continual external and inner assault of every kind; my ignorance has led him into a minefield of disaster. He also happens to be terribly sick. And yet not only does he not abandon me; every day he shows me more profoundly how he loves and believes in me, giving me every kind of encouragement and hope, even when he himself is afraid and exhausted.

Eryk came back and saw the tears streaming down my face and was alarmed. I told him why I was crying.

"You fool!" he said. "Don't you see that your love for me is healing me spiritually! Don't you understand that by standing with me and for me against almost everyone you have shown *me* that I am worth something? Don't you think I bless *you* every moment of every day? Our love for each other is birthing *both* of us together, in Her." Then he laughed, "And now I must cook some lunch. If we have to suffer lunacy after lunacy, let it be on a full stomach!"

———————

A part of me knows already that even if we are both killed tomorrow, the Birth has begun. The truth of our love—even if every trace of it were destroyed—has still been released along all the strands of the web of the Universe. No love can ever be wasted, I see that now, even if it seems to be annihilated in history, in time.

I cannot help begging for time for the Birth to be as full and complete as possible—but I know, today, that the inner miracle has already happened, that Eryk and I have been brought, with all our faults and frailties, and with many battles ahead, directly and consciously into the core of Her alchemy of Love.

ACT V

Terror and Grace

*

The cries of those free from pain are cold and dull:
The cries of the agonized spring from ecstasy.

RUMI

Look for the happiness of a lover of God—
All the joys of this world are nothing to it.

RUMI

Two nights later, on May 11th, I had an extraordinarily
vivid, poignant, and beautiful dream about Bede Griffiths,
who had died a year before.

We were sitting together in the calm South Indian sunlight in
his meditation hut in Shantivanam—the hut that he kept for himself a little apart from the ashram, surrounded by fields. He was
lying on the broken-down bed there, his face and hair lit up with
golden Light, an expression of the deepest compassion and welcome on his face.

"Is it really you? Can it really be you?" I asked, overjoyed at
seeing him so whole and serene.

"Of course it is me, dear boy."

He raised both hands and beckoned me to embrace him, and afterwards I sat by his side with our hands entwined together.

"What is happening is a terrible spiritual crime," he said, "but the Mother will see you through. Hold on to that certainty through everything. Never think of leaving your boy. He is a holy being and your love is holy, a Divine Grace, and a Divine opportunity. Live your love in such a way that you can help hundreds of thousands of others bring together soul and body, heart and mind, earth and heaven, and enter the Mother here in this world. This is the only way through for the future. A great healing of the heart must take place throughout humanity, and that healing can only come through a healing of the false split between body and soul. The body, sanctified by true love, ensouls itself; the soul, through true Love, becomes embodied. This is the alchemy of the Black Madonna and the force of the Sacred Heart; it is because the church has abandoned this secret that it is so lost and dangerous. I myself only glimpsed this secret in the last years—remember, my dear friend— how we talked of just this when I was alive?"

I nodded in wonder, gazing deep into his eyes.

"You and Eryk and the seekers of your generation will be able now to live this alchemical marriage, and so help bring in the reign of Love. Every dark power on earth will threaten you, because the marriage threatens all forms of temporal and spiritual power. But the Father-Mother has willed this triumph of humble Love. In the future there will be no need for Masters or gurus, only of loving spiritual friends who give away what they know in a spirit of generosity and adoration, without claiming anything for themselves.

"Two things are needed now more than ever—accurate and sober information about the mystical Path, marvelous but unromantic, and secondly, a turning of all beings *directly* to the Divine beyond all dogmas, names, and forms, in a spirit of total trust. Then, it is possible that the coming disasters will be averted."

I wept with joy and gratitude at the clarity of what he was telling me. I asked him to bless me, and he put his hands on my head and blessed me.

Then he said, "You are already blessed. The Mother and Christ are standing with you and by you and Eryk to hold you both up and give you courage. Do not tell anyone else but Eryk about this dream now; the time will come when you can share it with anyone who can hear it. But that is a few years off; there is much maturing to be done before you can stand behind what I am saying with your whole life. And that is what it will take. You know that, don't you?"

I nodded.

"I must return now to where I came from," he said softly, leaning over me. "Put your hand on my heart."

I placed my hand on his heart as he placed his hand on mine.

"Feel anything?" he said almost mischievously.

"No."

"Love more, love harder."

I closed my eyes and concentrated, and then it happened. Our hearts exploded simultaneously into one fiery sea of molten ecstatic joy. "We are both loving Love and Love is loving us both through each other." I heard Bede whisper, "We are each separate and yet one with the One, our individual selves, completely unique, and yet in communion through Love with every grain of sand, each waving grass, each star. This Separatedness-in-Union is the grace of Tantra and the mystery of the Trinity. In this sublime mystery we are all children and only those who have given up every form of power, every form of false hope, every form of false belief in themselves, in their mind or spiritual experience, can ever come into this Mother-Ground of wonder. In holding you I hold myself; in holding me you hold yourself. In receiving this dream, you receive the Real."

Bede laughed his wonderful warm, almost naughty, chuckling laugh that I had cherished so much: "Dear boy, am I making myself clear?!"

I woke up. It was three in the morning and the light of an almost full moon filled the room.

The attacks against us continued in venom; Eryk grew visibly thinner and sicker; my back grew so painful I had to give my classes on so many painkillers I prayed not to slur my words in public. Every day brought us new lies from Thalheim; the small group of devoted friends of ours who kept ringing under different names kept recording fresh lunacies.

We also learned from Rose Solari that when *Common Boundary* had rung Meera to ask for *her* version of what had happened, she, through Adilakshmi, had said flat out that I was lying about everything and that she had no prejudice whatsoever against homosexuals. In a grim but brilliant move, Adilakshmi had given Rose the name of the prominent gay devotee (one of the ones who had rung me insultingly at the middle of February). "Just ask him! You will see how mad Andrew is! Poor Andrew!" When Rose had rung him, this disciple had, of course, confirmed everything that Adilakshmi had implied, adding for good measure, "How could the Mother be homophobic if she is letting me, an openly gay man, speak for her!" Fortunately for us, Rose neither trusted nor wholly believed this disciple's testimony, but she had had to report it.

"Now the editors are saying," Rose told us, "that you must get someone else to testify on your side otherwise we cannot go ahead with the article."

"But people are terrified," I said. Then, "Can Eryk testify? He was there after all."

"I'm afraid not. People would always say that he was only parroting you. Anyone who has met Eryk for two minutes would know that this was not true, but we have to meet every eventuality."

Eryk and I knew that Rose would fight for our truth with everything she had; we also knew she had to honor the caution of her editors. Then I remembered Carol R., who had rung us in Paris. For two days I searched for Carol R.'s telephone number, which I had scrawled on the back of one of my notebooks. At last I found it and rang her. But she was not in. She was away on holiday, for a fortnight, the voice on the other end of the phone said. No, she had not left a number.

Two days later, Carol R. phoned us. I could hardly believe my ears when I heard her voice on our machine. Through a series of "coincidences," she had met a friend of a friend of ours in the South of France who had told her a garbled version of the horrors we were enduring and had given her the number of our friend who in turn gave us her number.

"Will you help us?" I asked her immediately.

"Of course. I know you are telling the truth."

"Will you speak to the journalist who is presenting the interview I gave to *Common Boundary*?"

"I will tell her everything that I told you."

Carol's voice was so simple and honest I started to weep.

"How can I thank you? Eryk and I will be in your debt for the rest of our lives."

She laughed, "Don't mind that. I am honored to help you. I can only begin to imagine what you have been through. The last months have been horrible for me, too, living through the breakdown of my belief in Meera. But I feel far stronger and happier now without her or any prop to lean on than I ever felt with her."

Later Gabriela rang and I spilled out to her my wonder and gratitude for Carol's courage.

Gabriela laughed. "Aha! And there you are always imagining you have been abandoned! Let those creeps of hers say whatever they want! Nothing can prevent the truth coming out!"

Knowing that Carol R. would testify for Eryk and myself gave us both confidence.

"Even if they do kill us," Eryk said, "the truth will now come out."

For three days life seemed almost normal. We both slept well for the first time in months; the weather was cloudless and warm; I enjoyed my classes for the first time that year, speaking freely and easily and without any drugs for my back. I even found myself able to pray for Meera and her deluded followers; fear at the evil she was prepared to do gave way, at times, to a deep pity for the danger in which she was putting her own soul and the souls of everyone who believed in her. Feeling pity for her came to me as a great relief; I had prayed to the Virgin to be free from hatred and bitterness, and to be able to see Meera as she is without the need to "demonize" or "despise" her.

This sweet respite was short-lived. On May 26th, Eryk's twenty-seventh birthday, we received the news that our friend Sandra, who had helped us so much at our wedding and made it so beautiful by her generosity, had cancer. We were only just starting to recover from the death of K.P. and were still intensely saddened by the profound suffering through which the whole Tarpar family was going; to hear that Sandra was now to go through a long—and possibly fatal—ordeal desolated us. Eryk's own fear of dying—and my fear of his death—redoubled; I listened to his every cough with scared attention. Sandra's pain and fear became our own; every day we waited for news of her tests and state of soul.

"Why Sandra now? Why does she deserve this?" Eryk would say over and over. "I believe and go on believing in Her but sometimes . . ."

He didn't have to finish the sentence.

At the beginning of June, another deeply disturbing event occurred. The friends who housed Gabriela when she was in Belgium (and from whose house she had rung us so assiduously) rang us in distress. One explained, "Gabriela would not tell you herself, but yesterday she almost had a fatal accident."

I had taken the phone. "An accident? What kind of accident?"

"She was walking along a street by a construction site. Suddenly, a sheet of lead fell and only missed her by about two inches. Even Gabriela was shaken."

Gabriela herself rang about twenty minutes later.

"I don't want you to be scared . . ." she began.

I finished her sentence for her. ". . . But the occult attacks have begun again. What happened was not an accident; it was a deliberate attempt to wipe you out. That's true, isn't it, Gabriela?"

She was silent, "Yes, it is true. The Force has not been completely eliminated."

I started to sweat and tremble.

"Oh my God, Gabriela, how much more do we all have to suffer in this?"

She was fierce with me. "Andrew, stop that kind of thinking. In this kind of danger, any kind of weakness or self-pity puts you in the power of the dark. You have to stay completely focused on the Divine."

"But, Gabriela, does this mean that the exorcism you had done has not worked?"

"No," Gabriela said firmly. "A great deal of the Force has been returned. But what was sent against you was immensely powerful. Some parts remain. It is as well to know that now."

"Aren't you scared?"

"No," she said firmly. "I am not scared. I know that the Virgin will see us through. I know it as I know I am a woman with red hair. I know it as I know that the best roses come from Bulgaria, and that the handsomest men are Rumanian."

"I believe you," I said.

"Don't believe me," she laughed. "Who am I? Believe Her. If She is allowing this to happen, it is only to make us more alert and vigilant, more concentrated."

"My nerves are shattered," I said.

"That is good," Gabriela said. "It is when you are shattered that you can be most open to God. It is when you are shattered that you stop relying on your own cleverness or insight or power and put yourself entirely into the hands of the Mother. Have faith."

But her voice was shakier than usual. Gabriela, who had always seemed so strong, was herself more shaken than she wanted to admit. That terrified me but also filled me with tenderness for her.

"Gabriela?"

"Yes."

"Promise me you will not walk near any construction sites, and that you will rest."

"I promise."

I told Eryk what had happened.

"If Gabriela says it was not an accident, it wasn't. She never exaggerated. In life she is very excessive, but about spiritual matters she is more precise than the driest scientist."

Then he started to weep noiselessly. "First Sandra, then this. Will it ever end? What is the point of living in this madness? What will happen next? A letter bomb?"

I shook him angrily, "Stop that, do you hear! Now you are becoming melodramatic and morbid! If you want to die, go out and shoot yourself but don't sit here like a patient in *Marat/Sade!*"

Eryk was not being melodramatic; on the afternoon of Friday the 8th of June a makeshift fire bomb was thrown through the front window of our flat on Page Street in San Francisco. I was out, walking, to try to exercise the muscles in my back; Eryk was in the front room with Louise, a friend from France who had been staying with us for a week. Suddenly, they both heard the screech of motorcycle tires, and a flaming Diet Coke can was thrown in and landed about three feet away from them. Fortunately, as it fell, the tin tipped over, and spilled some of its contents (which Eryk said looked like burning oil) onto the floor. Louise leapt up and smothered the flames with a blanket. Then Eryk threw what remained of the "bomb" out into the garden.

"I was almost disappointed," Louise later said. "Nothing happened. Clearly these people are as bad at making bombs as they seem to be at everything else."

We rang the police and they came and took the bomb away. Gabriela rang about half an hour after they left.

"Don't tell anyone what has happened," she said. "If you start making a fuss now the disciples will know that you are terrified and that is just what they want. Besides, the people you are dealing with are so crazy that they are quite capable of doing it a second and third time just to show you that they mean business."

I started to shout, "I can't shut up! I can't just let bombs float through my front room window and not say anything. Can't I even tell Rose at *Common Boundary*?"

"Tell no one. Louise knows and can witness it. That is fine. That is all you need. Don't tell anyone at the college; they will use the information against you. There are a lot of people at *Common Boundary*, too, who will say that you are crazy. They might even say that you yourselves planted the bomb in the garden; after all, it was badly made. I can hear them now: 'Andrew has gone so mad that he is even making his own home-made bombs and planting them in the garden to try and blacken Meera.' Remember these people can explain anything."

"But the police . . ." I started.

"The police are just doing their job. They don't know anything more than you do. And they have nothing much to go on."

Gabriela's cold logic calmed me down.

"I know what I am about to say will strike you as peculiar," Gabriela began, "but in fact all this craziness is a good sign."

"A good sign?" My voice shook with disbelief.

"The Force is desperate. It is trying everything it can. But it will fail. The bomb didn't go off, did it?"

"No."

"Well then!"

"All this is not exactly reassuring, Gabriela."

"Fighting the horror of evil is never reassuring. I thought you might have learned that by now. I know you have been praying for Meera. This is fine. But don't forget what and who she is and what and who the people are who are doing this. Don't let pity make you blind again."

"How long will this go on and are there going to be further attacks and accidents?"

"It will go on, but not for too long."

———

My classes and meetings finished at C.I.I.S. at the end of June. Both Eryk and I were relieved—Eryk, because every time I went out to teach he feared for my life; I, because the atmosphere of the Institute had become increasingly disillusioning to me. A few of my students had been thoughtful, sympathetic, and receptive of the radical new thoughts that the crisis was helping to crystallize. But in the Institute at large there was a vocal group of guru-worshippers who left anonymous insulting notes in my mailbox with scary regularity. By the end of the term I was just grateful that I had managed to maintain a sober "public front" and to give the best classes of my life, which later became the book *The Return of the Mother*.

Meanwhile, Rose Solari continued to fight for the interview I had given her and *Common Boundary*. At discrete intervals, we would talk and she would hint, with professional tact, at the madness she was encountering.

"What is really weird," she kept saying, "is the attitude of Meera's other gay disciples. Even the ones who were with you in Thalheim deny that they saw anything. I could tell they were, let us put it, generally 'not telling the whole truth,' but why the denial? I just don't get it."

Fortunately, Rose had talked to Carol R. and her testimony had placated the senior editors of the magazine, who were, understandably, still nervous about the impact of what I was saying. At the end of June, Rose rang to give us the news that the whole uncut interview would soon be going to press with a careful introduction by her, which would display the opposing points of view but make it very clear where she stood.

———

When Rose had told me, on several occasions, about the denials—
or worse—of Meera's other prominent gay disciples, I had at first
been scared and depressed—not just of but for them. Couldn't they
see how they were being manipulated? How much longer would
their denial keep them entrapped in a system which fundamentally
used and despised them? I heard over and over Adilakshmi's voice on
the telephone in January saying, "There is no future for gays in the
future of the Mother." Why were they still so desperate to cling to
Meera against the testimony of two people whom they must have
known could not be lying and against the proof of the various other
homophobic remarks that Adilakshmi had uttered? How could the
heads of Meeramma go on saying in public that I was lying when they
themselves helped me years before take out Meera's homophobic remarks from *Answers*? How could John and Jim, whose whole public
artistic lives had been bound up with Gay Liberation, who had seen
both Eryk and me in agony firsthand in Thalheim, and who had in
early January and February written us letters showing their fury at
what Meera had done, now deny that anything happened?

My tour finished in a grim, uneasy way in Santa Cruz on the last
weekend of July. The one piece of good news was that *Common
Boundary* would print the interview with Rose Solari verbatim.
Gabriela said, "I told you so! I told you!" and assured us that although there would be a massive scandal, we would be believed "by
the sane." Gabriela had added, "And why worry about the others?
There are still people who believe that Stalin was a great man and
that Hitler never wanted to exterminate the Jews."

Back in San Francisco, however, our nerves were in tatters. After certain of the gay disciples had come out against us, we began to receive more obscene calls and letters. Three times Eryk received hard gay porn magazines with "This should give you ideas" scrawled in red on the cover. Each time one of the sick parcels would arrive I would see Eryk blanch with fear and rage. "And what is worst," he kept saying, "is that I believe it is the gay disciples who are sending us this filth. How can they think so little of themselves that they need to make us into demons of depravity when we have affirmed our love before the world?"

Some of Meera's gay disciples had been "brave" enough to spit their venom at us without the mask of anonymity. In Chicago, in the middle of July, a plump, unctuously smiling self-described "super-psychic" came up to Eryk with his lover after my talk and said, "I see things I shouldn't really. I can't help it; I've had this gift from birth." Eryk waited icily. Eryk described how the man's face snarled into an ugly smile full of hatred as he leaned forward and whispered, "Andrew will abandon you soon. You have served his purpose. And the shock will kill you. Prepare for your death."

Another anonymous call warned us before my last engagement at Santa Cruz that Eryk and I would "at last receive what we deserved." Months of fear made me so nervous that when I was talking I had to grip the side of the chair so as not to be seen to be trembling visibly.

On the second day—a Saturday—I came out of my morning session to find Eryk sitting dejectedly in the car park. As I approached him, he looked up at me, tears streaming down his face.

"What has happened?"

"I don't want to talk about it," he said softly.

"You must talk about it. Tell me now."

As calmly as he could, Eryk told me that after my morning session, two middle-aged gay men had come up to him where he was sitting waiting for me. With great bitterness and fury, they had said to him, "We don't believe a word that Andrew is saying now or has been saying over these last months."

"What did you say?"

"I said, 'You can believe what you want. Andrew is not a guru telling you to believe anything.'"

"And then?"

Eryk paused, "One of them spat at me."

At first what Eryk said did not register.

"They did what?"

"One of them spat at me."

Eryk gazed at me with dark-ringed, infinitely sad eyes. "And then they walked away to their new BMW and drove off. Ah, the New Age!"

I couldn't say anything.

Eryk's voice seemed to travel across a vast distance. "Believe it or not," he said gravely, "I am not weeping for myself. For months we've both been thinking that we might be machine-gunned or bombed—what is a little spittle, after all? I am weeping for them. I looked into their eyes as they spat. There was so much terror there, Andrew, terror that we might be telling the truth and that their fantasy about the Mother of Mothers might be a fiction. They spat at me to be able to sleep calmly tonight. And who am I, God knows, to grudge anyone a good night's sleep?"

"I can't bear this. Why didn't they spit at me? Don't they know you are sick?"

"Of course they know I'm sick. They don't spit at you because I'm an easier target. What power do I have, after all? To them I'm

just a young gigolo whom they hope will die soon and stop disturbing their dream. In their minds, I'm a piece of trash. They can do
what they want to me, and in the name of the Divine Mother, too,
because for them I am less than nothing. In fact, for them I am
dead already. I see it all very clearly."

A weary smile slowly spread across Eryk's face, "You know what
an Old Testament person I am. Fire and brimstone and judgment. . . . Well, all this is changing me. I have been praying for them
waiting for you. I have been praying to the Virgin to grant them in
their love what She has granted us. Then they would *see*. I find I am
too tired even to think about vengeance; all this madness is too
sick; all I can think about is their healing. Only She knows how that
can come."

Then he said, "Do you think this horror will ever really end?
Or is this always going to be our life?"

"I don't know."

We sat silently in the full glare of noon.

Then Eryk said, "I forgive the two men. If they knew what love
can be, they would see that love in us. It would be as obvious to
them as if the sun suddenly came out at midnight."

ACT VI

The Pearl

✳

We have written of these blessings so that when souls become frightened by the wounds of so many trials they might take courage in the many blessings obtained from God through these ordeals.

St. John of the Cross

For almost a month, Eryk and I have been receiving messages that Thalheim is "desperate" to talk to Eryk. Pious, angry notes from "Meerons" all over America have reached us saying things like, "Mother loves Eryk ever specially and is longing to have the chance to tell him so." One of many accused me of so "brainwashing" Eryk that "he cannot reach out now when he needs it most in the crisis of his life to the love and endless compassion of the Divine Mother on earth."

By now Eryk and I had lived through so much that we simply graded the letters in different levels of lunacy. There were three categories: the mad, the bad, and the viciously ugly. We would have mock arguments about which belonged where, and give our toy tiger Balthazar the ultimate decision.

Eryk, especially, found this new "tack" of Thalheims hilarious. "Next the witch of Thalheim will be saying that she'd like to remarry us herself in a special satellite ceremony! Or perhaps she'll get up a whole media event—if I were Herbert, this is what I would advise—with thousands of gay men in white suits getting married by her all at once, like that mega-marriage the Reverend Moon did in Korea! If she had any sense, she would ask Madonna to sing and Gaultier to design the costumes! I'm going to write to her now!"

Underneath the bravura fantasy, however, I could see that Eryk was becoming more and more angry.

Then, at the end of July, when we were dining in our flat with Lucy, my manager, Eryk turned to me at dinner and said, "I've had it with all these 'messages.' If Meera and Adilakshmi want to speak to me so badly, why don't they just ring me? And why are they pouring out their so-sad hearts to anyone who rings, even to those who don't know us and have never been to Thalheim? Everyone, it seems, this month is getting the same sob story. I don't know who repels me more—the Thalheim crew, or the gaggle of idiots who believe any old rubbish that they say."

Suddenly, he leaned forward, his eyes ablaze. "Andrew, my passive days are over. What have I got to lose? I'm going to ring Adilakshmi now, myself."

"For God's sake Eryk. . . ." I was panicking.

I knew from the wild cold look in his eyes, however, that Eryk was unstoppable.

"Whatever happens, I'm going to have a good time," he laughed. "Why should they have all the fun, after all? Here you and I are, sitting in fear while they get to concoct and lie and manipulate all over the place. It just isn't fair! I want my share of the cake! I want to get into the action!"

He smiled at me, "What I am really dying to hear are the new lies. Why should we always get them secondhand? I'm sure that all this new business is about trying to separate me from you. They have been trying for months to separate you from me, in all the ways that we know. Now the Mastermind must have decided, well, that won't work; let's try the other way around. I know these idiots now as if I had made them. They have a comic-opera banality of mind, which doesn't make them less lethal, but at least makes them funny."

And we all started to laugh suddenly, wildly, until our faces were wet and bright with tears.

"Oh God, laughing feels so good," I said, still shaking.

"Yes," Eryk went on. "I bet you twenty dollars that the Divine Mother's anxiety to talk to me involved primarily the desire to tell me some ultra-horrible lie about you. They must have been thinking this up for quite a while; it will be as devastating as they can manage, and it will have to work. After all, Thalheim knows that the interview is at *Common Boundary* and will be out in September. If they can manage to destroy our love now just before you go public, then you—and I—but mostly you, darling, will look like a complete fraud, hysteric, and fake. I'm beginning almost to be grateful I was brought up in the corridors and salons of Paris. An early training in the evil of the world helps me now."

By now, I was swept up in Eryk's enthusiasm. It was the first time for months that I had seen him so happy.

"You know Thalheim's biggest mistake? Meera was so confident you would leave me, neither she or any other of her henchmen ever bothered to find out *who* I was. They think I'm just a sweet lost boy who hero-worshiped you and can be twisted around their little finger."

I started to laugh again. "My God," I said. "They should have met you—for just five minutes!"

"But they will one day know very different. I'm going to ring her now, Andrew."

Lucy cried, "Do it! You'll feel a hundred times better! Go on!"

Eryk stood up, adjusted his shirt, slicked back his hair, and became icy-calm.

"I'm ready," he said. "Follow me!"

My mind went white and I shook with fear and anger and excitement. Whatever would happen next, Eryk's refusal to be "passive" was already liberating. The fact that he could have the courage at all was also a wonderful sign—a sign that he trusted the Mother more and more deeply to protect him from the evil forces that had so tormented us both.

What followed was a conversation of over an hour which exceeded his wildest hopes. Eryk led an increasingly flustered, hysterical, and self-contradictory Adilakshmi (often, he said, audibly prompted by Meera) to reveal, beyond a shadow of any possible doubt, all the lies that Thalheim had ever said about us. Later that night, Eryk wrote down an extensive and hilarious account of his conversation.

"At the beginning, Adilakshmi denied that I had ever been to see Mother Meera at all: "'Nothing ever happened.'" After jogging Adilakshmi's memory about the evening she had stood outside Meera's house and told me to "'live a normal life and get married'" (Adilakshmi: "'Gay men are happier many times with children and wife, isn't it? I was just giving you advice because I love you'"), Eryk confronted her with what I had told him she had said in a phone conversation in Paris: "'Homosexuals have no future in the future of the Mother.'" In his account, Eryk goes on:

"Adilakshmi (suddenly chillingly harsh and aggressive, her voice trembling) replied, "'I don't want to speak about small details.'"

At this point, Eryk writes that Adilakshmi starts to become

more irrational. Forgetting who she is talking to, she tells Eryk that old girlfriends of his have been ringing her claiming that he is "abandoning" them. "But I have no old girlfriends," Eryk said. Adilakshmi becomes frantic, "But they are ringing and ringing."

Increasingly crazy, Adilakshmi at this point displays her hand. Let Eryk's account speak for itself:

"After a silence, Adilakshmi's voice suddenly brightens and starts to 'sing' again: " 'Eryk, dear one, we have heard that you have cancer, ser-i-ous cancer. We are praying for you.' "

E: " 'Oh thank you. I'm deeply touched.' "

A: " 'I must tell you the truth, dear one.' " (Very calm and steady suddenly): " 'The truth is, dear one, that Andrew wanted to leave you. He was bored with you. Yes, he was bored with you and wanted to leave you. So he came to the Mother and begged her to give him permission to leave you. Are you there? Did you hear what I said?' "

E: " 'I heard. If Andrew wanted to leave me, why didn't he just tell me? Andrew usually tells me everything even when I don't want to hear it. And why would he need Mother Meera's permission to leave me? Something else disturbs me slightly. Earlier in this conversation, Adilakshmi, you said that Andrew never went to see Mother Meera at all. Now you are saying . . .' "

A (frantic again, her voice rising): " 'Andrew was afraid, you see. Very afraid. Afraid, yes, yes. He came to see Mother and begged her to give him permission to leave you. But she is the Mother! Her love is great! She said, "No you must not leave him. A relationship is not like chopping vegetables." ' "

E: " 'But Adilakshmi, assuming that what you say is true—and why should I doubt it—why did you come out that evening of December 27 and tell me to leave Andrew, get married, and live a normal life? Why would you tell me that if Mother Meera did not want Andrew to break off his relationship with me!'"

Long pause. More Telugu. Meera and Adilakshmi's voice rising and falling, like demented birds.

A: "'I don't want to talk any more about this. You are happy with Andrew. This is good. This is very good. Why are you calling Thalheim then to talk about old things? We just want you to be happy. Mother is sending you and Andrew many blessings. We just want your happiness.'"

When the phone call was over, Eryk told us in great detail what Adilakshmi had said, imitating her accent, and sometimes doubling up with laughter.

"They are evil," Lucy said in the kitchen.

"I know they are lying," Eryk said, putting his arms around me and leaning his head against mine. "You have nothing to fear."

The full impact of what Adilakshmi had said was beginning to hit me and I could not speak.

Eryk laughed bitterly, "Did you notice exactly what Adilakshmi did? First, she said she knew that I had cancer. This proves, by the way, that Meera has known all along that I was sick—which makes her lies even more obscene. Then, *immediately* afterwards, Adilakshmi said, 'He wanted to leave you. He was bored with you.' Is that what an even half-compassionate person would say to someone they knew might die of cancer, even if it were true? That his husband wanted to abandon him and never loved him? She convicts herself by the cruelty of what she said and how she said it."

Eryk turned to me and kissed me. "I can begin to imagine what you must be suffering. To face such lies from people to whom you gave your whole being . . ."

I could still not speak. I nodded helplessly.

"You know what her plan must have been, don't you?"

"My mind is too shot," I said.

"Adilakshmi knew that if I believed her I would be so anguished and depressed it would probably kill me. She knows that cancer and emotional stress are related; she was relying on that. She knew that if I died hating and accusing you, you, too, would be destroyed. Either you would kill yourself, or in total desperation, return to Meera. I could almost hear her mind working, Andrew; it was very strange.

"Let me now go further and be what some Berkeley therapist would undoubtedly say was 'paranoid schizophrenic.' If you had returned to Thalheim, Meera and Adilakshmi would have found a way of finishing you off. You would either have become even more obsessed and fanatical than you were before, and so usable at will. Or more likely, you would slowly have gone mad and ended somewhere staring at a wall. Which Adilakshmi, no doubt, in her honeyed, singsong voice would have presented as a karmic punishment for your betrayal of the Divine One."

I sat down slowly at the kitchen table, too stunned by the clarity of Eryk's words to do anything but stare at my hands. After all we had endured at Meera's hands, anything, even far worse things even than Eryk had sketched, could be true.

"And this is the woman," I said, "that I believed was the Divine Mother on earth."

"I want you to know something," Eryk said. "I wasn't surprised that Adilakshmi told me you wanted to leave me. In fact I was half-expecting it."

"Why?"

"It is a lie I have heard quite a lot recently."

I looked up at him bewildered.

At this moment, Lucy coughed and said, "I don't think I can take much more this evening. Would you two mind if I went home?"

We kissed her and thanked her for her courage, and she left.

"What did you mean?" I asked Eryk as soon as she was out of earshot. "What do you mean it is a lie you have heard before? You never told me."

"There is a lot I haven't told you," Eryk said, exhausted now. "I wanted to protect you. You have been suffering so much I wanted to spare you many things. But now I think the time has come for you to face everything. You are strong enough and you know that I believe you and love you."

"What the hell are you talking about?"

"I'll tell you tomorrow. Tomorrow I'll tell you and show you. I'm not being mysterious, or coy. You've had enough for one evening. Trust me."

"Eryk, if I didn't trust you, I would be dead."

"And if I didn't trust you, so would I," he said slowly. "I'd have leapt off the Bay Bridge months ago."

The next morning, after breakfast, Eryk disappeared into our bedroom and returned with a blue plastic bag. He took my hand and led me into the front room, which by now was awash with glorious morning light. Without saying anything, he went to the stereo and put on Ockeghem's "Salve Regina."

"Sit, Andrew. Inspire yourself with the light and music around you. Pray to Her for protection."

His solemnity was priest-like. He closed his eyes. I watched his lips moving in prayer.

He came over to where I was sitting, leaned down and held my head tight against his heart.

"Forgive me in advance for having to put you through the suffering that is coming."

I trembled. "I forgive you," I said.

Then, he rummaged in the blue plastic bag and fetched out a khaki "artist's" notebook. Eryk put it on the floor in front of me.

"What is all this Eryk? What is going on?"

For one moment of blinding terror, I thought he was going to leave me and that the book contained his explanation. As if reading my mind, Eryk patted my head and whispered, "It has nothing to do with us. I am here and will always be here."

Then, Eryk, white-faced, and with his hands folded in his lap, began to speak:

"I'll try and make what I need to say as brief and as clear as possible. Last night I told you, after the call with Adilakshmi, that I was not surprised at the new lie, because I had already heard it. In fact I have been hearing it—and rococo variations on it—for two months now. I have almost become fond of it.

"Starting at the beginning of May—just two weeks after our wedding—a succession of those you call your 'brothers' and 'sisters'—some of the devotees of Meera and some of them just so-called old friends of yours—rang me again and again to tell me . . ."

He paused and closed his eyes.

"To tell you what?"

"Give me time, Andrew. This is one of the hardest moments of my life. These 'brothers' and 'sisters,' many of whom you have always talked of with love as your spiritual companions, rang me to tell me that you were a monster of cruelty and egoism; that you had destroyed the lives of everyone you had been close to; that you never loved me; that you were only using me as an alibi; that you had begged Meera to help you to leave me in December and my 'hysteria' had trapped you into staying with me and then marrying me. They rang again and again, from New York, from all round America, from Thailand, from England, from Israel. Sometimes they rang four or five times a day; sometimes I had a whole day to recover before they began again."

Eryk covered his eyes and started to weep.

"Every time the telephone rang, I felt like vomiting and sometimes did. Some of your 'brothers' and 'sisters' posed as my benefactors; they claimed to be trying to save me from you. They said, 'We love you, Eryk. We know you are pure and naive. We know you are dazzled by Andrew, just as we have been. He can be wonderfully convincing and eloquent and charming, but he is a killer. He is killing you. If you stay with him, you will die. Your soul and your mental health are in danger.' These were the worst, because they spoke in soft, honeyed voices that I could hear crackling with jealousy and hatred. Then there were the others, whom I started to prefer. They were more honest. They said to me, 'We hear you have cancer. You are going to die. You are going to die a horrible, painful death. We want you to die. You deserve to die. You are disgusting. Andrew doesn't love you anyway. Why stay around? Isn't there an open window near by? Why don't you just kill yourself now in some effective, painless way and spare yourself the trouble of dying slowly.'"

"How can this be true?" I cried. "How can this be true . . . ?"

Eryk stopped me with a short fierce shout. "These 'brothers' and 'sisters' you have been loving all these years—loving and writing blurbs for and introducing to gallery owners and editors and society matrons who could help their careers—all the flotsam and jetsam you surrounded yourself with all these years . . . can't you see they hate you, they hate your success, they hate your happiness with me, they hate me for making you happy. The Meera business is just an excuse. Many of them don't even believe in Meera; they are just using this madness for their own ends. When there is blood in the water, the sharks come in for the kill.

"After the first few calls, I asked Gabriela what to do. We wept together over the phone. 'I have seen a lot of evil in my life,' she said, 'but these people are the worst I have ever encountered.' Then she said, 'Andrew will not be able to believe you if you just tell him. He trusts you, but the truth is too enormous for him to stand and he will try to deny it. At this moment, too, you should not tell him. He has too much to suffer as it is, and it would send him mad. Wait until he sees almost everything about Thalheim clearly. Wait until he is a little stronger. Keep a daily journal of the times they called you and from which he can check if he needs to with the phone company. And into that journal pour everything they said in detail and all your pain and fear so he can see just what you endured for him and what they wanted to do to him and you. In these ways, you will give him, when it is time, the whole picture. Also you will have a complete record of everything that happened.'"

I gazed at Eryk, too scared to say anything.

The room swam before my eyes. It took all my strength to be able to focus on Eryk's face.

He stood in the door and turned. "I have been praying to the Virgin to give me the strength to forgive them. But I don't know if I will ever be able to. Christ said, 'Father, forgive them for they know not what they do.' But they did know, Andrew, what they were doing. And they did it because they knew."

I stared at the book a long time before doing anything. Then I knelt and prayed to the Mother. "Whatever I discover, Mother, let me stay sane. Whatever illusions I have to surrender now, give me the courage to do so without false sentiment. Whatever I have to face about myself and my past, give me the courage to face it without excuses or a paralyzing self-loathing."

Everything Eryk had told me was confirmed, over and over. There were no lengths my so-called closest friends and "spiritual brothers and sisters" were not prepared to go to ruin me, humiliate Eryk, and try and destroy our marriage, our hope, and our lives.

No lie was too outrageous, no insinuation too crass or obscene. There were details that Eryk left me to discover for myself, because he couldn't bring himself to tell me them. One close "spiritual sister," after trying unsuccessfully to get Eryk to believe that I had been betraying him from the beginning of our relationship, then said, "If Andrew doesn't shut up now he is going to find himself having serious problems. Thalheim has got ready a pedophile case against him, and if he continues to denounce Meera he will be denounced as a pedophile."

As I read, the versions dove-tailed into each other; it was clear that this vile symphony of sadism had been carefully orchestrated. (Gabriela later gave us the name of the person in New York who had been at the center.) C., the man I had loved for fifteen years and believed my oldest friend, rang and said to Eryk, "Get out now or you will die even faster. I haven't rung Meera but I know Andrew is lying and that she must be desolate." Eryk said to him, "You know that Andrew loves you more than his own brother." C. laughed. "You still believe what Andrew says about Love? Look what he has done to Meera, who loves him still deeply, I know."

Even more painful were the entries in the khaki notebook where Eryk had written down his horror and suffering during the long nightmare my "brothers and sisters" had made him endure:

Hell's address: 310 Page St. S.F., CA. 94108
A soft voice, male, in French with an American accent, "Eryk?"

"Yes?"

"You are going to die."

He burst out laughing and hung up.

Take me now but give Andrew a back and Sandra life.

If I jumped out of the window, everything would be in order—for Andy, for me, for them. Only the window is too low. I would only break a leg, at best.

"David" calls. He says he wants to talk to me about Andrew. I told him I didn't want anyone to talk to me about Andrew. He said, "You are going to die—that's sad." He didn't seem sad at all. On the contrary.

I said, "It is not sad to leave a world full of people like you."

My body is abandoning me. Sometimes after a call my legs betray me. Up to now I have had a chair or a wall to lean against. I want everything to go very fast. I don't want anything to drag. A. has enough problems. It is better I die very quickly.

This terror is destroying my intestines—if the Final Phase is to shit myself all the time I'd rather die now.

I dreamt I was attacked by monster crabs . . . one of them had Andrew's head. I couldn't tear it off my stomach. I wept because "they" had made me, despite my will, see A. as a crab—they are invading my mind. . . . The crab is the symbol of cancer, of course. I stroked A.'s forehead and begged his forgiveness. He was still asleep.

Last night I could not sleep—I went out—I fell in the corridor—I managed to crawl to the kitchen—there I felt better, just—Balthazar was on the table. I took him to smoke a cigarette in the garden. He is so kind. I thought of what C. said in his call from Thailand, "Andrew just married you for the publicity," and I wept and wept.

I spoke with Gabriela. "These calls are killing me. . . . I am going to die soon anyway." She said, "It is possible." We wept, then I said, "One minute costs three dollars. Do something other than weep."

I thought my childhood had taught me about evil. I had no idea before now how terrible human beings could be. Now I know what Musset meant when he wrote, "The world is a bottomless sewer in which monstrous seals climb and writhe on mountains of dung."

As the impact of what Eryk had suffered started to sink in, and with it the atrocity of what had been done against him, what astounded me most was Eryk's unfailing belief in our love. That was the only possible source of hope for me in so much anguish—that my husband knew who I was, knew the depth of my love for him and could not be shaken by anyone or anything. "I know," he wrote in the notebook, "that Andrew loves me with his whole heart. How could I not know after what we have been through together? None of these voices stinking of meanness and jealousy and hatred can convince me otherwise. If I have to die soon, and it seems likely, I will know that. It is enough. It is all I have ever really wanted—to be loved—and I am."

All I could think, as my mind cringed and all the illusions of twenty years of friendship were systematically first tortured then destroyed, was that in Eryk I had found what Christ called "the Pearl of great price." In his love, in his purity, in his loyalty, in his powers of discrimination and courage in the face of a storm of evil,

I had found a jewel infinitely more precious, in fact, than the world itself and all its games.

Halfway through the afternoon, Eryk came in to find me lying on the floor with my eyes closed.

"Are you all right?" he started to shout. "Good God! Are you all right?"

I opened my eyes and tried to speak, but no words came out.

"Forgive me," Eryk said. "I had to give you the book. You have to know everything now, so you can protect yourself if . . . if . . . I am no longer there. I wanted to be with you when you listened so you would know I don't believe a word they are saying. So you would know that I know you love me. So you would have my faith in you to help you live on, if . . ."

He didn't finish. He didn't need to.

I tried to say something.

"Don't try to speak," Eryk held me against him. "O my Baby Andy, they have tried to murder us both in every dimension and in every way. But She will not let them. And they cannot murder our love. Perhaps it is that which drives them so crazy."

The words came at last. "I think I could, in time," I said, "forgive them for what they have done to me. But what they have done to you I do not imagine now that I will ever be able to forgive. How can you ever forgive me for what I have made you suffer? If it wasn't for me . . ."

He cut me short. "If it wasn't for me, none of this would ever have happened."

"And I would have been lost in a dark dream all my life. Now at least I have the chance to wake up. If I can stand it."

"You can stand it. You are strong. Your true life is beginning. My love will always be with you, even if . . ."

We wept in each others arms.

———

That night, as I prayed before going to bed, I realized something I had never understood before; to forgive someone is not necessarily to reconnect with them. The Mother had shown me who the people who had rung Eryk really were to separate me from them forever, to separate me and Eryk and our life together from the range of their malice; I could whole-heartedly pray to forgive them, and try sincerely to wish them healing and even enlightenment, without ever needing to speak to them or see them again. At last I saw I was beginning to glimpse what Christ meant when he said, "Combine the wisdom of the serpent with the innocence of the dove." What my "brothers" and "sisters" had done amounted to torture; I had simultaneously to face that, face them, forgive them, and in my mind, to preserve myself, Eryk, and our love, separate myself from them forever, without hatred, yes, but also without any sentimental attachment or excuse that could keep me in any way "connected" to them or to the mistakes of the past.

Gabriela rang at about eight in the evening. It was four o'clock in Belgium, she said, but she had been unable to sleep.

I told her everything that had happened and everything I was learning.

"Forgive, yes," she said, "but do not forget. And never, ever see these people again. Have the courage to face that you can do nothing for them. Only God can help them now. If you allow them to come in again into your life, they will try and destroy you again at some later time. One life is now over. See that clearly and go on."

Then she said, "And now that you are beginning to *see* the meaning of this dying, let me humbly advise you to go back to your room and pray to the Virgin to let you see exactly where you encouraged and secretly, unconsciously, conspired with these false friends in their games. Ask Her to give you the strength to face your own responsibility for what has happened. This is the second part of the death. And you must ask for it to be done as fast, as ruthlessly, as clearly as possible. To defend the vision the Mother has given you and Eryk you will both need to be icily self-aware, and to have the clearest possible knowledge of the danger of your own personalities and past habits. You cannot allow the old Andrew Harvey to destroy in any way the future that the Mother is preparing for you. Your so-called friends wanted to kill him off; now you do it for them, in and under Her, and for Her work."

I knew Gabriela was giving me valuable advice. In my anguish, I had not yet dared to face my responsibility for what had happened: I was still, unconsciously, holding on to some part of "Andrew" to be able to deal with what had happened at all. I would now have to relinquish that grasp, and go naked and defenseless into Her darkness.

I returned to my room. Eryk went to bed. Hour after hour I prayed to the Mother to show me the real face of my false self, and to make me brave enough to will its death in Her. How could I ever be an instrument of Hers if I didn't allow Her to purify me? And how could I be purified if I kept back any horrible self-recognition? In the danger into which destiny had brought me, I realized that night that *any* lack of discrimination I still harbored, any vanity or exaggeration, would now be fatal not just for me and not just for Eryk but also for the alchemical tantric vision that the Mother wanted us to live and help transmit. I had no more excuses not to will my own conscious annihilation.

Because I asked Her with sincerity for the truth, I received it in terrible swift images and phrases, one after the other—in memories in which I recalled exactly how I had seen the cruelty and jealousy of friend after friend but deliberately ignored them and not from "goodness," as I would like to imagine, but out of a fear of being alone or rejected or worse, from a spiritual vanity, a belief that I could change them. I saw how my longing to shine in "sophisticated" circles had made me half-consciously accept the bitchiness and meanness that are the currency in those circles: I had lacked the courage to separate myself completely from the world, because I still wanted its rewards. I had, in fact, unconsciously played the double game that Meera was playing—pretending to be mystical, spiritually committed to a holy life, while continuing to live in the world and to want its excitements. Playing this double game had, I saw with despair, made me the perfect false apostle of a false Divine Mother. In my delirium of ignorance, I had believed I could live with "integrity" in all worlds and dimensions; in practice, I surrounded myself with the unhappy mediocrities which were now turning on me to destroy me and my love and life.

Their malice and lies, I saw, were presenting me with a sort of circus mirror, in which I could see myself as a cartoon figure, elongated, awful, pathetic, absurd. If I refused to look at what signs and angles *were* accurate, I would be trapped again in the vain, ambiguous, half-worldly, half-spiritual persona that had attracted such vicious flotsam to me in the first place; if I accepted and dared to look at what truths had been said, then I could, with Eryk's and Her help and grace, now begin to free myself from all those traits and obsessions that had kept me—against my better will and against even my own knowledge—trapped in a wilderness of mirrors.

I begged Her, again and again, to hold my face to this obscene mirror and not let me turn away, and not let me excuse anything I needed to dissolve and destroy in myself. And for long hours, I gazed and gazed, and held the whole of my life until then up to the driest and most merciless inquisition my mind and heart could stand. Each time I thought I would literally die from the pain of what I was seeing, I cried out to Her to give me Her strength to go on opening all the darkness in my nature to healing and resolution. I knew I had to be completely sincere now or never have a chance of being as authentic as She wanted me to be; I knew that the "deaths" that I had been handed in Meera and my friends' betrayals were *precisely* calculated by my karma and destiny to give me, if I was brave enough to embrace them, the chance to be born afresh in a far clearer and purer life. I knew that Eryk's love, a love that he had lived out to the end in the face of overwhelming suffering and cruelty, was the Grace given me to help endure what I had to end in myself, the mirror in which I could see the face his and Her Love were preparing for me to assume and wear. I knew, too, that I simply could not make this terrifyingly swift transition from one life to another on my own; I was not strong enough; *no one* could be strong enough; but then, no one was *asked* to be strong enough. The Grace of the Mother, Her Love, Her mercy, Her infinite tender acceptance of all human frailty, were, I knew, open to me and to everyone who call on them with a "contrite and broken heart."

As the hours passed and the night deepened, I felt each memory, and the awful recognition it brought me of my own ambiguity or vanity or cowardice, strip me of layer after layer of a self-esteem I hadn't even known was there, remove defense after defense, and then even the need to defend myself anymore. I surrendered to the Black Madonna, finally, completely. I went and lay down on the floor and spread out my arms and found myself saying inwardly and with the force of my whole being, "I know nothing and understand nothing. You must live in me now or I will not be able to go on at all."

I found myself—and I can describe it in no other way—"sinking down" through different levels of darkness, falling down, down, as if to the center of the earth or the hidden black center of the universe. At first I was terrified, but slowly, as I continued giving in and giving up to what was happening, I realized that the further I sank down into the always-growing darkness, the more deeply at peace I became.

Finally I reached a placeless place where everything was dark, where there was only black light that stretched infinitely in all directions. "I" was no longer either the Andrew who was suffering or the Andrew who had surrendered but this spaceless, timeless, formless, utterly peaceful and still, black light stretching throughout the universe.

I did not dissolve completely into this black light; I was "kept" conscious enough to "witness" that I was one with it and to savor the infinite peace and final safety of Its Truth.

The experience lasted about half an hour. When I "returned" from it still lying on the floor I was filled with a calm and unshakable confidence that whatever now happened, the "I" that I had known in my falling down to the black center of all things could never be destroyed.

I also "awoke" to the entire room around me awash in dazzling Divine Light. The vases on the wooden window sill glittered in white light; so did the threadbare carpet and the swirls of dust on the floor. It was as if the blackness I had been immersed in had "turned itself inside out" to reveal the divinity of all things and of the Witness in me that was now aware of it in a fuller, calmer, stabler, and more final way than ever before.

Lying in the arms of that darkness, in the arms of the Black Madonna, I did not "understand" why everything that had happened had to happen, I *knew* and *saw* its necessity and amazing and terrible mercy. I *saw* and *knew* why and how She had let me unravel my half-mad obsession with Meera until this crazy end, how and why She had allowed me to suffer everything I needed to of the consequences of what I had done (while always surrounding me with help and support and the truth of a few real friends like Gabriela), why She had destroyed all false loves so that, at last, I could be—would *have* to be—open to the miracle of Eryk's love and my love for him and the Love that held both of our loves in its dark arms. No pain of any kind accompanied these recognitions. Only peace, effortless peace.

At last I knew what Rumi meant when he wrote in lines I had always vainly thought I "understood" but now did not "understand" but "live":

Without destroying me, how could the Beloved pour me
    this treasure?
He had to throw me to the waves, for Love's Sea to sweep
    me away.

ACT VII

Beginning Healing

✳

Anyone who comes to know the state of annihilation is destroyed and made nothing. Yet God also streams him an existence from the heart of His own existence and adorns him with divine color. All qualities inside him and outside him are transformed. On that day, heaven becomes another earth altogether; and heaven another heaven.

IBN ARABI

FROM MY JOURNAL:
August 4th

Today is the feast day of Jean-Marie Vianney, Curé of Ars, the great French nineteenth-century mystic, who spent most of his life in Ars, a small village fifty miles from Lyon, and through his healing powers turned it into a place of international pilgrimage. For months, Eryk has been praying to him for healing alongside the Virgin.

We got up early and made a small altar in our front room and dedicated it to the Curé. As we began to pray in the fresh silence of the early morning, we both smelled an intensely sweet fragrance of rose. At first, it seemed to have no discernible source; then we realized it was coming from the shelf above the fireplace.

Eryk stopped praying, got up, and went to stand by the fireplace. He stood for a few moments, smiling ecstatically and breathing in the air. Then he reached forward and picked up the small and exquisite old Mexican statue of the Virgin in Splendor that he had found in a nearby shop and bought for me for my birthday. Slowly, he turned it round.

"Come and see! Come and see!" he cried. "There is a miraculous oil seeping from her back."

I leaped up. By now, the air had filled with an almost stiflingly powerful odor of rose. Eryk showed me the back of the statue—a stain the size of a small shoehorn was ooz-ing what seemed like a light rose-scented oil. Eryk put his right-hand index finger into it and made on my forehead the sign of the Cross; I did the same for him. Then I opened his shirt and rubbed my finger up and down his chest, along the contour of his lungs. Later, our friend Anne—whose birthday was also that day—came in for lunch and we showed her the still-flowing "stain" of holy rose-oil. She held the statue against her breasts and gazing at us both said: "Something wonderful will now happen."

The three of us knelt on the hard dark wood of the floor and prayed to the Virgin and her servant of Ars.

All I could find words for was, "End the evil of Thal-heim," and "Save Eryk."

FROM MY JOURNAL:
Later that night, too drunk with happiness and gratitude to sleep

When the Virgin first showed us—by the sign in early March that She was with us, and blessing us and supporting us—it was in a representation of Her where she was showing her Heart, her naked, fiery, bloody heart. Now, the representation of her that is showing Her protection is the "Guadalupe" surrounded by the sun's glory and standing on the moon. In the first, She was the "Mater Dolorosa" weeping with and for her children; here, today, She came to us as the Omnipotent Divine Mother, Mistress of the Universe. She is saying to us, "I will triumph. I am the Queen of hell and heaven and I will defeat all evil. Freedom and safety in My name are coming."

On August 8th, Eryk had an appointment with the doctor who was overseeing his cancer. He had missed the last two appointments out of fear and despair. "Why go at all and waste money when we both know what is happening?"

This time however, I bullied him into going. "We have to know," I kept saying. "So we can do whatever we can."

Eryk's appointment was at 2:30 P.M.; he did not want me to go with him, so I stayed at home, pacing the flat, restlessly praying. I knew that only a miracle could halt the progress of the cancer now: The suffering that Meera and her disciples had imposed on Eryk had driven him into a terrifying physical decline.

I spoke to Her in those hours more nakedly than I have ever spoken to Her—out loud, knowing She was there with me, with total directness. I said: "You cannot let him die.

You must not. I will not bear this, and you cannot want me to bear this. Surely you must want him strong and well, and our love to last and witness You. Save him."

The hours went by. Eryk did not return. I imagined the worst, even that in his desolation he had killed himself.

Then, at 6:30, Eryk walked up the stairs. He was very peaceful. He didn't say anything but just walked past me into the front room.

He still did not say anything. He knelt to the Mexican statue of the Virgin that had oozed miraculous oil, with his head bowed.

Oh my God, I thought, he is praying for the strength to tell me it won't be long now.

I looked at the small altar to the Curé of Ars, which was still decorated with flowers, and prayed wordlessly for the courage to endure whatever was coming.

Then Eryk turned, smiling a strange, calm smile. "The cancer has completely gone," he said. "Neither my doctor nor any of the others understand it. The Mother has saved me."

The news did not register for a few seconds. Then so much joy flooded me, I almost fell. We knelt and thanked Her. Although it was the middle of a Monday afternoon, a sudden silence seemed to fall on the world around us.

Two hours later, Sandra rang us excitedly from Houston, where she had been having tests in a cancer clinic.

"I am going to pull through," she said. "The tests are much better than anyone has expected! This old girl has a lot of life in her yet!"

FROM MY JOURNAL:
August 28th

Six days in our new apartment in the Richmond district in San Francisco . . . and already we feel at home in its white calm spaces. Eryk calls it, only half-jokingly, our "temple of love." We both know that She has given us this quiet and hidden sanctuary to heal in and to worship Her in every aspect of our lives. She is in every room in a statue or a painting. Two days ago we bought an old photograph of Fred Astaire and Ginger Rogers dancing in *Top Hat,* as a kind of prayer.

It took about ten days for me completely to "believe" the miracle of Eryk's healing. I have been so terrified for so long that he would die. It was only yesterday, when I saw him walk smiling up the stairs with his arms full of roses for the Virgin and groceries, that I finally understood. Eryk will not die. The relief was overwhelming: I didn't want to frighten Eryk by my tears and so left for Sutro Park, where, standing above the Pacific Ocean ablaze with August sunlight, I thanked Her again and again and wept with wonder and gratitude.

So far, thank God, no mad calls. Only a handful of people know our number. Slowly, slowly, I feel my nerves falling, and Eryk looks calmer every day . . .

Protect us here, Mother. Keep us safe.

From my Journal:
August 29th

Tonight, as we sat laughing and eating, hardly believing that we could be sitting together in our own place (and with Eryk healed), Eryk suddenly looked serious and said:

"We need to back to France next month; we must go on a pilgrimage to thank Her, and thank the Curé of Ars."

In two hours we had planned everything; just a few days in Paris, then to Ars and La Salette, where the Virgin began her great sequence of modern apparitions in 1846.

"It is important," Eryk said, "that as the interview comes out in *Common Boundary* we should be on pilgrimage to thank Her. Everywhere we stop we will pray that the interview helps people to get free of the madness of whatever cult they are in . . ."

I know what he is thinking but does not say. "And everywhere we stop we will pray, too, for our protection, when the storm breaks, as it will soon, very soon . . ."

When we left for Paris on September 12th we had spent three calm, tenderly domestic weeks in our new flat. The *Common Boundary* interview was out, with a shrewd and elegant introduction by Rose Solari; already some of the local masters, "power-Buddhists," and "New Age stars" who had either kept clear of us when our cause was in doubt or had been contemptuous or dismissive of us started to make unctuous overtones to us, claiming, of course, that they had always known we were telling the truth and had only kept on the sidelines "out of respect for our karma."

One famous American Buddhist, who had equivocated for months about whether or not we were fantasists, sent us an expensive bunch of roses with a quote form the Dhammapada; another initially denounced us, ringing up *Common Boundary* to say that publishing such "drivel" was an outrage; a week later, however, he had clearly heard that our case was being increasingly believed in because he wrote a flowery letter extolling our "intensity" and "courage."

"You couldn't put these people in a novel," Eryk keeps saying. "No one would believe you."

Several leading "spiritual figures" even claimed to have been at our marriage; some of them had, in fact, been invited but had been in Arizona or Hawaii or otherwise "unavailable." Now they were giving to mutual friends long, even elaborate descriptions of the ceremony they had avoided.

"I know such blatant hypocrisy is a good sign for us," Eryk said one morning, "but it makes me despise even more the whole so-called spiritual circus. The theater is more honest; no one in it even pretends to be sincere."

Several of the "callers" also rang and tried to reconnect as if nothing happened. Plaintive little cries of "Where have you been? Have I done something? Why aren't you talking to us any more?" echoed on our answering machine. Gabriela had told me that many of those who had tried shamelessly to destroy us would try just as shamelessly to contact us again. "Surely not," I had said, "they would have more dignity." She laughed wildly, "Dignity? Those people? Have you learnt nothing?"

Not everyone was for us, of course. Letters of denunciation and outrage poured into *Common Boundary*. Exhausted though we were, we were not afraid; we trusted the integrity of Rose Solari and the editors of *Common Boundary,* who had already resisted pressure to set our case clearly.

Gabriela said to me, "Think of the interview like an army of tiny ants invading a drawing room; you won't see anything at first but eventually all the furniture will crumble."

We arrived in Paris, disheveled and still nervous but already considerably stronger, on September 13th. My first few days back in my old flat were filled with strange pain; I had not realized until I returned to Paris to set about leaving it how deeply attached I still was to my European Parisian life. I knew it would be far better for Eryk and me to live and work in California, and I knew, too, that Eryk hated Paris because of the suffering and humiliations he had endured there—but for me to leave Paris meant another death in a year already full of deaths and harsh leave-takings.

What I finally understood was that I was not mourning the Paris that I had known but the demise of a dream I had never realized. I was weeping inwardly not for the Paris I had lived in but for the imaginary Paris I had wanted to live in and never found, the Paris of artists and creative passion and profound late-night friendships. That Paris had eluded me, perhaps because it no longer existed, and perhaps, as Eryk insisted, because it was only ever a creation of expatriate romantic imagination.

Exhaustion and the lucidity born of nine months of disillusion made me see my dream of Paris for what it was and had been, and although that made me sad I knew that no new life—especially the new life that the Mother was offering Eryk and myself—could be lived in the ashes of a false dream. And so, with a melancholy that sometimes infuriated Eryk, I said goodbye to all the cafés and galleries and museums and walks and gardens and friends that I had loved for so long, knowing that it would be many, many years before I would return, or could.

After two days back in Paris I wrote:

This journey on which Eryk and I have embarked is a piti-
less alchemy, dissolving everything I was attached to, even
this city I thought no force of earth could take from me. I
wander the streets that used to give me such simple ecstasy
and I am dull and dumb. For fourteen years I lived in Paris,
like Aladdin in the Thief's cave, but now the Mother has
rubbed Her lamp, and the jewels have revealed themselves
as paste, and the rooms I thought large and magical become—as perhaps they always were—narrow and full of
figures moving in a ballet of futile sophistication and cruelty. I can explain nothing of what I have lived or I am living to the friends here whom I once believed so intimate;
none of them have actively betrayed us, so at least the illusion of love survives as it cannot now anywhere else; but it
is time to go, to say farewell.

When I pray to the Mother to be able to leave grace-
fully and without making Eryk feel guilty I hear Her say to
me inwardly, "I am taking away everything, but you will see;
I will give you more than you can now possibly imagine in
return." I try always to remember what I know somewhere;
that the violence of this alchemy is necessary and inevitable
and can only bring more wonders in its train. But I am so
tired and my back is still one dark flame of pain.

From my Journal:
September 16th. Evening

Carol R. rang this morning at eleven o'clock. She was very happy that the interview with her testimony is now out and that "we would be seen to telling the truth." I could hear, however, from her voice that she was troubled.

"Is something worrying you?" I asked.

Then it all came out. For several weeks now, she had been receiving harassing calls.

Then she coughed and said, "I have something else to tell you too."

I froze.

"This morning Rose Solari rang me and asked me if I was Eryk's sister."

"What?"

"Yes, that is what she asked me. She was very apologetic about it, but someone had written to *Common Boundary* claiming that since I was Eryk's sister my testimony was fake."

"What did you do?"

"I laughed out loud. They will stop at nothing, these idiots. Apparently, they are running out of lies. And then I offered to send my passport, my birth certificate, and even to fly to Washington if necessary to convince everyone in person."

Tears came to my eyes at Carol's loyalty and courage.

"Was Rose convinced by what you said?"

"Yes, immediately. She is a sane and good person. You were very lucky to find her."

"It wasn't luck, it was Grace."

"I can see that. She said that no further proof was necessary but that she had had to check."

"Of course. I'm grateful that *Common Boundary* are taking their responsibility so seriously. That can only expose more completely Meera's lies."

Eryk had come into the room halfway and heard most of my conversation with Carol.

He took the phone, laughing. "I would be honored to be your brother but I have a sister of my own."

We tried to joke about what had happened, but the malice behind it had shaken us. We were both still too fragile to be able to take everything "lightly and funnily" (as one New Age "Master" had advised us, just before we left).

"Let us get out of Paris," Eryk said. "We were planning to go to Ars soon. Let us go tomorrow, and then on to La Salette."

I agreed immediately. I knew what Eryk was thinking— if the New York callers had found out Carol R.'s number, they would know ours and the calls might well start again in our Paris apartment. If we went on pilgrimage, we would feel safe, protected by the Presence of the Curé of Ars and the Mother; no one would know where we were.

FROM MY JOURNAL:
September 17. Evening in Ars

When I entered the church where the Curé had served for fifty years—now absorbed into a far larger, garish, late Victorian basilica—I was so winded by his Presence, by a great wild force, almost violent, of love, that I had to sit down. I have never on any of my journeys experienced such a fierce and overwhelming sense of holiness. I remembered what my friend Eva had told me of Rumi's tomb and how she had felt there "a volcano of Divine passion." I knew now what she meant.

Eryk came and sat by me, with tears in his eyes. "He is here. The Curé is here. Christ is here. The fire of Christ's Love is alive here."

Then he went to the side chapel where the Curé's body lies turned towards the world (in a glass case) with a half-smile. The second I looked at it, I wanted to laugh out loud, "He is not dead. He is only sleeping!" The Curé looked so calm, so real; the half-smile he wears is sublime in its tenderness and pity. His face seems to be fixed forever in the expression it wore as he, consciously, entered eternity.

I gazed for a long time at the Curé's wonderful, pain-wracked, pain-purified face, so austere and yet so filled in every line with love. "O my beloved friend," I kept praying to him, "reveal the love of Christ to me! Let its Fire burn in my heart always as it burned in yours!"

We left the basilica and went to a small shop nearby. There, almost immediately, I found a book for which I had been looking for months, in America, and recently in Paris, but without success: Louis-Marie Grignion de Montfort's *Secret of Mary*. I picked it up and, praying to the Curé, opened it. This is what I read:

"It is through the very Holy Virgin that Jesus Christ came into the world to begin with, and it is also through her that he will reign in the world . . .

"I say with the saints; the divine Mary is the terrestrial paradise of the New Adam, where he was incarnate by the operation of the Holy Spirit to work incomprehensible miracles . . .

"Until now, the divine Mary has been unknown, and this is one of the reasons why Jesus Christ is hardly known as he should be. If then—as is certain—the knowledge and reign of Jesus Christ arrive in the world, it will be a necessary consequence of the knowledge and reign of the very Holy Virgin, who birthed him into this world the first time and will make him burst out everywhere the second."

"And will make him burst out everywhere the second." The words went through me like a wind of flame.

So much of Eryk's and my journey was becoming miraculously clear. I returned to our hotel room alone, and kneeling begged the Curé and the Mother to help me understand more. I read on:

"Jesus Christ is for every person who possesses him the fruit and the work of Mary . . . when Mary has put down her roots in a soul she engenders there miracles of grace that she alone can work, for she alone is the fecund Virgin who has never had and never will have any equal in purity and fecundity."

Suddenly, I understood why, all those months before in early January, at the beginning of the atrocious and marvelous journey Eryk and I were on, I had been given—and by Eryk—in Banneux the "image" of the Christ for which I had been looking for many years. *Because now the Mother was going to begin to birth this Christ, this Sacred Androgynous Child of the Father-Mother in me and in Eryk together, through our Love for Her and for each other in the fiery dark womb of tantra.*

At once, the meaning of the miracle of the marriage of Cana became clear to me. The Virgin had asked Christ to turn water into wine at the marriage-feast; it was Christ's first miracle and She had prompted it. I had never until this afternoon realized why. Because she wanted Christ to change the ordinary, banal, possessive, attached aspects of human love and sexuality into an experience of Divine human love and Divine human ecstasy. Sacred Marriage, I saw, was an alembic of the Christ-transformation now offered to the planet.

I read on in De Montfort's *Secret of Mary*:

"Mary must break out more than ever in these last times in purity, force, and grace. Her power over the demons will flash out everywhere. It is a kind of miracle when a person remains firm in the middle of the fierce torrent of these times, and stays uninfected in the plague-ridden air of our corrupt era . . . It is the Virgin, in whom the Serpent has never had any part, that works this miracle for those beings who love her well.

"Anyone who knows Mary as Mother and submits to her and obeys her in all things will soon grow very rich; every day, he or she will amass treasure, by the secret power of her philosopher's stone. 'He or she who glorifies his Mother,' says Ecclesiastes, 'is like one who amasses treasure.'"

And then I read:

"Mary is the dawn that precedes and reveals the sun of justice. The difference between the first and second coming of Jesus will be that the first was secret and hidden, the second will be glorious and dazzling; both will be perfect because both will come through Mary."

I knew, reading that, to what the rest of my life will be devoted—to giving myself over to Mary so that Christ can be born in me, to trying, with Her Grace, to witness the miracle of her Divine Presence on earth, so that the fullness of the Birth that can be understood only when She, the Birth-giver, the Birth-power, is known in *all* of her power and glory and eternal splendor and tender concern for every living thing, is *known* everywhere. It is for this Work that Eryk and I met; it is in the realization of this Work that She has put us both—and will put us both—through so much: It is to pursue this Work ever more wisely and humbly that She has saved us and will save us.

FROM MY JOURNAL:
September 19th

Near midnight. In an inn in the mountains near La Salette. Eryk lying asleep beside me, smiling like a baby. Perfect, unshakable peace, older than all the worlds.

Today we took the long winding mountain road to the shrine and church of La Salette. There was a light sprinkling of snow on the fields and hillsides around us and on the road; the air felt finer and finer and fresher and fresher as we ascended. Neither Eryk nor I could speak; the sense of Her was so extreme, so evident, that only silence and prayer could be any kind of response. It was as if, as we wound higher and higher into the bare, stark mountain world where She chose to make her first crucial modern appearance—to two peasant children in 1846—we were being drawn deeper and deeper into the silence of her Immaculate Heart, that Heart of adamantine Love and purity that seemed also to live around us in the sheltering rocks of the French Alps and, finally, most wonderfully, in the exposed flank of the shrine itself, exposed on all sides to the winds and frosts and lights of heaven. It was only when we reached the top and when we were kneeling with our hands in the miraculous spring that she had caused to appear as a Sign of Her Coming, that Eryk smiled and said, "I didn't want to tell you. I wanted it to be a holy surprise. Today is the anniversary—September 19—of the Virgin's appearance here."

At the beginning of our "new life," we had been brought by Her Grace to Beauraing on the anniversary— January 3—of the last of her apparitions there; now, as one part of the journey was ending, and another perhaps even more mysterious one, was beginning, She had brought us to this infinitely pure, lonely, and sacred place on the very day that She had appeared there.

In my heart's eye I could see, clearly, the Curé's half-smile. Eryk leaned forward and made the sign of the Cross in the water of Her spring on my forehead. We linked our hands, intertwining all our fingers, and lowered them together into the freezing dark spring of the Mother. We prayed for humility, inspiration, protection against all evil, the power to witness to the world with our whole being the truth of the miracles She had shown us and done in us. Then, we prayed to the One who had appeared there to flash out the truth of Divine human Love in every heart and in every living being, now and very fast, so that Nature and the planet could be saved. Again and again we repeated the prayer that the Virgin dictated at Medjugorge:

Immaculate heart of Mary, ardent with your goodness, show your love towards us.
May the flame of your heart, O Mother, descend on all humankind.

At Charles DeGaulle airport, a bizarre and scary incident reminded us of all the darkness we had endured. One of the women who had been lying about us to anyone who would listen suddenly appeared out of nowhere and started screaming, "You have betrayed the Divine Mother! You have ruined my life." Eryk and I were about to board; suddenly there was M.—thin, hysterical, with great black rings under her eyes—screaming her nonsense at us. Was this coincidence? Had she laid in wait for us? It was impossible to know. After a moment's frightened helplessness, I replied to her as gently as I could and then turned to leave. She screamed after us, "You will die! You will die!"
Eryk muttered under his breath, "Too late, madam! You are two months too late!"

On Sunday, November 13th, I was scheduled to give a keynote address at the *Common Boundary* conference in Washington. The interview had been out for a month, in a fire-storm of controversy. In the circumstances I was nervous; especially since, on the 10th, just as Eryk and I were leaving for the airport, we had another threatening call which said, "When you get up to speak, keep your mouth shut or else."

In the early morning before I spoke that Sunday I wrote a prayer to the Divine Mother and dedicated it to Rose Solari for all her courage:

O Divine Mother
In this extreme danger
When we and all sentient beings
And Nature Herself,
Your glorious Body,
Face unprecedented misery and destruction,
Inaugurate in fierceness and tenderness
The splendor of Your Age of Passionate Enlightenment.
Bring us into the fire of Your sacred passion for reality,
Rejoin the severed mandala of our being,
Infuse our bodies each of those into mutual harmony.
Engender in the ground of all our beings
The Sacred Marriage,
That union between masculine and feminine
From which in each of us the Divine Child is born . . .

As soon as I had read it out loud and thanked Eryk and Rose before the thousand-strong crowd at eleven o'clock that morning in Washington, I knew that everything would be well.

For an hour I was able, with a calm and poise and joy I had never before experienced in public, to give my complete vision of the Divine Feminine and the role of the authentic Mother in the preservation of the planet.

I said that I saw the Sacred Heart of the Divine Mother as a vast sun of Flame that was now opening in full splendor in history's midnight. Five flames were always erupting from it. These five flames I had come to know were the five sacred passions that we each had to know, pursue, and live out in Her and for Her if we were going to achieve our full human divinity. I said that I believed these five sacred passions are:

1. The passion for the Divine beyond time and space and beyond all forms, for the Transcendent and Eternal Source.
2. The passion for Nature as the immanent manifestation of that Source, its sacred Body.
3. The passion of charity for all human beings and all sentient beings everywhere.
4. The holy tantric passion for one other being, lived out in the rigor of fidelity and consecration to the Divine.
5. Focusing and fulfilling all the others a passion for service and constructive and radical just action on every level in the center of the world.

I stressed again and again how I knew now that no intermediary priests, experts, or Masters were needed to live out these five great passions with the guidance and inspiration of the Mother; all that was needed (all!) was unremitting sincerity, humility, and the hunger to keep alive, through prayer and meditation and service, a *direct* connection with the Divine.

I said that I believed that the Divine Mother was returning in such conscious force and passion to the heart of humankind not to create any more dogmas or religions but to release everyone into their fullest truth and power in Her, to help everyone become the Divine Children, the Christs, we all essentially are: Only with such

a healed and empowered humanity could the great work of pre-
serving Nature, and so the human race, be done.

Such a "return of the Mother" could only, I made as clear as I
could, be revolutionary and involve a restructuring of all institutions everywhere to make them reflect the love and justice of the
Divine. Anything that blocked the *direct* relationship of the Mother
and human child had now to be done away with, because it served
in both blatant and subtle ways the enslavement of the human psyche and its humiliation. I did not mention Meera by name, but
everyone in the audience knew to whom, among others, I was re-
ferring when I spoke of the "false mothers, the Jehovahs in drag,
who are hijacking the power of the revolution of the Sacred Feminine for themselves." If only the return of the full Sacred Feminine
could balance and empower humanity, then it was crucial that we
understood the Sacred Feminine in as vast, complex, rich, and radical a way as possible so nothing in its revolutionary force could be
appropriated or dampened. The Era of Passionate Enlightenment
and of the Sacred Marriage of masculine and feminine in each of us
and at every level of society could only be lived by beings prepared
to go on an immense and costly journey beyond all inherited games
and dogmas and plans. "The Mother will help us and guide us directly through every ordeal if we turn directly and with our whole
being towards Her and dare to risk our lives in the service of Her
Heart of Flame."

At the end, there was a prolonged, loving, standing ovation—a
roar of joy. I looked at Rose, whose face had opened like a
sunflower, and at Eryk, so beautiful and pure and strong, with tears
streaming down his cheeks. I knew what he was thinking. Our
Child, the Vision of our "open journey" in Her, had just been born,
and now, because only Her mercy and Grace could have birthed it
in the first place, it would never die.

Part III

Coda

In early December 1994, after prolonged negotiations, Eryk and I won a legal battle against one of the chief protagonists of this story. Because I had to sign a "gag" order to finish the matter, I cannot give more details. However our victory sent a sharp signal to Meera and her cohorts that we were not going to be intimidated any longer; that any attempt to continue to defame us would have severe legal consequences; that Eryk and I were flanked by excellent lawyers on both sides of the Atlantic and had been given resources by friends to help us fight against any more libel or injustice.

The *Common Boundary* interview—and the *Yoga Journal* one with Catherine Ingram that followed it by eight months—gave, in simple philosophical terms, the essence of the vision I have shared more personally here. They were extremely controversial. An increasing

SUN AT MIDNIGHT

number of people, however, identified with what I was saying, especially those who had been through similar experiences and had never been allowed to speak out. The lid on the Pandora's box of guru abuse had been lifted, and no amount of denial, misquotation of the Scriptures, and jaded old rhetoric and prejudice could close it again.

Meera did not, of course, contact Eryk or myself. She was reduced to playing the Mater Dolorosa, sending absurd messages through strangers that "she still loved me" and that "one day I would understand." All this was for her disciples only and had nothing to do with any wish on her part to explain or expiate her actions.

The Meera cult continues, somewhat discredited and diminished, but still active. This is depressing but not surprising; the projections Meera, and all gurus, manipulate with such lack of scruple are extremely powerful and will die hard. I know, however, that the Mother will not be mocked; the end of the era of the false mothers and Masters is coming. They will all be unmasked eventually. Eryk and I have forgiven Meera and those who threatened to destroy us, but we are under no illusions about her or them.

In the last eight years a molten torrent of work of all kinds has flowed from the sufferings and revelations of Eryk's and my Dark Night. In *The Return of the Mother,* I made clear for the first time my knowledge that the revelation of the Sacred Feminine demands a revolution in our ways of doing and imagining everything, a rehauling of all elites, hierarchies, and institutions so that the Mother's love for all beings and for the Creation can at last be expressed in time to preserve the planet.

In *Son of Man,* inspired by what I had learned of the Christ during my ordeal, I fused together the latest knowledge of the historical Jesus with the testimony of the Christian traditions about the mystical Christ to birth a vision of the Christ-Force as a working for a revolutionary transfiguration of all the conditions of earth-life. In my anthology *The Christian Mystics*, I brought together the sacred texts that illustrate this vision.

In four books dedicated to Rumi—*The Way of Passion, Light upon Light, Love's Glory,* and *Teachings of Rumi,* I used everything I had learned in the dark fire of my own ordeal to present Rumi's extreme understanding of crucifixion by, and resurrection in, Divine Love so his wisdom could be available to everyone who wanted it.

In *The Essential Mystics* I collected together the finest and highest texts I know about the Sacred Feminine; in the *Essential Gay Mystics* I brought together for the first time the great homosexual figures of the world's mystical traditions and emphasized how many of them had been pioneers of precisely the kind of healing tantric awareness that had been graced to me and Eryk.

In *The Direct Path* I fused together everything I had learned in my Dark Night about the necessity and rewards of direct connection with the Divine and offered the practices and exercises taken from many different sources that I myself had used to endure and survive.

The great Grace of this labor has been that through it I have been able to give away everything that I was given, and to open to others the ways into radical Divine Life that were opened to me. I knew that the work had to be done fast: Only the living Grace of the Christ and the Mother could have given me the clarity or the strength.

I haven't only been writing during these last years; my work as a teacher has, through Grace, been tremendously expanded. Breaking from the guru tradition and speaking consciously as someone on the Path with no need or desire to claim "total enlightenment," I have been able to bring what I have learned to audiences in America and England. In 1999, through the Internet, TV, the radio, and personal appearances I was able to introduce "The Direct Path" and my work on Christ and the Mother to hundreds of thousands of people: Many human beings are now ready for a direct communication with the Divine and the radical life of service that flows from it.

What I have lived has woken me up permanently to the abuse of power in all its forms. I make no separation between "spiritual" and "political." All choices are potentially "spiritual" and the transformation the Divine is now asking of us demands a total revisioning of every area of our lives and ways of doing everything. My work has come to embrace all forms of environmental change, animal, gay, and feminist rights, and human rights of all kinds. One of Eryk's and my most cherished dreams is to dedicate forty acres that we bought in 1995 in northern California to the creation of a sanctuary for abused animals where there will be a temple for the Divine in all its "animal forms," and where victims of abuse of all kinds will be able to work with abused animals to recover hope and compassion.

The Dark Night of our time and the crucifixion of Nature is unavoidably driving more and more beings into an understanding that only a radical mystical activism—an activism that is fueled by mystical knowledge, passion, wisdom, and inexhaustible sacred stamina—can now begin to deal with the problems and challenges that face us and demand our most urgent attention. Much of the supposed New Age remains in a narcissistic coma, like the society it mirrors, but the terrors and recognitions to come—and they will come soon—will, I am convinced, shatter this. When they do, those that have allowed themselves to be birthed by radical heartbreak and unillusion into sacred action will be there to help and inspire others. I am neither pessimistic nor optimistic about the future; I simply offer my service and my life to the Divine and to the truth of our Divine humanity as tirelessly as I can. I have lived enough to know that the Divine can work miracles in the half-sincere; the motto I try to live by is St. Paul's "Love bears all things, believes all things, hopes all things, endures all things."

Eryk and I never started out to prove anything to anyone by getting married, but our marriage does prove, I think, the truth, dignity, and divinely inspired power of true Love, whether heterosexual or homosexual. I pray that what we have endured and discovered will encourage all lovers, whatever their sexuality, and embolden all those gay couples who know their love to be holy and wise to make their union sacred in and before God.

Eryk and I know what we have lived is not only a personal story: What Eryk and I experienced is being enacted on a vast scale in our contemporary history. The Angel of History is holding out to anyone with the heart and illusionless courage to look two mirrors; one black and the other golden. In the black mirror what you will see is the horror of billions of human beings living below the poverty line, an entire planet in psychological, spiritual, economic, and political chaos, abuse of power at all levels and in all institutions, and the holocaust of Nature.

Facing without illusion the horror of what we have done to ourselves, each other, and to Nature and the extent of the transformation we have to go through together in order to survive at all is humanity's last hope and greatest challenge, and most transforming imaginable possibility. Accepting the truth of what is displayed in the black mirror will necessitate going through, on a massive, unprecedented scale, and together, the Dark Night of the crucifixion of all our ideals—political, personal, and religious. In order to be able to preserve itself and Nature, humanity will have to lose all fantasies about itself—about its powers, its reason, its technology, its science, even its understanding of God. This will amount to nothing less than a conscious communal crucifixion. How will we as a race endure or learn from so devastating a process if the wisdom of the Dark Night is not universally known? How will we want to begin—let alone go through and survive—such a drastic searing and stripping unless we are also helped to understand that it will prepare for us, and in us, new life and new powers that spring directly from the Divine and can transform all of life?

This understanding is what the Angel of History's golden mirror is holding out to us. In it, all those who dare to look will see the truth of human Divine identity, the range and extent of the sacred powers of passion, creativity, and radical action that flow from it and a vision of the world as it could be—if instead of choosing power we were to choose to become servants of Divine Love and work with its nuclear intensity in the core of the real to transform the conditions and institutions of earth-life.

We must realize that both worlds—that in the black mirror and in the golden—are real. Will we go on choosing the vanity, pride, ignorance, and greed that keeps the world in the black mirror burning or will we choose "the resurrection adventure" in the golden mirror, and all the ordeals that make it possible and vibrant? I do not know. No one knows. Anyone who says they are certain we will survive or be "saved" must be blind or lying; anything at all can now happen. All prophecies in a time like this are straws in a hurricane.

I know which world and which mirror I have chosen to dedicate myself to. I know now that that choice demands and costs, continually, everything, but I know, too, that those who choose "the resurrection adventure" and to live out that choice in sacred, just action will be fed by living springs of truth and holy passion and the deathless energy of Divine Love Itself.

So I am saying to you; risk your Dark Night and the incineration of all your illusions so Divine Love can possess, invade, and transform you into its servant and remake you in your own essential beauty and power. Allow yourself to be transformed into a mystical revolutionary, one who will give his or her whole life to see that victory of justice and compassion in all arenas that alone can now secure our future, and the future of the natural world on our planet.

You have seen from Eryk's and my story that fear, horror, and suffering will be unavoidable if you choose to serve Love; you have also seen the depth and wonder of the protection Love will give you and the powers that will be yours to use when it has remade you. The treasures of all of the mystical systems now lie at your feet as do their sacred technologies and practices; use these treasures and employ these practices to make you strong, passionate, and indefatigable. May you be blessed enough to undergo all that is necessary for you to become a witness and servant of authentic transformation! May the bliss and clarity and power of revelation forge in you a holy and tireless passion to give all you are and do to the Great Work—that of protecting our glorious earth and the future that could, even at this late, dangerous time, flower on it!

January 15, 2002

Acknowledgments

✳

To Rose Solari, our "Solar Rose," bless you always.

To my agent and dear friend, Tom Grady, for all his stamina and generosity of spirit.

To my editor, Mitch Horowitz, for his wonderful sympathy and brilliant, precise editing.

To Joel Fotinos, my publisher, for his unfailing support.

To Anne Teich, for her constant kindness.

To Henry Luce, for years of friendship and protection.

To Gloria Cooper, for her tenderness and magical friendship.

To Doug Smith, for his loyalty.

To Carol Ricotta, for her strength.

Acknowledgments

To Francoise Bouteraon, for her goodness.

To Gabriela, for her wild and boundless courage.

To the Sircar family, for all they gave.

To all those who witnessed what happened, for their passion for justice.

To our lawyers, C.T. and D.S., for their wisdom and persistence.

To the San Francisco Police, Sheriff's office, Interpol, and various anti-cult organizations who wish to remain anonymous (here and in Europe), for their continuing vigilance and fearless support.

To Barbra Streisand, Donna Summer, Tina Turner, Maria Callas, Marlene Dietrich, my muses, mothers of courage and wild beauty.

To Purrball, Puli, and Princey, my darlings, proofs of Love.

About the Author

✳

Andrew Harvey is available for readings, lectures, workshops, and retreats. His agent, Nona Gandelman, can be contacted at *ngandelman@aol.com*. Harvey's website is *www.andrewharvey.net*. Eryk Hanut's website is *www.erykhanut.com*. A new website has been created by a group of psychologists and seekers to deal with the epidemic of spiritual abuse, and to give the abused a forum: *www.stopspiritualabuse.com*.